THE ROGUE'S KISS

Emily Bascom

MILLS & BOON®

First published in Great Britain 2006
Large Print edition 2006
Harlequin Mills & Boon Limited,
Eton House, 18-24 Paradise Road, Richmond, Surrey TW9 1SR

© Emily Bascom 2006

ISBN-13: 978 0 263 18917 9
ISBN-10:   0 263 18917 1

GW 28388526

Set in Times Roman 15¼ on 17 pt.
42-1006-84800

Printed and bound in Great Britain
by Antony Rowe Ltd, Chippenham, Wiltshire

THE ROGUE'S KISS

To my sister, Allie, for reading countless drafts and making cups of tea.

Chapter One

Spring 1741

Rain. Nothing but streets and rain. Glistening cobbles, rooftops awash with rivulets of water…everywhere, mist and rain.

Roisin had never experienced such rain. She leant her forehead against the window of her room, glass divided into diamonds by lead strips along which more rain dripped. She was used to the soft rain of her native Ireland. It was often torrential, even ceaseless, but the smell was different. The way it fell seemed somehow less hopeless. Perhaps because the window she was used to viewing the world from looked out on to fields and trees. Perhaps the hopelessness came from being far from home. Or, perhaps, because today was her life's worst.

Roisin was not Irish, although, if any had asked her, she would have claimed that distant green isle

The Rogue's Kiss

as her home. And her family seat in Kinsale, County Cork, had long been filled by the line of noble English ancestors now stretched behind her. Standing over her, she thought despondently, looking out once more at the downpour.

Roisin was nineteen and, after the death of her father eighteen months ago, her mother had decided it was high time for her to enter London society. It was not fitting, she said, for the daughter of the late Earl of Kinsale to have no experience of the wider social world; he would have wanted his only daughter to have every opportunity. So it was that she was here, in an inn somewhere in London, en route to the house of her mother's brother and his wife. She had never met either, nor the daughter who was said to be of a similar age to herself, yet she must depend on these people to be her new family. She had not been allowed to travel with a maid as she had requested. Instead aged Aunt Millicent, who was really her mother's aunt, not her own, accompanied her. The journey had been a long one, made no shorter by her aunt's prattling conversation. Roisin was beginning to believe she would be forcibly married off within a month of this new London life.

Aunt Milly slumbered now in the chamber next door. They could not, she had professed, disturb the family at this hour. They would rest, refresh themselves and continue on the morrow. They had gone to bed directly after a rudimentary supper, no room for discussion.

Secretly, Roisin was glad. She had not wanted to come to England, because she very rarely agreed with plans that involved her squeezing herself into corsetry of any kind. She would much rather have stayed at home in Cork, riding and hunting with her three brothers.

Her wishes had been steadfastly ignored by her mother throughout proceedings. While Lady Melville knew full well what these wishes were, she was not one to sit by while her daughter turned slowly into a savage, running about the hills. Roisin, she said, would thank her once she saw what London had to offer.

Roisin, having seen, wanted to go home.

In the darkened glass of the window, she caught a glimpse of her reflection. Her red-brown hair was loose after her day of travelling, curling itself gently around her shoulders as it dried. The skin against which it lay was pale and—to the constant chagrin of her mother—lightly freckled as a result of her time outdoors. England, if it was to be like this always, would soon remedy that, reflected her daughter, meeting her own eyes in the window. Those eyes, a light hazel-brown with flecks of green, suddenly filled with tears.

Abruptly, she stood, tired of her own malaise, and

looked about the room. It was cosy enough, though small. Picking up her candle in its carved wooden holder from the windowsill, she moved further into the room, towards the bed. At least the sheets were clean.

She sank on to them, her slender figure sagging with fatigue and another wave of despair. Was it always to be like this? Coerced into leading the life of a pampered lady? She had been content where she was, surrounded by the gentle hills of Kinsale. The society she had known had been that of country nobles—hunt balls and relaxed evening dinner parties. She knew nothing of London and whatsoever went on here. It was half in her mind to run away.

She sat, thoughts far away.

Outside, coaches clattered past. Rain dripped. Escape beckoned.

Roisin frowned. Run away. Could she? It would not, in truth, be running away. It would be going home. If she could return the way she had come, to Bristol, on to a ship…Could her mother harden her heart to send her back to London if she made her way so far?

The thought that had been waiting in the shadows of her mind during the five-day journey from Ireland burst into life. Roisin jumped to her feet.

She would go. What really mattered was freedom to choose—she wanted this at any price. No flouncing about at parties, no fluttering her eyelashes at eligible men to please her mother. Roisin was under no illusions—she knew she had no alternative but to find a husband. But not like this—not like a prize heifer at a London show, to a man who would stifle her. She wanted to see the world and choose a husband on her terms, when she was ready.

She carried enough coin in the purse her brothers had given her to buy at least three nights in any accommodation she could find and after that…well, in the money pouch was also all the jewellery she owned. It was still hers, after all—she was not married yet. She was certain a buyer would not be hard to find in one inn or another—all sorts of people travelled on these roads.

She could not, of course, use the carriage they had hired to bring them thus far. The driver would be abed by now and, besides, he would tell her aunt exactly where her runaway charge had fled… Furrowing her brow in a most unladylike manner, Roisin considered how best to escape. She just needed a tale to spin for the innkeeper…

Minutes later, having gathered her belongings, she was face to face with him.

'What can so young a lady need a carriage for at this hour?' he asked. Roisin arranged her features into a look of worry.

'My aunt bids me carry a message across town for her. It is of some urgency.' Knowing from his face what he was about to say, she added, 'She insists I take it in person. Now, please, arrange a fresh carriage for me, my good man. Do not disturb our driver—his horses need rest for the morning.'

'You go alone, my lady?'

'It is not your place to question me!'

She disliked speaking to the man this way, but she could see her haughty manners impressed him. He thought a while, then nodded.

'I will send my boy in search of a carriage, if you will wait.'

Roisin thanked him, pressing more than was necessary into his palm as an incentive. She waited on a bench in the corner of the inn, trying not to look nervous, while the few men still hunched over tankards of ale eyed her curiously.

She must trust to the innkeeper's polite nature that he would not investigate and wake her aunt. Not, at least, until she was far enough away. She had no idea how long it would take to reach Bristol—but she was determined to go faster than they had on the way here.

'Madam—the carriage is outside.'

She looked up, smiling at her host. 'Thank you. And, please, do not disturb my aunt. This is a worrying time.'

He nodded, her eyes conveying a certainty that she did not feel. She passed him another coin, gushed her thanks and promised her return—then stepped out into the rain.

It had lessened somewhat, but the coachman who turned to look down at her still wore a heavy woollen cloak. He nodded in greeting. Roisin made sure the door of the inn was firmly closed before she spoke.

'I need to go as far to Bristol as you will take me,' she said.

'Bristol?' He considered, eyes deeply sunken into his thin face. 'There's an inn at Hammersmith,' he said at last. 'I can take you that far and you could likely hire a carriage from there in the mornin'.'

She nodded. 'My thanks. Please, I need to get there by the fastest possible route.'

He hesitated. 'That may not be the best—'

'Please. It is a matter of great importance.' Again, she pulled a coin from her pocket.

'As you wish.' He jumped down from his box and opened the door of the carriage for her. Gathering her skirts, Roisin climbed in. The driver threw the door shut, climbed up again and called to his pair of horses. They began to move.

Roisin looked behind her, through the smeary window. She half-expected the door to burst open and the innkeeper to emerge, shouting and shaking his fist. Instead, the inn stood silent in the driving rain, few lights in its windows. She could only hope it stayed that way.

With a sigh, she leant back against the well-upholstered seat and offered up a silent prayer. All she wanted was to get home.

Deep in a clump of trees, the rain dripped through the leaves on to a very different figure. He wore a cloak, pulled tightly around his tall frame, and his face was shadowed in the darkness surrounding him.

The air was silent, any animals that would usually be foraging having taken cover from the onslaught. He had seen few people on his way here, which suited him, for that meant few had seen him. This was not a night to be at large.

Beneath him his horse moved, restless. She knew from long experience what was to come and, like himself, was impatient to accomplish the deed. The sooner it was done, he reflected, the sooner he could be warming himself beside his fire. He turned his head, ever listening, waiting for the sound of an approaching coach.

Nothing.

No mail coach, its precious load heavily guarded. No stagecoach, packed with travellers laden with funds for their journey. Not even any private carriages, carrying wealthy ladies and their husbands to social events.

Only the night and the ever-falling rain.

This was not the time to depress himself further by contemplating his situation, yet he found himself doing exactly that as he waited. There had been a time in his life when he would have laughed heartily at any dog who dared suggest that he would ever find himself here. He would have condemned his own actions, perhaps. No more. He had learned much in these past months. He knew how circumstance could change a man.

A sigh escaped the dark figure's lips. The man he had been would, in all truth, have died before attempting such an act. He had been a gentleman. True enough, in many respects he still was…but he doubted any of his victims would see him that way.

He shook his head and his shoulder-length hair, tied at the nape of his neck according to fashion, showered droplets. His horse, disturbed by the movement, blew softly to herself, shaking water out of her own mane. He put out a hand to caress her soaked neck, words of comfort far from him this miserable night.

He wished he were home.

Roisin pulled her cloak more tightly around her and stared dismally out of the carriage window. It had stopped raining some time ago, and just lately they had left the cobbled streets and were proceeding through what appeared to be country, from the trees she could make out through smeared glass. Branches brushed the carriage, which lurched on the mud road. Roisin could feel every pothole. She had not thought

London so small that they could have left it already. If they had, however, it was no bad thing. She was exhausted.

She put her head against the rocking, uncomfortable side of her seat and fell into a doze, into a dream of rolling hills and wind in her hair. Good, brisk Cork wind, the wind she had grown up with and never asked to leave. It felt almost real and, for a brief while, it was.

She was awakened what seemed like minutes later as they went over an especially large hole in the road, almost biting off her own tongue as the whole carriage dipped.

It was still dark. She did not know how long she had slept.

Roisin put a hand up to her mouth to stifle a yawn. Her body felt like it would no longer hold her upright. They must have been driving a fair while. This inn could not, surely, be very far now.

She was about to knock on the roof to ask her driver when something black rushed past the window. She jumped into alertness as the horses screamed, the carriage swinging to one side. Then, with a jolt that threw her on to the floor in a tangle of skirts, it drew to an abrupt stop and all was still.

Roisin, somewhat dazed, crouched in the dark and listened.

There was a short whinny from a strange horse, and

the sound of boots hitting the ground as a rider dismounted. The silence was broken only by her own breathing, and the soft rustle of her skirts as she slowly raised herself back on to the seat. There was a figure outside. Suddenly afraid, she tensed, heart pounding, eyes closed. She waited.

She knew what was happening. She might be a naïve country girl, but she had heard tales of highwaymen. She was about to be robbed.

Footsteps came towards the carriage. Hastily, Roisin pulled off her ring—the only jewellery she had worn on this long journey. It was an emerald. Her father had given it to her on her eighteenth birthday and she was not going to have it stolen from her. With only a moment's thought, she thrust it deep into the best hiding place she could think of, just as the door was wrenched open.

The man outside appeared tall despite her raised height, broad of shoulder and lean of body. His face was obscured by a mask that covered everything but his mouth, with holes for his eyes—colourless in the gloom. He stood looking in at her with something like surprise.

'Good evening, my lady.' His voice was disarmingly gentle, a light Scottish burr softening the slightly mocking tone.

Roisin swallowed hard.

'All alone on such a perilous road?' He held out

his hands in an imploring gesture, lace cuffs white in the gloom. 'Do you not know that there are high-waymen about?'

'I know it all too well,' she said, her voice almost steady.

He inclined his head. 'Then I must assume you were expecting me. Kindly step out of the carriage a moment, my lady.'

'I would prefer not,' Roisin replied quickly.

'Then I am afraid I will have to ignore your wishes.' He held out a hand to help her. Roisin, after a moment's thought, decided it would, perhaps, be better to obey. There was a possibility she could run once she was outside.

'Very well,' she said coldly. Ignoring the hand he offered, she stepped out of the relative warmth on to a muddy dirt road. The light from the lanterns affixed to the sides of the carriage was the only thing that separated her from the total darkness where he stood, face obscured.

She looked around, expecting to see the captured yet comforting bulk of the man she had hired. There was no sign of him. 'Where is my driver?'

'At the next crossroads by now,' he said, looking amused. 'I have never seen anything on two legs move so fast.'

'Gone to get help,' Roisin assured him.

He raised an eyebrow. 'Perhaps.'

Roisin felt her heart sink. She knew he was probably right—she would never see that wretched man again. After all, he had no allegiance to her.

Her eyes must have betrayed her sudden desperation, for he gave a wry smile. 'Well then, my pretty one, let us not stand here wasting each other's time all night. You will have heard how it goes, no doubt: your money or your life.'

He could not have been more right. It was like all the tales she had ever heard. He stood, expectant, waiting politely—disarmingly so—for her to hand him her purse. But she could not—how then would she ever get home?

'You'd not kill me,' she told him, only a little doubtful.

He nodded, eyes sparkling. 'Aye, true enough, I never kill anyone. But…' His eyes were on the low neckline of her gown, where the tops of her breasts were just visible.

'But…what?' Roisin tried to stifle a rising panic. Would he ravish her and leave her for dead on this cold road? The tales that filtered through to Ireland made no mention of such atrocities, but they must have been censored for her innocent ears. In truth, she had no idea what men like this did to their captives. She knew there was fear in her eyes.

His smile grew. 'You mistake me. I want only that jewel that you placed there before I arrived.'

'Which jewel?'

'It looked like a ring.'

Oh, God. He had seen. 'I…do not…recall…'

His expression stopped her. He moved further towards her, his face, lit now by the lanterns, coming out of the shadows. The first thing she noticed was that his hair appeared to be his own, not a wig as with most men. Although his eyes were dark, it was an unexpected tawny red—the colour of the fox cubs that she often watched playing in the fields behind her family home. It distracted her for a moment. She could not remember the last time she had seen a man with such hair. He wore no hat, having swept it off, just a ribbon that tied the hair back at the nape of his neck.

'I have need of a warm fire and a good meal tonight,' he was telling her. 'The ring will provide me with both. Now, shall I fetch it, or will you?'

Roisin met his eyes. Now she knew why they were called gentlemen thieves. His politeness might yet be his downfall. She steeled herself. 'Please, be my guest.'

Again, that look of veiled surprise. He raised his eyebrows. 'If that is what you wish, my lady…'

'It is.'

He nodded. 'Very well.'

His hand reached for her, the lace of his cuff brushing her skin. Then his fingers, cool from the night air, were on the curve of one breast, the place where one of his sex had never laid a finger. Roisin squared her shoulders. Their eyes met and she could tell nothing from his look. A smile played across his lips, as, slowly, he began to move his hand lower, towards the shadow between her breasts.

And then he stopped, frozen just as he had been, only his expression changing.

'Is something the matter?' asked Roisin coolly.

He swallowed. 'Uh…'

She adjusted her pistol so it fitted more snugly into his crotch. 'Do I look like I've just got off the boat?'

He nodded, disbelief fresh in his eyes. 'Aye, you do.'

Roisin smiled. 'Well, I have. But I brought this with me. All the young ladies are wearing them in the country these days.'

He was still frozen in place. 'I…apologise for any embarrassment I may have caused…'

'Thank you. Now take your hand away from there.'

He did so, quickly, stepping back.

'I am much obliged,' Roisin told him, straightening her bodice.

She was about to speak again when her feet were kicked out from under her and, hitting her head on the carriage door, she fell to the ground. Next thing she knew there was a pistol pointing at her and her own was out of reach, gleaming in the dark under the wheels. Dazed, she was aware of his hands searching her pockets. By the time her head stopped reeling, however, he was standing over her once more.

Her situation seemed to amuse him. There was mud on her hands and on her dress. How could he treat her so?

'Again,' he said quietly, 'I have to apologise.' He was holding her purse. Roisin struggled into a sitting position.

'I need that!'

'As do I.' He adjusted his pistol, mocking her, offering her his hand. 'Come, let's not be at odds.'

'Odds? You are stealing my money!' she cried, batting away the proffered hand.

He shrugged, showing no sign of having heard her. 'If you prefer to stay in the dirt, I will take my leave.'

'But—'

He bowed, then turned and walked towards his waiting horse, tucking his pistol safely away. Roisin made a dive under the carriage and, by stretching, just managed to grab her own.

'Halt!'

He turned as her shout echoed back from the silent road. She pointed the gun at him and braced herself. Desperation steadied her, with the knowledge that he *could not* be allowed to take her money. 'Stay where you are.'

He laughed. 'Do you even know how to load that weapon?'

'It's already loaded,' she said, teeth clenched.

Again, surprise. 'Really?'

'Bring my purse back.'

'Why?'

She frowned, frustration taking hold. 'Because I will shoot you!'

'Of course you will.' He turned and began to walk away. Roisin took a deep breath and pulled the trigger.

She was not expecting it to be so loud. The force of the huge bang drove her backwards against the carriage, smoke issuing from the barrel of the gun. Gasping, Roisin threw it from her. It landed on the ground with a heavy thud.

Silence.

A long, horrible silence.

Then an almost inaudible groan.

Roisin forced herself to look over at the heap on the ground that had been her attacker. He lay, half on his back, half on his side, and she could see the rise and fall of his chest as he took deep, gasping breaths. He was not dead, then. She was not sure if that was a good thing or not...

'God's death...' he murmured, raising his head. 'You shot me!'

From somewhere in the depths of her, Roisin found her voice. 'I told you I would.' Making her careful way forward, she retrieved the pouch of money and jewels from where it lay a few feet from him, wanting to escape as soon as possible. His dark eyes followed her movements. Trying not to meet them, she strode back to the carriage, and was about to pull herself up on to the driver's seat when he stopped her with a cry.

'Wait! You can't leave me!'

'Why?' She turned back.

He had propped himself up on one elbow and was looking after her. 'Because, lass, I'm wounded. If your friend returns, I'll be captured and left to rot in a cell—you'll have murdered me!'

'You said yourself he won't return,' she pointed out.

'Then I'll bleed to death here in the road!'

'That's none of my concern…' Roisin swallowed as she saw the blood seeping darkly through the shoulder of his shirt.

His eyes were filled with pain. 'Please.'

'You were going to kill me!'

He shook his head. 'Of course I wasn't.'

'Well…' She hesitated. 'Are you badly hurt?'

'Look!' He held up the hand he had been holding clamped to the wound. It was smeared with red. 'Please. Help me. I beg you.'

'Oh…' Roisin resigned herself. She could not leave him here, knowing that if he died it would be her doing. She could be arrested for murder… With a sigh, she crossed to him, bending down beside him to try and take stock of his injury. 'It doesn't look so—'

She stopped short, gasping, as she felt the cold steel of a gun beneath her jaw. This time his eyes were not amused.

'You should not be so soft-hearted,' said the highwayman.

'But…'

'I think we are even now, yes?'

The gun was still choking Roisin. 'Are you going to kill me?' she asked between her teeth.

'No,' he replied. 'But I'll have to take you with me. You may be of use.'

'I will never go!'

He bared his teeth in a pained smile. 'That was not a question, pretty one.'

Before she had time to argue, something hard collided with the back of her head, and the world disappeared into a void. She fell face first into the mud and knew no more.

Chapter Two

When Roisin awoke she was lying on a hard, uncomfortable bed, in a cold room lit by candles. She lay, somewhat dazed, eyes only half-open. It was not yet day, and raining again, if the water that dripped in upon her through a few small holes in the thatch above her head was anything to go by. Wherever this was, it seemed to be run-down and deserted…the perfect place for a highwayman to make his lair.

She groaned, suddenly aware of her headache.

'You're awake, then.'

The voice came from her left. Painfully, she turned to look. The highwayman sat in a battered chair, watching her. He had removed his shirt, revealing a firmly muscled chest and upper arms. Roisin, who had never seen a man in such a state of undress, felt her eyes linger on him despite herself.

The candlelight turned his skin to tawny gold, and played on the hard lines of his body and its light dusting of hair as her eyes moved along it. For a moment, she felt a sensation she had never experienced before—a strange tingling as if her body knew something she did not. Confusion reminding her where she was at last, she forced herself to concentrate on her plight and dragged her gaze away.

He had crudely bound the top of his arm in a rough bandage that looked like it had been made from something not very clean. The colour was vaguely familiar…

She raised her gaze to his, and flushed crimson when she saw him watching her intently. He had obviously mistaken her dazed state—brought on, surely, by shock—as something more.

He was still wearing the mask, and for a moment she studied her own reflection in his eyes. Her red-brown hair hung haphazardly about her face—a face streaked with dirt—and there was a cut on her left cheek. She felt like she had been dragged here and, upon reflection, decided she probably had.

The highwayman did not smile, although she could have sworn there was a sparkle in his eyes. 'Welcome to my home.'

'It's as crude as you are,' she told him, voice weak as she pulled herself into a sitting position.

'A fine way to speak after I took you in.'

'Took me in!' she yelled. 'You abducted me, you dog!'

For a moment he said nothing. His eyes were mocking her again. She disliked his attitude.

He said, 'The two are much the same. I apologise for the knock on the head… It was the only way to take you without a fuss.'

Roisin shot him a look of hatred, her fear overcome by anger. Then she noticed her dress. It was filthy and—if that had not been enough to render it unwearable—a strip had been torn irregularly from it at the bottom.

'What have you done to me?'

He shrugged. 'I needed a bandage.'

'Ugh!' said Roisin in disgust.

There was a silence in which she sat, hands in lap, not looking at him. The full extent of her plight was only just filtering through into her bruised head. No one knew where she was, least of all Roisin herself. She might be miles from civilisation, in a hut with a half-naked man who, despite what he said, could be a murderer. Oddly, she was more annoyed than frightened as she looked at her kidnapper.

He cleared his throat. 'Now that you are awake, would you do me the service of—?'

'No,' she said immediately.

He looked taken aback. 'I have not yet told you—'

'I care not,' she said firmly. 'I will never do you any service.'

'I need my wound dressed properly,' he said quietly. 'That is the reason I brought you here.'

'Then you must take me back again,' she retorted, 'and leave me by the road as you found me, for I will not—'

She stopped as her eye caught the 'bandage'. Country living and sisterhood to three boys with no sense of physical danger had given Roisin a thorough grounding in how to deal with such things—apparently a skill this man did not share. Blood soaked it—he had not bound the wound correctly…probably had not washed it… And it did not smell pleasant.

'Did you never learn how to dress a wound?'

'I have never needed such knowledge.' He was looking at her again. 'I have never been so outwitted.'

Their eyes met for a moment, and he gave her a wide, wicked smile. The light of the fire picked out the red in his hair. His face—what she could see of it—was very dirty.

'Take off that mask,' she said suddenly. 'If I am to be held prisoner I want to see my gaoler.'

'That is exactly what you must not do,' he said evenly. 'My apologies. The mask stays on. Now, please, the wound.' Again, that smile.

Flustered, she looked away. 'Very well. I will clean it if you let me go.'

'You have my word.'

'That means nothing to me,' muttered Roisin. But she slid off the bed none the less. 'You had best lie down, then.'

He removed the pistol from his belt and made a great show of leaving it behind him on the table, then lay down on his good side on the bed, head raised as if to keep an eye on her.

She thought then of attempting escape, but, when she glanced again at the wound a pang of guilt went through her. She would help him first, then run if he refused to free her of his own accord. Added to everything, he was once again harbouring her purse.

Slowly, she unwrapped the bandage. He closed his eyes, teeth clenched as it peeled away from the bloodied flesh beneath. It seemed the shot had passed cleanly through his outside upper arm, for which she was profoundly grateful. She did not feel in the mood to go fishing about in some stranger's shoulder today.

He was breathing harshly, clearly in pain. 'A woman should not be trusted with a gun,' he muttered, face turned away from her.

'I hit my mark, did I not?' she snapped, pulling on the last piece of cloth. It unstuck with an audible ripping sound. The man gave a cry of pain, his face screwed up.

'God's teeth, woman! Have a care!'

'You have a care!' she retorted. 'I am helping you!'

She dropped her eyes from his and carried on working. He had placed a bowl of water by the bed for her, and she set about cleansing the wound of the grit and dirt from the road.

'Do you have a name?' he asked eventually.

'Of course I have a name,' she said brusquely.

'Might I inquire…?'

'Roisin.'

He considered. 'Irish.'

She nodded.

'But you aren't Irish.'

'No,' she said shortly. 'I live there.'

'Ah. I see now.'

Sharply, she looked up. 'And what, pray, is that supposed to mean?'

He laughed. 'Nothing, lassie. Nothing.' He was looking closely at her. 'Just Roisin?'

'As far as you are concerned, yes.' She did not want to put ideas of ransom into his head by telling him that she had a title. She should have lied, told him she lived in England. He must have concluded that her family were landed gentry as it was.

She continued to work, vowing to keep herself to herself.

'My name is Ewan Hamilton,' he volunteered. 'You may have heard of me in these parts.'

'No,' she lied. His name had been mentioned as a notorious criminal at the inn. But she did not wish to inflate his ego by letting him see that he was well known.

He seemed surprised. 'Well, you are new here.'

'Hmm,' said Roisin. Sighing in resignation, she

pulled her skirt up a little and tore a strip from her still-clean petticoat. 'I might as well complete the job,' she told him curtly.

There was a short silence in which he watched her.

'I don't mean to offend you,' he said softly. 'And I apologise for ruining your dress.'

She was not sure how to cope with him now that he was looking at her in a more friendly way. 'It was already ruined,' she said gruffly. 'It was not designed for crawling in the dirt.'

Ewan smiled. 'Neither were you, by the look of you.'

'What do you mean by that?' She paused in dressing his wound, guarded.

'Only…' he shrugged '…that you seem to be a lady of some standing. It puzzles me that you have to travel alone. What kind of father would allow his daughter out unchaperoned?'

'It's none of your concern,' Roisin told him.

She returned to her work, tying the bandage neatly and looking about for something to cut the loose ends with.

'Here.' Reaching down, he pulled a dagger from his boot, flicking it from its leather sheath. His fingers brushed hers as he handed it to her. They were filthy.

'Thank you.' She cut the cloth with ease—the blade was very sharp. 'Not too tight?'

He shook his head. 'The pain is much less.'

'Shame,' she could not resist muttering.

He took back his dagger. 'Are you always so unpleasant?'

She snorted. 'Obviously no one ever explained to you how to treat a lady.'

He frowned. 'Why do you say that?'

'I hardly need to elaborate,' she retorted. 'Just look at the way you have treated me!'

'You were not going anywhere. In all likeliness I did you a favour.'

She sat up straighter. 'I was *going* home!'

'But you probably would never have arrived. There are bandits on these roads.'

Roisin gritted her teeth. 'If I was not aware of that fact before, then I certainly am now.'

He gave her a long look. 'You were running away, weren't you?'

'From what?' She was on her feet now. 'I am my own mistress!'

He grinned. 'Mistress? You're nothing but a girl.'

'I would hold my tongue if I were you,' she began, hand going to her pocket. There was nothing there. He brought out her pistol.

'Such workmanship. I could not resist.'

'That is mine.'

'Board and lodging,' said the highwayman. 'You cannot live for nothing in the real world, my lady.'

'Fine,' she told him, seething. 'Then I will take my leave. Good day to you.'

She gathered up what was left of her skirts and made for the door, her hair falling in her face. She managed only a couple of steps before he was on his feet behind her, and she was grabbed roughly around the waist.

'Let me go!' She turned to face him, at which point he transferred his grasp from her hips to her flailing wrists.

'Wait,' he said, softer now. 'I do not mean to upset you.'

She gritted her teeth, trying to free her wrists. 'I am not upset, sir, I am leaving.'

'It's not yet light,' he protested, 'and you will soak yourself to the skin.'

Roisin stopped struggling. He was indeed tall when standing upright, over a head taller than herself, and she had never considered herself particularly small.

'Then what, pray, will I do until morning?'

He gave her a lopsided smile. 'I'll take you back to town myself at first light. You only have to wait an hour or two.'

She looked up at him. Could she trust him? It seemed she had little choice. 'I can see no alternative,' she said at last, dropping her gaze. 'Now, please, let me go.'

He released her wrists and stepped back, easing himself on to the bed with one hand as if his wound was causing him pain. He eyed her for a moment, head to one side, hair brushing his bare shoulder with its clearly defined muscles. Roisin swallowed.

'You may put your shirt back on now,' she said.

He smiled. 'I apologise if my state of undress disturbs you.'

'It does not disturb me in the least,' she snapped.

'Indeed?' He raised his eyebrows.

Grabbing the shirt from the chair behind her, she threw it at him. 'You will catch cold, sir. Besides, it is not seemly.'

'Ah, not seemly, aye.' He replaced the torn and bloodied shirt, easing it over his wound and fastening the buttons gingerly with one hand. Roisin found herself relaxing slightly now he was decent once more. 'You are a lady, then?'

She frowned. Would he not let the subject drop? Perhaps he did harbour thoughts of ransom. 'Why do you keep asking?'

'You said I do not know how to treat a lady.'

She sighed. 'My family own land in Cork and are wealthy, yes. But I am worth little.'

He smiled. 'I had not thought of exacting money from them. I am curious as to how their daughter comes to be wandering the highways around London alone. Going, says she, back home.'

Exhaustion and a throbbing head allowed Roisin's guard to slip. She brushed her hair out of her eyes, shrugging. 'I find London unsatisfactory. Not what I am used to. You, sir, must surely understand what it is to be far from home.'

'Far from home?'

She nodded. 'You are Scottish, are you not?'

'Aye,' he said quickly, dropping his gaze. 'Aye. Far from home. You are making for Ireland, then?'

'I am no longer making for anywhere,' she told him, tears of frustration suddenly threatening, 'since I now find myself penniless.'

The look he shot her was one of sympathy, unthinkable though that seemed.

'You may yet find London to be to your liking.'

'I think not.'

There was a pause then as, embarrassed, she attempted to control her rapidly unravelling emotions. She wished he would not be kind to her—at least when he was mocking she had anger to protect her. She could feel him watching her as, taking a deep breath, she straightened her back and raised her chin.

'It is none of your concern, at any rate,' she told him stiffly. 'Kindly keep your opinions to yourself.'

'Believe me,' he said quietly, regardless, 'it is safer to stay where you are.'

She made no reply.

'I wonder,' he added, 'that you did not get robbed on your way *into* our fair city. Do not test fate by trying to leave again.'

All at once her misery was forgotten in sheer disbelief. Roisin stared at him, agog. 'I am…incredulous, sir, that you would have the…' nearly speechless, she faltered, '*audacity* to—'

He smiled. 'You mean you don't want advice from a highwayman. Trust me, lass, I'm the best one to give it to you.'

'I have *been* robbed!' she threw at him. 'By you, if you will have the grace to recall. And now I have nothing, and nothing to lose—so I may as well walk back home!'

He was up off the bed again, catching hold of her as she made for the door. 'No.'

'Stop this!' Again, she struggled. Again, he held on. 'How is it that you are so concerned as to my fate?'

'Because you are a young, beautiful woman,' he said, 'and you will be alone in a city full of men far worse than I. Now cease this!'

Roisin ceased. She stared up at him, stunned into silence.

In the silence, he laughed. 'Do not look at me as if I have grown an extra head. What I say is true. All of it.'

Something was in his eyes as he looked at her. Something new and unlooked-for. He stood very close to her, so close that she could see that he needed a shave. She held his gaze for a long moment, not knowing whether it was more dangerous to speak or be silent. After what seemed too long a time, he seemed to remember his manners.

'Please,' he said softly, but with an edge to his voice. 'My arm pains me—stop leaping about and allow me to sit down a while, wench.'

Roisin broke free. 'Sit all you like!' She shoved him backwards on to the bed, crossing her arms stubbornly as his eyes reproved her from behind the mask, his hand going again to the wound. She did not like the way he made her feel—vulnerable and inexperienced in the world. She would not let him dictate to her, vagrant as he was.

'Take me back,' she commanded. 'If you are such a gentleman, do as I say. Now.'

He sighed. 'Daylight is but—'

'No!' She was growing desperate. 'Take me back, or I will leave alone.'

He looked at her, as if considering whether she would do so. To prove it to him, she turned her back and, for the third time, headed for the door.

'Very well.'

When she turned he was on his feet. There were lines of exhaustion around his mouth, but he protested no more, merely picking up her cloak, which lay on a chair further into his hut. She had expected him just to toss it at her, but instead he fastened it around her shoulders with deft fingers, lifting her hair out of the way. She did her best to ignore his closeness, waiting with lowered eyes as he donned his own cloak, pulling on also his tricorn hat.

'Come then,' he said, opening the door.

It was still dark outside, and a light rain fell like mist, but there was light on the horizon, she saw with relief. The highwayman's horse was tied up outside what looked to be some sort of disused shack. It was all but falling down, with moss and lichen growing all over it. It was still too dark to see much to either side.

'Where is this place?' she asked.

He cast a perfunctory eye over his hovel. 'We are well outside the city, never fear. Come.'

All around them was wood. He mounted his horse and, turning in the saddle, held out a hand to help her up.

'I apologise for the lack of ceremony,' he told her, 'and you'll have to ride astride.'

'I am well used to it,' she assured him coldly, attempting to pull herself up behind him. It was, however, not such an easy matter to mount a horse in a day dress. She was used to her riding habit, which allowed her more freedom. The full skirts and under-garments of this dress hampered her considerably.

'Do you need assistance?' asked the highwayman after a time. From his voice she heard that he was laughing at her.

'I can manage, thank you,' she told him frostily. And she did, eventually. Once up behind him she was out of breath, and her ankles in their embroidered stockings were visible below the hem of her dress. Too annoyed to care, she placed her hands on the saddle, beneath her, gripping the leather.

Shaking his head, he removed them and placed them on his hips.

'You'll have to hold on tighter than that.'

Beneath her hands she felt what she had already seen in the hut—he was lean and well muscled, probably from years of riding around the law. She was indeed forced to tighten her grip as he clicked his tongue and the horse moved forward. They rode in silence, the road beneath them soft earth, trees all around. Roisin wanted to close her eyes and sleep, but knew if she did she would slide from the horse and fall. Perhaps, she thought with an inward sigh, that would not be such a bad thing.

The rain fell lightly on her face, and she pulled the hood of her cloak up to cover her now tangled hair. If she had not been in such a position she would have considered this wood, with the first stirrings of birds before sunrise, a lovely place. She began to feel calmer, her thoughts starting to order themselves.

Now was the first opportunity she had been given to think, and she spent most of this time regretting her impulsive escape earlier in the evening. Perhaps she should have found a way to leave in daylight, when the dangers of the road were less. The whole inn was likely to be awake and searching for her now. Her aunt would not be pleased, and the story was bound to make its way back to her mother.

She sighed aloud. Her plan could not have gone more wrong.

'We shall have to go the way we came,' said the highwayman over his shoulder. 'There's more cover.'

He did not seem to expect an answer, and they rode on in peace.

It occurred to Roisin, through the mists of her tired mind, that he was taking a risk by returning to the scene of his crime. Not that she was at all concerned for him, she reminded herself. He deserved to be at Tyburn like all his kind, with a noose about his neck. Is that not what they did with highwaymen and kidnappers? As she thought it, the idea made Roisin feel strangely guilty. This man had not hurt her. Not yet, at any rate. Why should she wish ill on him?

Even as her mind formed the thought, two figures became visible on the road ahead. They were standing by their horses and appeared to be arguing. She felt the highwayman's back tense and he pulled the brim of his hat down over his eyes. He eased his horse into a slightly faster trot.

'Not a word,' he muttered to her over his shoulder, mouth barely moving. 'Or we will both be the worse for it.'

Frowning, Roisin lowered her eyes, hiding her face

as best she could in her cloak. She did not know why she complied with his wishes, she only knew she did not like his tone. He seemed edgy suddenly, and this made her afraid.

They passed the men, who barely glanced at them, poring over a map as they now were. Despite herself, Roisin watched them out of the corner of her eye, and felt the relief in the body of the man before her as they passed by unaccosted.

'What was the meaning of that?' she hissed once they were out of earshot.

He seemed just about to reply when a shout rang out behind them and their heads both whipped around together. The two men had mounted their horses and were rapidly approaching, shouting to them to yield. They did not look friendly.

The highwayman swore as he spurred the horse into a gallop, with Roisin clinging on to him for dear life, eyes wide at this unexpected complication. For a time they gained speed, and the cries grew less threatening. It was only when there was an explosion behind them, and something narrowly grazed Roisin's shoulder, that she began to be really afraid.

'They're shooting at us!' she cried.

His jaw tightened. 'I can hear that. Hold on!'

With that he pulled sharply to the left, swerving away from the track and into the trees beside them. Roisin gasped as branches whipped past, some ripping her clothing, even threatening to unseat her. Then, ridiculously, he pulled the horse up abruptly and leapt off, pulling Roisin down with him. Her left ankle twisted painfully beneath her as she landed, but he supported her around the waist with one hand, giving the horse a hard slap on the rear with the other. It bolted, vanishing through the trees within seconds. By this time, the highwayman had already flung both himself and Roisin to the ground beside the track, where thick bracken grew.

'Lie still,' he hissed in her ear.

She did so, with his body half-covering hers, her face pressed into the ground and one of his hands on the back of her head. It occurred to her for one moment to fling him off, to run out to her saviours. But she remembered the looks on their faces. Would she be any better off with two such men? So, along with the pressure of the man beside her, fear held her where she was. Fear and a strange unwillingness to leave him alone to his fate.

They had been there what only seemed like a laboured breath or two when thundering hooves signalled the arrival of their pursuers. The noise grew steadily louder, and Roisin felt her fellow fugitive press himself further into her back. Then the riders were upon them, a flash of horses' legs and cloaks passing so narrowly that for an instant she thought her head would surely be trampled. It was not. They passed, the noise of hooves retreating into eventual nothing.

Still, they lay.

Roisin licked her lips. Her breathing sounded hugely loud in her own ears and she wished she could quieten her wildly beating heart just by telling it to hush. The highwayman's hand was still pressing her head into the dirt. She moved a little and he applied more pressure.

'Ssh,' he said, very softly.

She discovered she could feel his heart beating against her, where his chest was pressed against her arm, trapped under him. They lay for what seemed hours more. Slowly, both pulses returned to normal. At last, very, very gradually, he raised himself on to his elbows and peered over the bracken. Beckoning for her to stay low, he moved into a crouch, went a little way towards the path, then, after a time when she could not see him, returned.

'They're gone.'

For a moment she could not move, just lay with her face in the mud for what seemed the hundredth time that night. He offered her his hand.

'Come, you have to get up. They'll be back once they realise there's no one on that horse.'

Roisin pushed herself up, ignoring the hand. She felt unsteady on her feet.

'Roisin? Are you all right?'

She rounded on him, fear turning to anger. 'What was that? Who were those men?'

He looked evenly at her. 'They were thief-takers. Bounty hunters. Perhaps you are unaware that there's always a huge ransom for highwaymen. Dead or alive.'

'And what are we to do now?' she all but shouted at him. 'We have no horse, we are stranded in the middle of a *wood*—'

For a moment he only eyed her, his gaze turning cold.

'This is no wood,' he told her. 'It's the outskirts of London. And if you go a little that way—' he pointed in the direction the men had gone '—you'll find an inn and a man who'll help you. I've brought you this far, I want no more of you. Good day to you, ma'am.'

Her mouth fell open. 'You robbed and kidnapped me!' she cried. 'You brought yourself here, do not accuse me as if it was all my doing, you…you dog!'

'Do not think I don't regret the moment I laid eyes on you,' he said quietly.

'Then leave me!' Roisin's eyes blazed with anger as she flung out her right arm to show him the road. This was followed by a cry of pain as she realised that this arm hurt. She turned her head and saw a rip in the fabric of her dress where the arm joined the bodice— one of many, but this one with blood oozing from it.

She touched it gingerly, wincing as her fingers grazed the wound. The man had been a good marksman—the ball had almost hit her, merely glancing off her shoulder as it passed and leaving a bruised scratch.

'Let me see,' said the highwayman, still present despite his protestations.

'Get away from me!' She batted his hand away, turning to stalk off. The weight landed on her tender ankle, however and, with another cry of pain, she fell backwards into the bracken once more.

She lay, looking up at the trees, and could only be thankful that it had not been face first this time. All her strength was gone and she could easily have slept where she fell.

The silence was broken by the deep chuckle of the man who now stood above her. Roisin watched, anger draining despite herself, as the chuckle grew into a soft laugh. She gave him a grudging smile and, this time, took the hand he offered.

She stood, testing her weight on the ankle, steadying herself against him. It occurred to her that she was no longer afraid. Something had taken place along the road, and they were not now kidnapper and prisoner. They were equals.

'Something tells me you are not having the night you had wished for,' he said.

Roisin gave a laugh that was half-sob. 'I understand your regret at meeting me,' she said.

'Because the feeling is mutual?'

She shook her head. 'Now you are in more danger than I.'

'You may be right.' He looked around him. 'We must continue carefully.'

Despite her better judgement, Roisin protested, 'No. I will make my way alone. You must leave this place now if you wish to leave it alive.'

He shook his head. 'I gave you my word—'

'I release you,' she interrupted. 'If, as you say, the distance is short, I can manage alone.'

He looked at her for a long moment, eyes unreadable. Then, placing a hand in the pocket of his now-battered waistcoat, he pulled out her pistol and handed it back to her. 'You may quickly make your way to safety from here,' he told her. 'Take this, and leave the road if you hear anyone coming.'

She nodded, looking into his face. 'Thank you.'

'Do not hesitate to shoot as you did with me.'

She smiled. 'I have learned that lesson well, sir.'

'I dare say you have.' His eyes sparkled, though his face remained impassive. 'I will go then, if I have your leave.'

'You have it.'

'Tell no one you have seen me,' he said, suddenly serious.

For reasons she could not fathom, Roisin shook her head. 'I would not.' As the words left her lips she knew they were true—and she was surprised. After all he had done to her, she wished him no harm.

He seemed to understand this, for he smiled.

Then, unbelievably, he stepped forward and kissed her.

Roisin stood, paralysed as his lips grazed hers and her senses sprang to life. She had never been kissed by any man before—but she was willing to bet her inheritance that the men she had known back home would never presume to such a kiss. Not out of wedlock, at any rate.

His lips were soft against hers, gentle at first, then more insistent as the kiss deepened. Her body seemed to know what was required and, despite her best intentions, responded. He was pressing against her, one hand behind her head, in her hair, the other at her waist, holding her captive. She placed a hand on his chest—to push him off, she told herself—and felt the hard muscle beneath his shirt.

She could not believe, in the few instants the kiss lasted, that this was she, Roisin. And then her thoughts dissolved, as did her knees, and she merely stood, kissing him back and barely realising.

After all eternity, he pulled away. 'Forgive me,' he said, eyes locked with hers.

She parted swollen lips to reply, but could think of nothing to say. Then, with a small bow, he turned and headed into the trees, disappearing from view.

For a long time, she stood, pleasure mingling with disbelief. The sky was lightening around her. She looked down, taking in the torn fabric of her dress, her ruined shoes, the mud everywhere, and the blood still trickling down her arm. He had given her back her pistol, but not her purse. He had dragged her about the countryside, mocked and assaulted her in the most grievous manner, then left her to find her own way home. She was penniless, abandoned and alone, with no idea where she was.

Roisin allowed herself, just for a moment, to smile.

Then she went in search of help.

Chapter Three

Twenty-four hours and much hysteria later, Roisin stood at another window, looking out at another street. Her uncle's house in Knightsbridge was a tall white town house, relatively new and very ordered inside. Her own room looked out over the street, with a large window. It was good, she had already discovered, for standing and gazing at the world. Everything looked very civilised from here. It was almost as if yesterday had never taken place.

But Roisin's mind ran over and over the details, magnifying each one.

She had made her way to the inn that the highwayman had told her about last night, her dishevelled appearance causing a furore. The parish constable had been called and Roisin coddled by the innkeeper's wife, a bored-looking woman who obviously viewed such events as high drama. The carriage, it transpired, had been found abandoned, and the connection made between it and a hysterical Aunt Milly, shrieking that her niece had been carried off by highwaymen. Roisin, after having her small wound treated by a doctor, had been reunited with her aunt at some delicate hour of the morning, only to spend the rest of the time up until breakfast trying to explain herself. It had not been easy as, in the light of day, her reasons seemed foolish even to Roisin herself.

Although she had told no one the identity of the highwayman, her driver had found the constable himself, shouting about a red-headed vagrant on the road out of town. The reward for the capture of Ewan Hamilton had been raised to fifty pounds. Remembering the thief-takers of the night before did strange things to Roisin's stomach.

Not nearly so strange, though, as the memory of his kiss.

She raised her hand to the cut on her cheek. She was clean now, her hair neatly dressed and pinned under a lace cap…but this cut told her it had really happened. Even it had already faded, healing slowly.

As did her emerald ring, sparkling newly cleaned on her finger. When eventually she had thought to check she had found it still there, wedged between her body and her linen stay. He had not, then, availed himself of the opportunity her unconscious state had provided, though he must have remembered it was there. She had not been wrong about him, it seemed. Thief though he undoubtedly was, he did have some morals.

A knock on the door of her room pulled her out of her reverie. Turning from the window, she smiled as her cousin opened it a crack and slid into the room.

'Mother said I'm not to disturb you,' she said softly, coming to stand before Roisin, 'but I have so many questions.'

Catherine Penrose was very different from the stuffy town-dweller Roisin had anticipated. She was of the same age as Roisin, but appeared much more worldly-wise. Female confidantes were not within her sphere of experience, yet she was beginning to think she had found one in this long-expected cousin. She had been given little chance to talk to the girl as yet, however, for her uncle was adamant that she should rest.

'How is Aunt Milly?' Roisin asked distractedly.

'Better.' Cathy pulled a face. 'She still spent the whole day talking of what she feared had happened to you. Mother had to frown at me several times to stop me grinding my teeth from sheer boredom. And she insisted on veal for dinner.'

Despite herself, Roisin smiled. 'I should not have behaved so. Will she be returning to Ireland?'

'On the morrow, she says. London is apparently a dangerous, hellish place, not the oasis of culture she had hoped. She wants to be away from it as soon as possible. Father is having to lend her a carriage for the whole journey to Bristol because she refuses to trust a hired driver after the trauma she has suffered!'

Roisin nodded, sorry for the angst she had caused her aunt—but wishing that she too could leave. She did not think, however, that Aunt Milly would ever be persuaded to travel with her wayward niece again.

Cathy took her cousin's hand and pulled her over to the bed.

'Enough of Aunt Milly. You must tell me all about it, Roisin. When you arrived yesterday I thought you had come straight out of the wilds. Your dress torn, your hair everywhere…it was most romantic.'

Roisin gave her a small smile. 'It didn't feel so at the time. I was very frightened for much of it.' She grimaced. 'Your mother must think I am very ill bred.'

'Never mind Mother.' Cathy sat up, face alight. She was very lovely, her blonde tresses pinned up and curling prettily around cheeks now rosy with excitement. However, Roisin was beginning to suspect that those huge blue eyes hid a mischievous soul, despite appearances. They were wide now with barely contained curiosity. 'Was he very handsome?'

Roisin dropped her gaze. 'I…could not see. He wore a mask—his face was hidden.'

Brief disappointment, then 'But he must have been, think you not? I hear highwaymen are often fine specimens of men.' Cathy paused for a moment, apparently to picture this vision. 'And he carried a pistol?'

Roisin nodded, not mentioning that so had she. It seemed wise to avoid any more trouble for the time being. Mrs Penrose would probably not welcome such an unladylike niece into her home.

'It is all so very exciting,' breathed Cathy. 'We have never been robbed. Father always avoids such roads—and now he says he will appoint an armed guard. Think of it!'

'Would that I had had such a thing,' Roisin said half-heartedly. She wondered what the highwayman would think to being discussed so—then immediately questioned this thought. She cared nothing for him. What he had done for her he had done because he had given her his word.

'I know we shall be the greatest of friends,' Cathy was saying now. 'I will introduce you to everyone, as Aunt Camilla wishes.'

Roisin smiled again, a wave of dismay washing over her. Her mother would indeed be pleased that Cathy was such a sociable girl. With any luck she would be able to marry her daughter off within the year. To a stuffy husband with a town house such as this, Roisin thought. No more open hills, no more rides with her brothers.

She hoped Ewan Hamilton was spending her money wisely.

'Roisin?'

Cathy's voice jerked her thoughts back to her body. 'Will you come?'

'Come?'

Her cousin rolled her eyes theatrically. 'I have just told you! To the theatre, tomorrow night. Drury Lane. Mr Garrick stars in *Richard III*—it is a revelation, they say. Everyone will be there and we have a box, of course—do say you will. I do so want to show you off.'

Roisin looked at her. What choice was there? 'Of course,' she said. 'I will be pleased to go.'

In the end, of course, she *was* pleased to be going. Despite her distaste for parties, Roisin had often wondered, as she read accounts of it, what it would be like to actually visit the theatre in Drury Lane. Cathy's indomitable enthusiasm had rubbed off on her, so by the time she stood before the mirror in her room, with the maid lacing up the last fastenings on her gown, she was almost excited.

It was one of her best dresses, of a rich dark green silk damask that picked out the green in her eyes and made her skin look like porcelain. It was in the fashionable sack-backed style, with a train falling behind her from the neck to the floor, skimming her skirts. Underneath it she wore her finest silk stay, a new pair of stockings—and the side-hoops that pushed out her skirts at either side of her waist. She was still a little unsure, however, about the low-cut bodice, with its ruched ribbon edging, which exposed the top half of her bosom.

She twisted first one way, then the other, checking her reflection. The maid had dressed and powdered her hair, pinning in tiny wax flowers to compliment the patterned silk of her dress. The overall effect was pleasing, Roisin decided. Her left ankle, in its high-heeled silk shoe, was still a little tender. She must try not to disgrace herself by tripping over.

'Roisin?' Cathy stuck her head around the door, then entered, grinning broadly. 'Oh, you look love-ly—you will put me to shame!'

Roisin doubted it. Cathy was herself dressed in pink silk, with lace at the cuffs of her three-quarter-length sleeves and on her bodice. Her hair too was piled up and powdered in the modern style.

'The carriage is waiting,' said her cousin. 'Shall we go?'

They were accompanied to the theatre by Cathy's mother, Mrs Penrose. She was a quiet, graceful woman who enquired after Roisin's health and care-fully avoided the subject of highwaymen as they con-versed. Cathy, holding her cousin's hand, grinned excitedly at her.

The Drury Lane Theatre was already filling with people by the time they entered, the vestibule buzzing with the murmur of many conversations.

Their cloaks were taken, and Roisin put up a hand to check her hair. She wished to appear less dishevelled this evening than on her last foray into the world. The sight of so many people filled her with a nervous fluttering. She was not used to such crowds, and was sure she would never be able to think of anything to say. Cathy, still holding Roisin's hand, grinned with excitement.

'I must introduce you to everyone.'

There followed a line of faces and names, which she knew she could not hope to remember if she met with the same people later in the evening. From the way people looked at her she was aware that her tale had been told already, along whatever grapevine of gossip that networked London. She smiled politely and remembered what she could.

Cathy knew many of the other young girls present, and seemed to have much to say to each. Roisin, at a loose end, looked around her, scanning the crowd in vain hope of a familiar face.

Across the room, someone else was standing by himself.

He was tall, taller than many men around him, and he stood with his back to the velvet-patterned wall. His dress spoke of wealth—knee-length waistcoat in deep red silk, velvet breeches, white powdered wig. His face was set as he stared into the middle distance, strong jaw clenched. Roisin nudged Cathy.

'Who is that man?'

'Man? Where?'

Roisin inclined her head in his direction.

Cathy broke into a smile. 'Oh, Kit?'

'Kit?' A man with such presence did not look like such a small name was enough for him.

'Handsome, isn't he?'

He was, Roisin reflected, possibly the most attractive man in the room; even from this distance she could see the admiring glances other ladies threw at his broad-shouldered form. The displeasure on his face somewhat spoiled the effect.

'He would be more handsome if he smiled a little,' she murmured.

Cathy nudged her. 'I'll introduce you. Come.'

They threaded their way through the crowd to where the man stood.

'Lord Westhaven!' Cathy smiled at him. 'I should have known such an evening would not pass you by!'

The man looked at them as though only just aware of their presence. For a moment he looked distant, then he gave Cathy a controlled smile. 'Miss Penrose. You look lovely this evening.'

His voice was deep, the clipped tones speaking of his impeccable breeding.

To Roisin's surprise, Cathy blushed a light pink that matched her dress perfectly. 'You are always so kind.'

Remembering Roisin, she pulled her forward. 'My lord, allow me to introduce my cousin, Lady Roisin Melville. Her father was the late Earl of Kinsale.'

Dark eyes moved to her face. Her breath stopped on the way into her lungs. He smiled again, with no hint of recognition. And yet…

'Roisin, this is Christopher, Lord Westhaven.'

Lord Westhaven. It suited this forbidding figure much more, thought Roisin, as he raised her hand to his lips in a formal greeting. 'Lady Roisin. I have heard much about you in the little time you have been with us,' was all he said. He did not seem overly interested in her—his tone was one of a man making small talk. 'I trust you are recovered?'

She inclined her head, withdrawing her hand. 'Completely, thank you, sir.'

'He was such a brute to her,' Cathy told him, eyes wide. 'Have you seen the papers?'

'It is in the papers?' Roisin was dismayed.

'Indeed.' Lord Westhaven looked, if possible, even less impressed. 'There is a touching description of the young heroine of the piece and her plight.'

Roisin felt herself turn crimson under his steady gaze. 'It was…I had not…' She trailed off, unsure of what she was trying to say. He had accused her of nothing, yet something in his tone made her feel she should be ashamed.

Cathy put a comforting hand on her arm. 'We'd

best take our seats. I trust we will meet again later, Lord Westhaven.'

He bowed formally as Roisin was led away, her thoughts in turmoil. What had the papers been saying about the incident? Had Ewan Hamilton been painted as some sort of monster? He had not harmed her in the slightest and yet… Everyone seemed to have quite a different idea of what a highwayman was like…

'Kit is not his usual cheerful self tonight,' Cathy was saying. 'I fear something is troubling him.'

Cheerful? Roisin could think of several words to describe the rather cold person that was Lord West-haven. Cheerful was not one of them. But she held her tongue as they were ushered into their box, the padded door and then the thick velvet curtain closing behind them and cutting them off from the rest of the theatre. She began to relax again, the prospect of a real play claiming her mind. Below and to either side of her people were taking their seats in boxes and in the pit, dressed in an array of colours. The women all wore dresses in the latest styles, looking far more sophisticated than those Roisin knew at home. She admired the different hairstyles as they moved below her, forgetting all else for a moment in her fascination.

'Cathy, Roisin, news!'

Mrs Penrose entered, her usually composed face flushed with whatever secret she had to tell. One look at her expression disquieted Roisin all over again. 'Lord Chief Justice Webbe is here,' she said, seating herself between them, 'and he has told several people that Ewan Hamilton is captured this very night!'

'Captured?' Roisin hardly recognised her own voice, so dry was her throat.

Mrs Penrose nodded. 'He resides at Newgate as we speak, waiting to be tried. They say he will be hanged at the next Tyburn day. If he is convicted, that is,' she added offhandedly. 'But all seem sure he will be. Indeed, how could he not?'

'Less than two weeks away!' Cathy clapped her hands excitedly. 'Roisin, you must be beside yourself with relief. Oh, Mother, can we attend? We must go to the trial as well, surely?'

Roisin did not hear her aunt's reply, for she was on her feet, muttering something about needing air. She went swiftly along the plush corridors of the theatre, down the stairs and into the vestibule, brushing past the doorman with a muttered excuse.

Outside the air was cool on her face, and the stone of the theatre supported her back as she leant against the wall. People walked past her; Drury Lane bustled with city dwellers. Roisin stood, her breathing shallow, trying to make sense of the thing she had been told.

She had been certain he would get away. He seemed so ready to deal with the dangers of his lifestyle, she had thought it natural he would be able to evade the thief-takers, desperate as they must be to bag a prize of his worth.

He was to be hanged.

She was not sure why it affected her so deeply.

No, she told herself, that was a lie. If she was going to lie to herself, what hope was there? He had been, after everything, kind to her, had risked himself to take her home. She would not wish him dead.

Roisin looked up as the main doors to the theatre swung open again with a crash and a man half-ran on to the street. She only just recognised Lord West-haven, for he was already pulling off his powdered tie-wig, looking around for a cab as he did so.

As she watched, he turned, saw her and froze, something guarded instantly awakening in his eyes. They looked at each other, each noting a certain lack of composure.

'Lady Roisin?' He advanced towards her, and she saw that his hair was actually a striking raven black, cut short as was the norm to accommodate the wigs which men wore in daily life. He ran a hand through it now, which tamed it but little.

Roisin met his eyes. 'Lord Westhaven.'

He did not seem pleased to see her. 'Are you unwell?'

She shook her head. 'I know not, sir.'

His eyes narrowed. 'You have heard Hamilton is to be hanged, then?'

She nodded. 'The whole theatre knows, it seems.'

'You do not seem overly pleased.'

Hurt, Roisin faced him. 'Why would I be pleased? I would not wish such a fate on any man.'

He looked at her for a long moment. Then he nodded, turned to leave…and stopped. He stood, seeming to hesitate—and turned back to her just as she was sure he was about to walk away. 'May I see you home?'

'Why?' she asked, before she could stop herself.

'Like myself, you seem to have lost your appetite for drama.'

Just for a moment, she smiled. 'No, thank you.' Because she could not resist, she added, 'You seem to be in a hurry to leave.'

'Nothing that cannot wait.'

Something in his eyes and in the speed of his answer told her that this was a lie. Looking into their depths, she had that feeling that she had seen this man before.

He knew. He said, 'Is something the matter?'

'Yes,' she said, although she knew she ought not. 'When we met—when I first saw you…I thought you were him. But you are not. Is that not foolish?'

For the first time, he gave her a genuine smile. He had a kind face, she thought, despite its harsh lines. 'Not foolish at all. You have endured much.'

Roisin lowered her eyes. 'You must forgive me for speaking so. I am not myself.'

He nodded a little stiffly, as though not knowing how to respond. 'And I may not escort you home?'

More than anything she wished to be away from the theatre and its curious eyes. She knew that he felt this. But he was a man she had known for minutes—and experience had taught her well what happened when one rode alone with young men.

'I should stay and see the play,' she told him. 'Thank you, sir.'

He bowed. 'Then I will take my leave.'

A carriage had drawn up across the road and he hailed it, running across the street and climbing in, wig flapping like a dead thing in one hand.

Roisin stayed outside the theatre, eyes following as the driver cracked his whip and it pulled away. It was not him. His voice was different, as was his manner. His hair was merely black, not that distracting red. It was not him.

Because he was at Newgate.

Closing her eyes momentarily, she turned and went back into the theatre.

Kit glanced backwards as the cab carried him away from Drury Lane. She was still there, back to the wall, perhaps wishing she too was far from that place. He knew how she felt, because he guessed what the encounter with Ewan Hamilton had done to her. Highwaymen were a romantic dream to women, not the harsh reality of which he was so painfully aware.

Sitting back now and tossing his hated wig at the opposite seat, he ran a hand over his face. The news of his brother's capture had brought a bolt of fear-tinged nausea to his stomach. It was like being shot.

Kit had feared such a thing would happen. The business of robbing coaches was a risky one and no criminal escaped the combined efforts of the watchmen, bailiffs and thief-takers for long.

He clenched his jaw. If there was not something he could do… The thought shut itself off in his mind. There must be, he told himself. If this damned driver ever got them to Newgate.

It seemed an eternity later that they clattered through the cobbled entrance gates, the horses drawing to an abrupt stop. Kit leapt out, paid the driver and made for the shadowy figure that waited in the entrance to the gaol. Before them the gate loomed, its spikes black and menacing in the light that came from beyond. The door was of heavy oak, held together by iron bolts. The sight filled Kit with dread.

'I wish to see the highwayman, Hamilton,' he said shortly. 'Fear not, I can pay.'

He handed over the visitors' fee and, guided by the gaoler, made his way into the depths of the prison. It was not a place he was familiar with, but he had heard the stories. The walls were damp to the touch as they proceeded, the corridors dimly lit with lamps spaced few and far between. Straw covered the floor, having overflowed from the cells. It smelled neither fresh nor clean. Every now and then Kit saw a rat scurry along the wall beside him as he walked. Eyes gleamed through the bars of the cells. Eyes of rats, and eyes of prisoners.

'Here.' The gaoler was a man of few words. He had stopped before a cell, pulled open the huge door and beckoned Kit forward. 'I'll come back for you.'

Kit stepped into the condemned cell, trying not to wince as the door swung shut behind him.

'Kit.'

His brother was manacled to the wall, but stood a little way from it, his tawny-red hair falling loosely about his face. They stood, looking at each other for a moment. The younger man's mouth lifted in a half-smile of greeting.

'Newgate is an efficient place,' he said. 'I have not been here three hours, yet they've had me on the whipping block already.'

Kit stood, silent. He could see the red smears across the back of the white shirt that his brother wore. Now he understood why he did not lean against the wall.

The younger man sighed. 'So ends the wild ride of Ewan Hamilton.'

Kit dropped his gaze.

'I'm sorry, Jamie,' he said softly.

'They would have caught me eventually,' said James Westhaven. 'Remember how Dick thought he was invincible? He ended up here, just as we all will, and it is already two years since he was hanged.'

'You are not like him.' Kit knew that Richard Turpin had not been the gentleman immortalised in the legends that already formed. 'He was an ill bred mongrel.'

'Ill bred or nay, I have done similar deeds.'

A silence. From somewhere, water dripped. Someone screamed in the depths of the prison. James's breathing was harsh and laboured.

Kit looked around him and saw there was a chair in the shadows of one corner. 'Here.' Picking it up, he took it to his brother. 'Sit.'

The younger man looked relieved as he lowered himself on to it, taking care not to brush his back against the ill-finished wood. 'My thanks.'

'Why lie you in the condemned cell?' Kit asked. 'You have yet to be tried.'

James smiled. 'They seem to be trying to tell me something. My conviction is, I think, a foregone conclusion.'

'Why say you so?'

'They took pains to assure me that this was the case.' James met his brother's eyes. 'I think they thought t'would make me more ready to confess. The coachman has identified me, they have witnesses to previous robberies and…' he met his brother's eyes '…it is by no means my first such offence.'

There was something else in his face, that he did not tell. Kit leant over him. 'And have you confessed?'

His heart seemed to stand still when the younger man shook his head.

'Thank God.'

'It makes no difference, Kit. They know it was me.'

'But it was—'

'Kit.' A pale hand grabbed him by the arm, and he did not recognise the look on his brother's face. 'They know it was me. Leave it at that.'

Kit straightened up, running a hand through his hair until it stood on end.

'We will get you out,' he said softly. 'More dangerous criminals than you have bought their pardons. That is what we will do.'

James gave a short, bitter laugh. 'Do not think I have sat idly waiting for your arrival, elder brother,' he said, not harshly. 'I have five hundred pounds to my name, and they will not take it.'

'I can raise another five,' said his brother eagerly. 'That should be far more than is—'

'Kit. I am given to believe that, in my case, there will be no way out.'

Kit froze. 'What..?' He leant heavily against the wall. Its cold clamminess did nothing to remedy his state of mind.

James's eyes were on his face.

'That's ridiculous! If we raise enough...I'll rob a mail coach.'

The younger man laughed. 'Well spoken, Kit. Then we could languish here, brothers both.'

'Why would they refuse? There was no murder!'

James sighed. 'My gaoler was kind enough to inform me that the Lord Chief Justice Webbe is a friend of the woman Roisin's uncle. He does not take kindly to the affairs of his niece becoming public gossip. They feel too many highwaymen are walking free of the law. They have, I believe, decided to make an example of me.'

'She cannot have prompted him,' Kit said quickly. 'Her reaction at the theatre...'

His brother shot him a look. 'Taken with her, were you?'

'It matters not!' Kit pushed himself away from the wall and began to pace. 'Think, Jamie, if we can raise enough money, surely—'

James smiled. 'What is not already sold?'

'The house.'

'No.' His brother was firm. 'There is not the time, and if there were...I have done this for our birthright, Kit, for Oakridge. Give me your word you will not attempt such a thing.'

'Brother, your life is—'

'Your word. Please. Do not undo these years.'

'Very well.' Kit nodded.

'And give me your word that you will come here no more.'

'I cannot!' Kit was astounded. 'You are my brother—'

'And any who see us will know it!' James shook his head. 'I sometimes think I was given all the share of brains for both of us.'

'Jamie.' Kit took his brother's head between his hands in desperation. 'You will be hanged if we cannot find a way out of here. I will go now to see Webbe— have you forgotten, Jamie, that he was a friend of our father? Colonel Penrose is not the only man in this town with influence, and by God, I will make sure—'

'And then what? You tell him who I really am— that you are brother to a criminal? You expect him to believe you had no knowledge of this? You will hang with me, as my accomplice, and then who will take care of Oakridge? And even if they believe such a foolish tale, you will bring our name into disrepute!'

'You think I care about our *name* if it will save you?'

'I care,' James said softly. 'Our father would not have wanted it that way, and neither do I.'

'Our father,' Kit began heatedly, 'was a—'

'Whatever he was,' cut in the younger man, 'he went to his grave respected. And, in a different way, so will I.'

'This is not a game!' Kit shook his head, amazed.

'Look where you are, Jamie! There is no place for chivalry here!'

'I am not a boy,' James said softly and, indeed, for a moment he looked much older than the brother who held him. 'I have had these hours to reflect. It is unmanly to scavenge so for a way out. I will die the death I deserve, as so many have done before me. I will not confess, and I will make no gaudy speech at the gallows. But I will do what any man in my place would do. These are my wishes. My *last* wishes, Kit. And you must give me your word that you will stay away.'

'I thank God that our mother did not live to see us here,' said Kit quietly.

'As do I. But we acted as we thought we must. And I do not regret my life of danger, nor the circumstances that led us here. I do not blame you for allowing me to do what I wished. But I will have your word that you will reveal to no one our relationship. And you will stay away from here.'

'Jamie!'

'Please. I have little enough control in this, at least give me your word when I ask for it.'

Anguished, Kit closed his eyes. 'You want my word? As what?'

'As a gentleman. As the man our mother raised you to be.'

Kit sighed. 'A cheap shot, Jamie.'

'But a good one, brother.'

For a moment they smiled at each other, still men who had shared a childhood, despite the turmoil around them.

'You want my word?'

'Just your word.'

'Then you have it.'

'And you will not see the Chief Justice, or be next door in the Old Bailey to see me tried and sentenced.'

'Jamie—'

'Kit.' His brother's face was a study in calm.

'Fine.' Jaw clenched, Kit straightened up. 'If you are determined to die like the stubborn dog you have always been—'

'Thank you.'

There was a long silence, in which Kit did not trust himself to speak for fear of the impotent, direction-less rage within him.

'One more thing,' said James.

'What more can you possibly ask of me?' Kit was almost beside himself. 'Must I stand here all night and make promises that I will always regret?'

'Be at Tyburn,' said James. 'I would not die alone with a crowd of strangers. But keep your head down. And bring Roisin with you. I would see her.'

For a moment Kit could not move. Then he was on his knees before his brother. 'I will be there. And I swear to you that I will not rest until our home is secure, whatever I must do.'

'Give me your word also that you will not die as I will. Do not be a fool, Kit. Whatever you do, it must not be this. Have sons for both of us.'

'One last time, I give you my word.'

'If you go back on this, I shall haunt you,' said James.

Kit smiled. 'I believe you would.'

'Now go, before I change my mind,' his brother said softly. Then, as Kit got to his feet, his face lit up in that old, wicked smile. 'Who knows, I may yet be found innocent.'

Kit paused. As their eyes met, James looked suddenly very young.

'No,' he said, barely audibly.

'What?'

'No, I cannot do it.' Kit's voice was stronger this time. 'I don't think you realise what you're asking of me, Jamie. I cannot go about my life and watch you die.'

'Kit, you just gave me your word!' Jamie raised himself painfully to his feet.

'And for anything else I would not go back on it, you know that. But you are my brother and I will not let you die when I have not even tried to save you.'

'No!' The chains strained as Jamie leant forward. 'It will not work! We will *both* die!'

'I cannot. I am sorry to ruin your fantasy of a noble death, but this is reality.' Kit strode to the door.

'Where are you going?'

'To see Webbe. I will make him see sense.'

'He is a High Court judge—he has no sense!'

'At least I will have tried.'

'And what of Oakridge?'

'Oakridge can go to the devil!'

Jamie swung out and grabbed a handful of his brother's shirt, jerking him hard round to face him. 'Tell me you do not mean that,' he said, very quietly.

At the look in his eye Kit let out a long sigh. 'Jamie. You know I would give everything for Oakridge, to see it as it was, for our children. But I cannot let you die for it. It is too much.'

'Should not I be the one to decide that?'

'What manner of brother would I be to let you? What manner of man?'

For a moment, he thought he saw tears in the younger man's eyes. 'You have always been the best of both.'

'I will not let you go to the scaffold. I must at least try. You have imposed all these conditions on me— allow me at least this, I beg you.'

Silence, as they faced each other.

Jamie sighed. 'Can you not respect my wishes?'

'You would do the same in my place and you know it.'

Another pause, then a small nod from Jamie. 'Do what you must, then, but for God's sake do not put yourself in danger. Remember you have promised me as much.'

'I will remember.'

'Goodbye, Kit.'

'Not goodbye.' Kit leant his forehead against that of his brother, black hair touching red. He closed his eyes. 'Forgive me, Jamie.'

'I will forgive you whatever you ask, as long as you keep your word.'

'Then forgive me everything.'

James slapped his brother on the back and leant out of their embrace. 'There is nothing to forgive.' He fumbled in his pocket and brought out a battered hip flask. 'Now, come. Let us drink together.' He raised the flask. 'To freedom.' He sipped deeply, sighed with satisfaction, and handed it to Kit.

'To freedom.' Kit, smiling as the old Jamie reappeared momentarily, took it and drank. It was whisky, and the taste warmed and steadied him. He handed back the flask and fixed his brother with certain eyes.

'I will see you again.'

There was something strange in Jamie's eyes as he looked at Kit. 'I dare say you will. But if it is at Tyburn, brother, pray for my soul and bury my body.' His lips curved upwards. 'If my head finds its rest on a spike outside the hanging ground, my ghost will walk for sure.'

'Do not lose hope, Jamie!'

'I never have. Now go, I have other visitors to entertain.'

Their eyes met for one last time. Then, turning, although it hurt him almost physically, Kit pounded on the door with a fist into which all his pent-up feelings flowed. It was opened by the surly gaoler. Resisting the almost overwhelming urge to put the other fist in his face, Kit strode out of the condemned cell, past the odious man, and out. He did not look back again.

Kit made his way swiftly out of Newgate, hoping Webbe would agree to see him at such an hour. He had to save Jamie's life, or live with his brother's blood on his hands for ever. He walked a few yards along the darkened street, and stopped, looking around for a cab to take him there. None was apparent. He sighed with frustration—they must all be ferrying rich, drunken fools to and from the theatre.

His head came up as a thought occurred to him, and he fumbled for his pocket watch. He had left Drury Lane but an hour ago—and had he not seen the Lord Chief Justice himself in the packed theatre? Perhaps, if he could reach him during the interval, he would allow a few moments.

It was worth a try, at least, and he did not think himself in any state to wait until the morning.

At that moment a cab appeared and Kit hailed it, clambering inside with a brief shouted instruction to the driver up on the box. Settling in his seat, Kit brushed himself down and retrieved his wig from his pocket. He must marshal his thoughts in preparation, he told himself, attempting to block out all thought of Jamie in that cold cell.

It was a short drive and Kit leapt out as soon as the carriage halted, thrusting a handful of coins at the driver and not waiting for his change. He strode through the entrance and bore down on a young usher.

'Is Lord Chief Justice Webbe here tonight?'

'I believe so, sir.'

'Has the interval begun?'

'Not yet, sir,' stammered the youth, seeming somewhat overawed by this gentleman making demands of him. 'It begins very shortly, sir.'

'Thank you.' Kit headed for the stairs that he knew led to the judge's box. Behind him he heard the youth try half-heartedly to stop him, but paid no heed. Walking along the corridor until he located the box he needed, Kit pressed his ear to the closed door. He could hear faint voices from the stage which, after only a couple of minutes, gave way to applause as the first half ended. Kit stepped back, hearing movement from within the box.

The door opened and several ladies left, chattering excitedly to themselves, the scents of powder and perfume lingering as they made their way down the corridor. They were accompanied by two gentlemen Kit did not know. He stepped forward as Justice Webbe emerged behind them.

'Your honour?'

The older man looked at him with some surprise. He was rounder and more bald than Kit remembered—but it had been some years since he had gone shooting with the late Lord Westhaven. 'Christopher Westhaven, is that you?'

'Forgive my intrusion.'

'Nonsense. Come in.' He shook the hand that Kit extended to him and retreated back into the now empty box, gesturing Kit to follow. 'I declare, you look more like your father than ever, sir. What brings you here?'

'I have a favour to ask.' Kit glanced out at the rest of the theatre, where the audience were milling about, hailing each other and proceeding outside for the interval. He spotted many people he knew, but no one seemed to have noticed him here.

'Indeed?' His late father's friend perched himself on a chair and motioned for Kit to do the same. 'Shall I have some refreshments brought up?'

'Do not trouble yourself, this will not take long.' Kit cleared his throat. 'It is about the highwayman, Ewan Hamilton.'

'Ah!' The older man grinned broadly. 'Wonderful arrest! Best since we collared that vagabond Turpin. I dare say that'll bring 'em out at the next Tyburn day, eh?'

Breathing deeply, Kit tried to quell his anger at this response. 'Quite,' was all he said.

'You don't agree?'

'That is why I am here. Hamilton is an acquaintance of mine.'

'Is he?' Bushy eyebrows rose. 'I must say I'm surprised!'

'He is not quite the man people take him to be,' Kit muttered. 'I am led to understand his request to buy his pardon has been denied.'

'Yes.' Less jovial now, Webbe fixed Kit with a beady stare. 'There's been rather too much of this skipping out on justice recently, Lord Westhaven.'

'I am given to believe that yourself and Colonel Penrose have a long history together.'

'What are you suggesting, sir? That he has asked me to use my influence somehow?'

'Of course not,' Kit said hastily. 'I meant merely to say that I understand your personal wish to see justice done in this case.'

'Indeed—and Hamilton is a notorious highwayman. That alone would be reason enough to desire his conviction. If he is pardoned, we both know what will happen—he will be back on the road within days.'

Kit leant forward. 'What if I could assure you he would not? I would stake my reputation on it. He will never be heard of again, you have my word.'

'Stake your reputation?' The older man's eyes narrowed. 'Why ever would you be willing to do that?'

'He was a friend of my father's in better days for both,' Kit said carefully. 'As, indeed, were you, sir.'

'Then your father seems to have made friends from all walks of life—some more worthy than others.'

Kit nodded. 'Indeed. It would mean much to his memory were you to assist me, sir.'

There was a pause. Justice Webbe looked faintly embarrassed. 'I suppose you were not aware that your father went to his most immortal rest owing me several thousand pounds.'

'My God,' Kit muttered before he could stop himself. He swallowed hard. 'Forgive me. I was not aware of it.' His thoughts churning, he looked down at his hands. Was the full extent of his father's ruin never to be known by his sons? How was he to deal with this latest debt? 'I can but promise you that the debt will be repaid,' he said quietly. 'It may take me some time, sir, but—'

'I don't want your money,' Webbe interrupted. Looking up, Kit saw what looked like sympathy in his eyes. 'The only reason you were unaware of it is that I have not brought it to your attention. Your father and I were friends in, as you put it, better days—I do not wish to sully that memory. I merely mention it because I do not think I owe him any more favours, even if I was willing to intervene as you suggest.'

'I see.' Kit felt his best bargaining tool dissolve before him. Cold fingers of despair clutched at his heart as he thought of Jamie, awaiting a punishment beyond all imagining. He must regroup and do his best now, with whatever presented itself. There might yet be a compromise if no pardon was granted... 'Will you be presiding over that case?' he asked softly.

'In all likelihood, yes.'

'Then, as a favour to myself—'

'Why would you presume I would grant you a favour?'

Kit's jaw tightened. 'I would not. Yet I must ask. Could you not give some other sentence than hanging? Hard labour, perhaps?'

Justice Webbe looked at him steadily. 'You are suggesting we sentence a highwayman to hard labour? How, then, do you suppose I will avoid becoming the laughing-stock of my profession?'

'Transportation, then.' Kit felt himself growing desperate and tried to keep the note of panic from his voice. 'Send him to America. He will be removed from society, unable to re-offend even if he wished to. Transportation is a viable option.'

'At whose expense?'

'At mine, if need be!'

'You have the money?' It was not said unkindly.

'I will find it.'

The older man shook his head. 'Lord Westhaven, people want to *see* justice being done. Just today I sentenced a man to death for stealing one piece of silver. What will the public think if I allow a man who has perpetrated multiple crimes to escape with any less?' Kit knew some of his inner turmoil must show in his face, for Justice Webbe sighed. 'At any rate, he has not yet been tried. It seems a little premature to be discussing the punishment of a man who may yet be found innocent.'

Kit looked levelly at him. 'I do not think either of us believe such a thing is possible.'

'Then, if the court decides—in the face, I must add, of much evidence—that he is guilty, we must do our duty to sentence him accordingly. Whether, for whatever reason, you can vouch for him if he is pardoned is of no consequence. Some criminals have too high a profile to allow such things.'

Kit spread his hands. 'Is there nothing I can say?'

'Young man, I think you have said rather too much already,' Webbe replied. 'I would not wish to see the name your father built for you tarnished, so I shall pretend I did not notice how ardent your wish to save this criminal appears to be. I shall also—and this is my favour to you—ignore any suspicions I may have that you are more involved here than you admit. I am not a fool, Lord Westhaven, but neither am I a monster. You know, as I do, that I cannot help you. Let us leave it at that.'

'Your honour—'

'May I give you some advice as a friend of your father?'

Wordlessly, Kit inclined his head.

'I suggest you say no more about it, to myself or any other person. People talk, and they will wonder exactly what your relationship is to this man. Especially as you look rather like him around the eyes.'

There was a pause. Then Kit rose to his feet. 'Thank you for respecting the spirit in which I came to you. I trust you understand why I had to try.'

'I do. But I must warn you against trying again.'

Kit met his eyes and knew he had allowed this man to see too much to risk going anywhere else. 'Thank you for seeing me. I apologise for interrupting your evening.'

'Not at all. I trust I will not see you in court?'

'You will not.'

Exchanging a brief handshake, Kit left the box and walked with haste down the corridor, eager to put as much distance between it and himself as possible. He felt physically sick. He had not saved his brother, after all his rash promises at Newgate. And Justice Webbe had as good as told him that he suspected who Ewan Hamilton really was… He must trust to the older man's honour that he would say nothing.

Kit stopped abruptly as he caught sight of his reflection in one of the ornate, gilt-framed mirrors that were everywhere in this frivolous place. He did not see that, for once, his wig was perfectly straight and that the set of his chiselled jawline only emphasised his dark good looks. He saw only what Webbe had seen, a dark brown gaze and well-formed brows: *rather like him around the eyes.*

This was what he would see every time he looked in the mirror, then. Jamie looking back at him. Reminding him of how he had failed.

Unable to look any longer, he turned and made his way down the staircase, blind to his surroundings and deaf to any greetings as people passed him, taking their seats once more for the second half. So it was that when he crashed headlong into a lady coming the opposite way he had to grab her by the arms to avoid knocking her over altogether.

'I'm sorry—'

He broke off, realising the woman before him was Roisin Melville. He removed his hands from her as if she had burned him.

'Lord Westhaven.' Eyes wide with surprise, she looked up at him.

For a long moment, his eyes bored into hers, as a hundred things raced through his mind; a hundred possibilities and regrets, all discarded in an instant. For a second at least, all that registered in his scarred consciousness was that she was very beautiful. He wished, without knowing quite why, that it had not been her involved in this mess—that she had not been the last woman Ewan Hamilton had robbed, the cause of his undoing.

Then he brought himself roughly to his senses.

With a muttered 'Excuse me', Kit stepped around her and fled the theatre as though the devil himself was at his heels.

Behind him Roisin leant back against the wall, open mouthed, and watched him go.

Chapter Four

Ewan Hamilton was tried at the Old Bailey the following week. News of the verdict flew through town minutes after it had been passed. It was told from mouth to mouth, travelling through London until it reached Kit, with a knock like the hand of Death himself at his library door.

He turned from the book he had been pretending to read. 'Come in.'

With agonising slowness, the doorknob turned and John Farham stepped into the room. He was a tall, well-built man a little younger than Kit, and had been his manservant for many years now. In fact, friend was a better word. Had he not paid John's wages, Kit would have called him that always. It was this man whom he had trusted to attend the trial and report back. Although he, with the rest of London, knew what the verdict would almost certainly be, a thin thread of hope had kept him dangling all morning.

'Well?' His throat was dry. It made his voice sound ragged.

John's hazel eyes told him before his lips could. 'Guilty.'

Kit's chest tightened. 'Did she give a statement?'

John shook his head. 'She was not there. Gossip is that her uncle prevented it. He does not want her to undergo such a public ordeal. That the coach-driver gave his evidence was enough.' He paused. 'The judge sentenced him to hang.'

'When?'

'A week hence, at Tyburn.'

Kit sat very still, realising he was unable to speak as everything receded into a fuzzy blur at the corners of his consciousness. John said something that he did not hear, then a glass of whisky was pushed into his hands. He drank it in one draught. Its warmth spread through him and, slowly, the world returned. John was watching him. Kit took a deep breath.

'How did he take it?'

'He bore it well. He did not look ashamed.'

'And how has he been treated? Does he look ill?'

John paused. 'Not ill, exactly. Perhaps one could say more…' He trailed off, at a loss, hazel eyes troubled.

Kit's hand tightened around the glass he held. 'Be honest with me, John.'

There was a pause. The younger man said, 'The

effects of Newgate are visible. If I had not known it was Jamie before me, I would not have recognised him.'

Kit looked up for the first time. 'You look like you could do with a drink yourself. Did you manage to see him before the trial?'

John nodded. 'There were a great many people in his cell—I do not think anyone noticed me overly. He read the note you sent and sent this back.' He handed Kit a grubby piece of paper, unsealed, and sighed heavily. 'I think I will have a drink.'

He poured them both a double measure as Kit read his brother's hasty scrawl.

Kit,

You have not failed me—do not think it for a moment. I know you have done all you can, but some obstacles are insurmountable. I go to the death that fate has allotted me with no bitterness, and nothing but love for you, and the greatest relief that you are safe.

Remember always your promises. You must do all you can to keep our home—but for the one thing that landed me here. Secure Oakridge, fill it with sons who bear our name, and I will rest easy.

Forgive me, my beloved brother, for it all, and do not think to blame yourself. I do what I do out of

love—and, of course, the stubborn belief that I am right. I will see you on Tyburn Monday.
God be with you always,
  Jamie

Kit let the letter fall and took the glass John offered him. 'He does not say "I told you so",' he said, attempting a smile. 'I suppose I should be thankful for that.'

John smiled. 'I think he was amazed you had escaped with your life.'

'Fortunately for me Webbe is a reasonable man.' Kit drained his glass a second time. 'Part of me wishes he had not been so kind.'

'Well…' John's tone was bracing '…I, for one, am glad he was. I do not relish the thought of finding another job.'

Kit gave him a half-smile that died almost immediately. 'I will need you with me at Tyburn.'

'I had not assumed otherwise.'

His master plucked Jamie's note from the floor and stared at it a while. 'How I will find the courage to attend I do not know,' he said quietly. 'God knows where my brother gets his.' Taking a deep breath, he rose to his feet. 'Come, John. There is much to organise.'

Roisin heard the news via her uncle, who had attended the trial. He seemed satisfied with the result, saying repeatedly that justice had been done. She was grateful to him for sparing her the horrors of telling her tale in front of a court that included Ewan Hamilton himself. Yet she was not glad at the verdict. Far from it, in fact. She had wept into her pillow that night, wishing that she could have helped him. Her testimony would only have damned him—she could say nothing without admitting that, yes, he had robbed her, he had carried her off. She only wished she could have told them that it was another man. But the man who had driven her on that night had identified him.

All she could do was lie awake, regretting her idiocy at running away, her foolish decision to shoot him—which she had confessed to no one—and ever coming to England at all.

So it was that she was pale and quiet at breakfast the next morning, picking over her food as everyone else made conversation. She kept feeling his kiss, over and over again, inside her head. She wanted to leap from her chair, knock over the breakfast table and run screaming into the street that this was all wrong—that she was sure he was a good man; that he did not deserve to hang. But it would do no good. They would say she was hysterical with shock, that the experience had damaged her. So she lowered her eyes and sipped half-heartedly at her tea, her mind in limbo.

Her attention was drawn back to the table when a maid entered, bearing the morning post on a silver tray. There were a couple of letters for the Colonel, one for Mrs Penrose—and one for Roisin. Surprised, she took it, breaking the unfamiliar seal.

'Well?' Cathy was expectant, watching Roisin's face. 'Who is it from? An admirer, perhaps? A prospective suitor?'

Wordlessly, Roisin handed her the letter. She did not quite know what to think.

'It is from Kit! He is going to the hanging, and he wants us to go with him,' Cathy told her parents, nudging Roisin expectantly. 'Will we go? Do say we will, Roisin. You must see this to its close.'

Roisin was silent. Suddenly she wanted more than anything to attend the hanging. It would be unimaginable, she knew that—but something in her told her that she had to see Hamilton again, if only to stop herself from thinking the thoughts she had about him. She needed to see him in broad daylight, for the criminal he was, she told herself firmly. It was not because she wanted to look into those eyes again.

'I would like to attend,' she said to Cathy. 'If you will come with me, of course.'

'I certainly will!' Cathy replied. 'It is all so exciting! We must write directly after breakfast and take up Kit's offer.'

Roisin nodded. She wondered what had prompted him to suggest they go together. Perhaps Cathy was right and he was drawn by the spectacle, preferring to see it with others. But she remembered their meeting outside the theatre at Drury Lane, and, later, how he had stared at her inside. He seemed to understand the way she felt, and something had certainly upset him that night. She could not imagine him watching a hanging with heartless relish.

Perhaps she should just take the letter at face value—a kind offer by a friend of her cousin. He did seem to know Cathy well, after all, despite his somewhat strange behaviour towards herself.

She would reply with her thanks, and take up the offer. She would be grateful to have them both with her at any rate, for something told her it would not be as gay as Cathy seemed to think.

In fact, she had a feeling it would be quite the opposite.

The day of the hanging dawned bright and clear, in perfect irony for all concerned. Roisin, in a grey-patterned dress that expressed her mood, sat with Cathy in the parlour and waited for Lord Westhaven to arrive. Nerves clawed at her stomach, as they had all morning—and all the night before. She had not been able to stand the sight of her breakfast, just about managing the cup of tea that had been set before her. She watched as the clock dragged its hands past each minute in turn, half-listening to her cousin as she excitedly wondered what the day would bring. Cathy had never been allowed to attend such an event before, it seemed. Roisin was not surprised. She was not sure now that she wished to see today through in the company of a stranger, but she supposed they would have been unable to attend without Lord Westhaven's escort. He would be discreet, at least. He seemed that sort of man.

His knock rang through the house at precisely the time he had said he would arrive, not a minute either side. Cathy jumped up to greet him, doing all the talking in the familiar, chatty way that she adopted with him.

Roisin followed them outside as he handed Cathy into his carriage. Her cousin was thanking him effusively for inviting them, eyes sparkling as she settled herself within. Roisin waited on the steps of the house, hands clasped a little too tightly for ease.

He glanced up at her and bowed slightly. 'Good morning, Lady Roisin.'

He looked as she felt, she realised with a jolt, though he was trying to appear cheerful. She wondered again why he had wished to attend the hanging.

'Lord Westhaven.' She inclined her head. 'I trust you are well.'

'Quite, thank you.' He did not seem it. 'I must apologise for my behaviour at the theatre. I had some urgent business to conduct—I was preoccupied, and I fear I was rude.'

'There is no need,' said Roisin. She had not realised

business could cause a man to look as he had looked that night. Today, however, he seemed more composed—though no less distant—so perhaps whatever had troubled him was at an end. 'I…um…trust everything is resolved?'

He nodded stiffly. 'It is.'

'Thank you again for your kindness in escorting us,' she began, but he waved her aside with a dismissive hand.

'I was planning to attend already—it is no inconvenience.' He evidently felt the keenness of her gaze, for he added, 'I have an interest in matters of the law,' by way of explanation. 'I wished to see the infamous Ewan Hamilton for myself. Morbid curiosity, perhaps.'

She nodded. 'Nevertheless, it was thoughtful of you.'

He said no more, offering her his hand to help her into the carriage as he had done with Cathy, who now waited impatiently.

They started off at last, Cathy prattling incessantly. Lord Westhaven was outwardly attentive as she told him snippets of gossip about people whom Roisin did not know (and about whom, she suspected, he cared just as little). However, he was subdued, so much so that Cathy, in the middle of a conversation, broke off to enquire, 'Are you quite well, Kit? You look shocking.'

Despite her mood, Roisin swallowed a smile. Trust Cathy to be so blunt. Her presence certainly cheered things, if nothing else.

He also appeared to be amused. 'As you ask, I have been feeling a little off colour. Something I ate, perhaps.'

'You poor thing.' Cathy was all feminine concern. 'You must get more rest, Kit.'

'It seems to be going around,' was all he said. Roisin felt his eyes on her.

Conversation ceased. Roisin longed to close her eyes, but did not wish to be rude. Instead she looked out at the passing houses, and the growing number of pedestrians.

'We must walk from here,' Lord Westhaven explained as the carriage drew up. 'The crowds will make it impossible to drive.'

Roisin looked out at the packed street. 'They are all going to see the hanging?'

Cathy laughed. 'Of course. Tyburn Mondays are national holidays, Roisin. Everyone comes out to join the throng.'

They alighted from the carriage and joined the crowd, who were all headed in the same direction. They filed into a huge yard, two sides of which were taken up with the large spectator stand where the more affluent viewers bought seats. The scaffold stood eighteen feet high at the centre of everything, with people thronged about it at ground level, talking loudly and excitedly.

'This way.' Lord Westhaven placed a hand at the elbow of each cousin and guided them towards the grandstand. They mounted it by way of steps, until they found a spot where the three of them could sit comfortably. Roisin was amazed to see how many well-dressed, wealthy people were present there, their faces as flushed with excitement as the common folk below them. She began to feel even more uncomfortable.

The gallows below them stood alone, the hangman smoking his pipe and leaning against one of the posts, uninterestedly eyeing the crowd. It was huge, the top a triangle formed of three beams, each supported where they met by a post that reached to the ground. Although she had never beheld anything like this, Roisin knew that several men were often hanged at once. She suddenly wished she had not come. She did not wish to see men die, even faceless criminals. She swallowed hard.

Down in the main yard she could see entertainers—jugglers and clowns—amusing the throng until the hangings began. Men with carts moved among them also, selling gin and what appeared to be rotten apples. It was like a festival.

'Quite a spectacle, isn't it?'

She turned her head. Lord Westhaven did not look like he relished the sight either.

'Do people like to watch men die?'

'Of course.' He smiled ironically. 'The eight or so annual Tyburn days are the height of London culture. Just look at your cousin.'

Roisin looked. Cathy was gazing around her eagerly, obviously excited by the admittedly electric atmosphere. She could not be thinking about what everyone was really here for, surely? No one could. They were just caught up in the excitement. Weren't they?

Suddenly there was a change in the crowd—everyone looked towards the roadway that was being kept clear for the carts bearing the prisoners. Sure enough, here came the first, a cart containing three young men, all beside themselves with fear, by the looks on their faces. They were horse thieves, from the shouting that was going on below—the deputies of the Country Sheriff telling the crowd who was who. A chaplain walked before the cart, reciting prayers. A few apples were thrown at him.

The cart reached the scaffold, where it was driven underneath the gallows. The men, their hands bound, had their faces covered with white cloth bags. Nooses were placed around their necks and Roisin caught her breath. The crowd was cheering. The hangman prepared them, checking the ropes and fussing around them. Then, at his signal, the driver of the cart cracked his whip and it was drawn swiftly forward, out from under the feet of the thieves. The ropes tightened as, one by one, they fell.

Roisin put her hands over her eyes to block out the sight as the crowd laughed at the 'dancing' men.

'Oh, God,' she murmured. He would meet that same fate. She could not bear it.

'Are you all right?' Lord Westhaven's hand was on her arm. 'Do you want to leave?'

She shook her head, eyes firmly meeting his, turned away from the scaffold. 'I'm fine.'

Bizarrely, she could have sworn she saw relief on his face. Or perhaps it was her confused brain, dizzy now with the heat and the noise.

Cathy's eyes were wide as she beheld the spectacle. 'It is not as I imagined,' she said softly. She did not look distressed, just a little taken aback.

Prisoner after prisoner came out to be hanged. Some seemed popular with the crowd, who cheered them as they processed. Others had apples and other rotting fruit thrown at them, accompanied with jeers. Roisin wanted to be at home, far from this place.

You wanted to attend, she told herself firmly. It was as Cathy said—she must see this thing through to its end. If it ever would end.

At last, an announcement came from below that here came the highwayman, Ewan Hamilton. A cheer went up from the waiting crowd. Knights of the road were the most popular prisoners, it seemed, garnering respect even from their fellow criminals. Roisin, feeling Lord Westhaven tense beside her, craned her own neck to see the cart.

And there he was.

His shoulder-length red hair was tied back as before, his face now unhidden by any mask. Even from this distance she could see it was him. His eyes, his mouth, all were the same. His hands were bound behind his back, yet he stood erect in the cart, head held at a proud angle. No one threw rotten fruit at this prisoner.

He was dressed in a scarlet waistcoat and a three-pointed hat with matching trim. There was lace at his cuffs and at his collar, as there had been that fateful night. Roisin smiled, remembering.

His eyes searched the crowd, even as he was drawn along, his head turning from one side to the other. Then he looked up at the spectator stand, past Roisin for a second—and then directly at her. He smiled.

She felt herself weaken as his eyes met hers. He was going to his death, and she must watch it, when it was partly—no, more than partly—her fault. Her breath caught in her throat. He did not look away.

Roisin felt hands on her shoulders. She looked around to see Lord Westhaven close behind her, his face grave. She was grateful for his support.

The cart drew closer to the gallows, coming at last to stand in place beneath the scaffold. Lord Westhaven's grip tightened on her shoulders. The hangman moved toward him, linen bag in hand. Ewan Hamilton, stepping forward, removed his hat and bowed low, to the delight of the crowd. Several ladies near the front threw flowers. He gave them that wide smile, then, looking up at Roisin again, winked broadly. Behind her she thought she heard Lord Westhaven make a small sound in his throat.

The smile Ewan wore faded slowly as he looked up at her. For a moment she thought there was fear in his eyes. It was gone as quickly as it had appeared.

Then the highwayman placed the bag over his head, and the noose around his neck. Roisin held her breath, her chest constricting in horror at what happened before her.

The horse was whipped. The cart flew out from under him, and his body fell into nothing. Roisin could not tear her eyes away this time. The sight, she thought, would invade her thoughts and haunt her dreams forever afterwards.

In the whirl of noise and the crush around her she found that tears were running down her face. Her hands were on her shoulders, gripping those of the man who stood behind her. She pulled herself free, turning away from the gallows, towards Lord West-haven. He was not looking at her, eyes still fixed on the scene below.

His face was ashen.

As she stared at him, he turned his head and met her anguished gaze. For a moment they looked at each other. Out of nowhere, she wanted to be in his arms, sheltered from the cheering and the screams. He seemed unable to move, however.

'Lord Westhaven?' For a moment her own grief was forgotten. He looked near collapse.

With a visible effort, he came back to himself. 'Forgive me. I had not expected…' His voice trailed off. Looking around for Cathy, Roisin saw her standing a couple of feet away, crying quietly. She looked over and met Roisin's eyes.

'He was very handsome, after all,' she said quietly.

'Yes.' Roisin took her hand. 'Come, Cathy. Let's go.'

Her cousin nodded mutely, and Roisin was about to voice their request to Lord Westhaven when a tall, broad-shouldered man drew near, shoving his way through the crowd. He had lost his wig and his light brown hair was mussed and sweaty. He grabbed Lord Westhaven by the shoulder.

'Kit. We have to go.' He noticed the women standing, watching, acknowledging them with a nod. 'James has had an accident. They sent me to get you.'

Lord Westhaven stared at him as if he had accosted them in a foreign language. He was very still.

'What kind of accident?' Cathy recovered her tongue for all of them. 'Is it serious?'

'Something to do with his horse.' The brown-haired man looked fraught. 'Kit. We can lose no time.'

'All right.' Lord Westhaven came back to himself and took each woman by the arm. 'My carriage will see you home. I will go with John. I'll take you back to—'

'Kit, there isn't time!'

'You go on ahead. I'll follow.'

John hesitated. Then, shrugging, he strode off again, elbowing people out of the way with little regard for their displeasure. Roisin and Cathy followed Lord Westhaven as he, too, began to force his way back the way they had entered. The grandstand was packed, but they were able to thread their way through the rows of benches and on to ground level.

It was here that they experienced a problem. People were packed into the yard, waiting to see the next hanging. They jostled each other, not taking kindly to the three people shoving through haphazardly. Lord Westhaven grabbed each lady by her hand, trying to keep them all together as the tide of bodies moved either side.

A huge man moved in front of Roisin. She found herself cut off, wrenched free from Lord Westhaven's hand, being carried in the opposite direction by people pressing forward for a better view. She caught a glimpse of Lord Westhaven as he disappeared.

'Stay there!' he shouted.

She nodded, wondering, as he and Cathy disappeared, how exactly she was supposed to do that. The crowd was like an entity all itself, moving constantly, with people rubbing up against her from all sides. A woman, her face painted garishly, almost pushed Roisin over as she threw herself forward into the fray. Before them the gallows was being prepared for the next hanging.

Roisin could not breathe. The smell of sweat and liquor was all around, stifling her senses. She tried to exert some force on the bodies around her, to go in the right direction, but at times she was turned right round just from the sheer force of people pressing, moving, against her. She began to lose her bearings.

In the end she did the best she could to do what he had said. It was like treading water, moving from side to side to let the crowds pass her by, trying to stay in one place. There were shouts around her as another criminal was rolled, in his cart, beneath the scaffold. A man, raising his arm to gesture, caught her across the face with his elbow. Pain rippled across her cheek. One hand to her (surely splintered) jaw, she tried to make herself as small as she could.

Someone grabbed her arm. Startled, she tried to wrench free. The grip was fierce and, turning, she saw why. Lord Westhaven was standing behind her. He smiled wryly.

'Do you want to remain here so badly, then?'

'No!' She turned as much as she could to face him. 'Get me out!'

He stood like a man chest-deep in mud, bodies surging around him, as if considering the best course of action. Then he reached for her waist.

Roisin knew a second before it happened what he was going to do.

She cried, 'No!'

But it was too late. Picking her up, he hoisted her over his shoulder in the same way she had seen the coalman do to one of his sacks. One arm curved up her back, the other rested under her buttocks, as he shoved his way forward. Roisin, terrified that he would drop her from his great height, held on to his shoulders and prayed.

It was easier this way, she found. People made way for them—some even shouted lewd comments after them. Grimly, he carried on.

Gradually they emerged from Tyburn, on to the streets where the crowd was less.

'Please,' begged Roisin in his ear, 'put me down before you do yourself an injury!'

He did so, sliding her body down his until her feet touched the ground. Roisin found herself looking up into his face, very close. He was out of breath, his wig crooked, showing hair underneath the same shade of black, but shorter. She felt hands on her waist, steadying her, yet somehow she was unable to take her eyes from his face. A tingling passed through her as his dark gaze took in her dishevelled state, and she found herself oddly short of breath. He still held her close, partly through necessity as the crowds pushed past, partly for a reason she suspected had nothing to do with their situation. His eyes were bottomless, drawing her in, until, dizzy from his proximity, she blinked hard and, unaware of her action, shook her head slightly.

'Are you well, Lady Roisin?' he asked, and for a moment she could see nothing except how his lips formed themselves around the words.

Then—remembering his hands on unseemly parts of her body as he had carried her—she abruptly came to her senses, realised she was still most unnecessarily pressed against his chest…and was suddenly mortified. Dropping her eyes, she pulled away.

'I can walk unaided from here, thank you.'

'A fine way to thank your saviour.' His voice held no mirth, but his eyes showed the shadow of a smile. 'The carriage is this way.' He propelled her before him, and they reached it in no time.

Cathy was hanging out, despite the protestations of the driver, looking for them. When she saw Roisin she cried out with joy, 'Thank God! Are you all right?'

'Fine.' Roisin turned to Lord Westhaven, unable to quite look at him. 'Thank you, sir.'

He nodded, and she noticed he was distractedly massaging the top of his arm with one hand.

'Have I hurt you?' she said, concern leaping into her eyes.

For a moment he looked puzzled, then followed

her gaze and dropped his hand. 'It is nothing, I assure you. You weigh very little.'

Suddenly shy, she lowered her eyes. When she looked up again, his man was at his side.

'I must go,' he said, his expression clouding over. 'My brother…'

'I hope nothing serious has occured,' she offered.

'My thanks.'

She reached up then, without thinking, to straighten his wig. He caught her hand on its way back to her side and their eyes met once more. He looked indescribably sad, just for an instant. Her heart contracted as misery, momentarily forgotten, flooded back. His thumb moved against the soft skin of her palm.

Roisin's lips parted, but, before she could say another word, he was gone.

She stood, gripping the door of the carriage for support—a rock in a surging sea of humanity. It seemed for a moment that all but she were filled with life.

Cathy was urging her to get in. She pulled herself up into the carriage and slumped on to a seat. Cathy pulled the door shut and knocked on the roof for the driver. They started forward, slowly, through the crowd.

Roisin was out of breath. Her hair was loose down her back and her dress was torn, the hem ripped from where someone had stood on it. She was too shocked by the hanging, and her irrational reaction to Lord Westhaven's rescue, to feel anything but the most extreme exhaustion. Her limbs felt heavy, as did her head.

'Thank goodness Kit was with us.' Cathy was staring at the crowds. 'Imagine if we had been alone!'

Her cousin could not answer.

'That was awful,' said Cathy quietly, after a reflective pause. 'He was so brave. And it made no difference, in the end. He died the same way they all did.' She held out a hand to Roisin as her cousin's face crumpled. 'Oh, I'm sorry. I did not mean to—'

She left her seat and came across to Roisin's side of the carriage, face pale, arms outstretched.

They held each other all the way home.

Hours later, under the trees that gave Oakridge its name, Kit found himself piling the last spadeful of earth upon his brother's grave. Beside him John stood silently, eyes fixed on his master's face. Kit stepped back and surveyed the mound. His expression showed nothing of the turmoil that must be within, but suddenly, to the man who had known him long, he looked ten years older.

'He is at peace now,' John said, feeling the helplessness of such a statement even as he made it.

Kit did not like to think of his last glimpse of his brother. The hanging had been worse than he had imagined. The way the smile on Jamie's face had faded as his eyes shifted from Roisin to Kit, and realised that they looked their last… Only the need to protect Roisin—both from the crowd and from the truth—had held him together. He had kept his promise. Jamie had looked into her face. And he, Kit, had stopped her from being trampled, which was a blessing in itself.

But the memory of events once she was safely delivered to her carriage chilled him.

It had all been so undignified: the rush to the gallows, the money they had handed over to the men who were supposed to dispose of the body…transporting Jamie home in a covered cart. Death should not be this way.

Kit sighed. At peace. He hoped so.

A deep sigh from his manservant broke the silence and Kit, glancing at him, put a hand on his shoulder. 'Forgive me. I forget in my selfishness that you mourn him too.'

John, who had seen both brothers grow up even as he had become a man himself, smiled at his friend. 'He died like the gentleman he was.'

'He was carried away by ideals—he didn't know what he was doing,' Kit said quietly.

'He knew,' John replied.

Kit shook his head. 'I should have sold the wretched house. I should have tried harder. There must have been a way—'

'There was nothing you could do. He knew that. He wanted you to live.'

'How are you so sure?' Kit's raised voice echoed off the trees. 'Why must you always have such faith in me, John? How can he make such a choice for me? I should have done…something more! And now he is dead—and for what? I am no nearer to extricating myself from this damnable mess!'

There was a long silence. The trees above them rustled in a breeze that Kit barely felt. His mouth was dry.

'Forgive me,' he said.

'For what?' John gave him a half-smile.

'You know what it is to lose everything. And you bear it with such dignity.'

He spoke the truth, for John had been a rich merchant's son until his family had fallen on hard times and he had come to Oakridge as manservant to its heir.

'You helped me when fate robbed me of my inheritance,' John said softly. 'I would not see the same happen to you. You will find a solution, Kit. As Jamie knew you would.'

Kit closed his eyes, ashamed of his outburst. He had enough to contend with without making an enemy of his only friend into the bargain.

'He should be buried in hallowed ground,' he muttered.

'He lies in the land he loved,' was the gentle reply. 'What ground could be more hallowed?'

Kit looked at his manservant. 'You are right, of course. But at this moment the knowledge gives me little pleasure.' He sighed. 'I thank God no one was present at Tyburn who would recognise my brother for who he really is. You saw no one, either?'

John shook his head. 'You know how Jamie shunned polite society.'

Kit knew indeed. His brother had had many friends, but all common-born. He had always hated balls and parties, not to mention the theatre and other such outings, preferring an evening at a roadside tavern to any of the events Kit had tried—and failed—to make him attend. He would be surprised if anyone in the circles he mixed in would be able to put the West-haven name to his younger brother's handsome face.

But they had cheered him. Even in his grief, Kit had felt a stab of pure pride for the way his little brother had gone to his death—the wicked smile, the wink to Roisin. Jamie had died as he had hoped he would have the courage to. For that Kit was glad—if such a word could be used under such circumstances.

'I have carried out your instructions,' John told him, breaking the silence. 'In a few days the tale will spread through town that a hunting accident has claimed the life of James Westhaven. With luck no one will make the connection.'

'You are a true friend,' Kit told him. 'Forgive my ungratefulness. I only hope I can play my part convincingly.' He dropped his gaze and for a moment looked indescribably weary. 'I think I shall stay clear of society for a while.'

'It has been a long day.' Reaching out, John removed the spade from his master's hand. 'You should rest a while.'

Kit nodded. 'You are right once more.' He began to walk away, towards the house, then turned. 'My thanks again for your support, John.'

The other man inclined his head. 'I wish it were not needed.'

'As do I.'

Kit's body ached all over as he walked up the grassy slope to the magnificent white-stone building that was Oakridge House. He loved his home as much as Jamie had… Yet how could he live on here, thinking what his brother had sacrificed?

By making a sacrifice of his own, it seemed. Kit's mind roamed back across the past few days to rest on the promises—seemingly unending—that he had made at Newgate. Firstly, attending the hanging. Well, he had done that, and it had almost killed him. But he had done what he said he would—Jamie's body lay safe in the earth.

Secondly, that he would not die in the way James had. That meant no more money was to be gained by illegal means. He could not pick up where his brother had left off.

Thirdly, that he would protect Oakridge: pay the debts that their father had left them and ensure that there was money to upkeep the house.

If you go back on this I shall haunt you. Kit heard again the voice of his brother, more than half-serious. He would find a way to get the money.

Since their father had died and the huge extent of his gambling debts became known, the brothers had made this vow, to themselves and each other. They would not see their family home sold, they swore. So Jamie had taken to the highways as Ewan Hamilton. He had lasted longer than many. Kit felt a twist of hopelessness as he thought about it. As heir to Oakridge he had been provided for by his father—but the money lay tied up in trust until his birthday two years hence. Kit knew not how he would survive until that date. That had been their plan—to pay the debts so the trust money would not be endangered. And they had nearly succeeded.

And now… Kit closed his eyes. He almost wished sometimes that the house would be sold. It hung around his neck like a necklace of guilt which he had woven for himself. Like a noose.

He leant against the pillar topped with a stone acorn that stood at the bottom of the stairs up to the house. He could no more sell this place than he could sell a part of his own body, he knew that. But it was a house that was best when echoing with many voices. In his childhood it had been so—Jamie and himself had raced between the suits of armour; had hidden beneath antique tables...

Kit froze as a thought came upon him.

Family. That was where the key to this problem lay. Or, more specifically, with a wife. London was filled with rich, single, young women. He would marry money, as the rest of his generation seemed to do. As he should have, perhaps, years ago.

Jamie had flatly refused to do such a thing, of course, any time they had talked about it. They had both seen what a sham their parents' marriage had been, the late Lord Westhaven having married his wife much more for her fortune than her dark beauty. Though they had been but boys when their mother died, they had seen with hindsight the way she had withered under Lord Westhaven's treatment of her. Lonely and unfulfilled, she had nursed an increasing contempt of her husband—while he carried on with a score of mistresses increasingly ill concealed from his growing sons. Thinking about it, Kit found it more than slightly miraculous that society as a whole had not realised what manner of man the late Lord Westhaven had been.

No, that was a tale for him alone to tell, now. As if he ever would, to anyone.

Jamie had known full well that to marry for love was probably more unusual than to marry for convenience. Yet when the need for money arose for the Westhaven brothers, he had preferred a life of danger and mystery. Like his brother, Kit had not wished to give up the chance of happiness with a wife he loved in order to marry one he did not. They both had looked forward to their sons exploring Oakridge as they had done.

Kit frowned. Now it seemed they had been idealistic and naïve, and that chasing a fairy tale had cost Jamie his life. Now there was no other way. He must either enter a loveless marriage or lose his home, though he had watched others do it and swore he never would.

He knew, also, without really exploring his thought processes, who would be the perfect woman for such a marriage.

Roisin Melville.

The thought of her as his wife did not displease him. There was something about her that made him feel…he knew not how. With a stirring of arousal deep in the pit of his stomach, he remembered her when he had pulled her from the crowd—hair loose, eyes huge, dress rumpled… An island of loveliness in a river of pain. And the way she had looked at him suggested that she was not immune to him as a man.

He suspected marriage to her would not be such a

chore, once they got to know one another, for she was beautiful, indeed, but also unlike the twittering women it was his displeasure to know on the social circuit. She was from Ireland—used to country living—perhaps she would find Richmond and Oakridge to her liking.

Yet, could he woo her? Could he bring himself to profess love to a woman he barely knew, and expect her to believe him? Could he drag her into this mess, with all the secrets and unsaid things that lurked in every corner of his home?

Kit saw again his brother's face on the scaffold and knew the answer. It seemed he had little choice. He must do whatever it took to keep his word.

He would marry Roisin.

Chapter Five

It was one week now since the hanging. Roisin had slept late every morning and lain still when awake, eyes fixed glazedly on the light falling through the closed curtains. She had not wished to see anyone. If she shut her eyes the whole scene played itself out before her, every detail fixed in her mind. She could not forget the eyes of the condemned man boring into hers. He looked at her as if he had never seen her before. And yet, it was him.

She had wanted to stay in her room, hiding. Read a little, perhaps sleep a little. At first they had let her do this, and no one had bothered her in the aftermath of the hanging. Mrs Penrose had seemed content to have Roisin sit by her in the study, sewing or reading and talking seldom, while Cathy called on friends. But today, after Roisin had breakfasted alone in her room, Cathy had sought her out, had cajoled her until she agreed to an outing. There was no use in moping, she said, it had been long enough. Roisin must get some fresh air into her, forget about the horrors of Tyburn day. Secretly, despite her tears at the end, Roisin suspected that her cousin had rather enjoyed the spectacle. But she had relented.

So they had borrowed Colonel Penrose's carriage and spent the morning shopping. Cathy had treated herself to a new pair of gloves and a pair of satin slippers to go with her latest fashionable gown. Roisin, admiring the lovely things in the shops and giving her opinion dutifully, wished she could go home.

It was only as they stopped for tea and cakes in an airy tearoom filled with grand-looking people that she started to think less of herself. They had been eating scones and cream when Cathy spied some friends entering. She had excused herself, gone over to greet them—and returned with wide, serious eyes.

'Roisin.' She seated herself with a thump, one hand coming across the table to clasp her cousin's. 'There is the most awful news. James Westhaven is dead.'

'Dead?' Roisin frowned. She remembered Kit's face at the hanging, the grey colour of his skin as he beheld events. Then, as the news had arrived about his brother's accident, his hasty retreat. Something had seemed very wrong, but this?

'I have just had it from Felicia Stephenson. A riding accident last week—it is all over town, they say. There was no fancy funeral, he was buried quietly at Oakridge Park.'

'Oakridge Park?'

'Kit's family seat in Richmond.' Cathy's face crumpled in concern. 'Poor Kit. No wonder there has been no word from him lately. He must be distraught. I had never dreamed…'

Roisin nodded. She remembered with a wave of sympathy the pressure of his hands on her shoulders, supporting her. Her wordless grief for a criminal she had hardly known now seemed so foolish next to this—a man losing his brother.

'What manner of man was he?' she asked.

Cathy shook her head. 'I know not. I met him only once, several years ago. He was not often in society.' She lowered her eyes. 'I do not even recall his face. But he was uncommonly close to his brother, by all accounts. Roisin, do you think we should call on Kit?'

'No.' Roisin thought of her own desire to be alone. 'He would not wish to be disturbed. We could write, perhaps, expressing our condolences.'

'You are right.' Cathy sighed heavily. 'Do you mind if we leave? I have quite lost my appetite.'

Roisin, who had never had one to begin with, agreed.

They did not speak much in the carriage home, each thinking their own thoughts. Cathy sprang out as soon as they arrived, hurrying up the steps and through the front door to impart the news to Mrs

Penrose. She halted in the hall, however, and Roisin, following at a slower pace, saw the flush that suffused her face. She was holding a small white calling card, having picked it up from the silver dish on the hall table.

'It is Kit's,' she said breathlessly. 'He *did* come—and I was not here!' She stamped her foot in frustration. Roisin took the card and turned to Simpson, the butler, who had opened the front door to them and was now hovering.

'When did Lord Westhaven call, Simpson?'

He barely had to think. 'Around ten thirty this morning, ma'am.'

'Just after we set out,' wailed Cathy. 'Oh, Roisin!'

Roisin laid a comforting hand on her arm and turned back to the butler. 'Thank you, Simpson.' Nodding to indicate that he could leave them, Roisin waited until he was out of earshot. 'Cathy,' she began gently. 'Is there…an understanding between you and Kit?'

Cathy shook her head, colour rising once more in her cheeks.

'But you care for him?'

'Perhaps I am foolish to do so.' Cathy sighed.

'Does he care for you?'

Her cousin shrugged her slim shoulders. 'I know not. He has always been kind to me. I merely wished to see him today to tell him how sorry I am. I *am* foolish, aren't I?'

'Of course not.' Roisin gave her a reassuring smile. 'You cannot help the way you feel.' She knew from experience that this, at least, was true enough.

They could talk no more then, for Mrs Penrose found them whispering in the hall and hurried them along to change for dinner. Roisin thought long on what her cousin had said as they ate, quiet once more. Her aunt and uncle, as they had before and would again, put it down to the shock of the past week—but could not account for Cathy's silence. Neither girl ate much. Too many cakes, Mrs Penrose commented later to her husband. It did little for either the appetite or the temperament of young ladies. She would have a word with Cathy.

The girls sat together in the front parlour when the Colonel had retreated to his study and his wife to the tapestry she was embroidering. They each immersed themselves in a book—there seemed little to say now that they had the opportunity to say it.

It was just growing dark when there was a rap on the door. Roisin looked up from her book and met her cousin's gaze. They listened as Simpson went to attend to the visitor. Some moments later he gave a perfunctory knock and leant his upper body into the room.

'Lord Westhaven,' he said.

Cathy all but leapt to her feet. 'Show him in, please, Simpson. And ask Nancy to bring us some tea.' The butler nodded and retreated. Cathy straightened her skirts and patted her hair, a flush rising in her face as she met her cousin's gaze.

Roisin too rose as the door opened once more and Lord Westhaven entered. He looked drawn, she thought, the firm line of his jaw tighter than usual, the black of his mourning clothes making him appear pale. He seemed too big for the daintily furnished room as he inclined his head towards them both.

'Miss Penrose. Lady Roisin. I apologise for the lateness of the hour.'

'Nonsense.' Cathy went forward. 'It is barely eight o'clock.' She took his hands in hers, her blue eyes growing even larger than they already were, though that seemed impossible. 'Kit, we were so sorry to hear about James,' she said gently.

Roisin, watching her, thought suddenly what a lovely wife her cousin would make. She herself had none of Cathy's social graces—she would never have known what to say. Instead she nodded, murmuring something similar.

Lord Westhaven looked uncomfortable. 'Thank you both.' He took back his hands from Cathy and put them behind his back. He seemed not to know how to respond, so fresh was the grief with him.

'Won't you sit down?' Cathy was all understanding. Roisin felt useless.

'Thank you.'

They seated themselves.

'How are you?' asked Cathy.

He shrugged. Again no response seemed to find his lips. 'Destroyed,' he said eventually, a small, mirthless smile following the quiet statement.

There was an awkward silence.

'Forgive me,' he said. 'I do not mean to depress you. I merely wondered…' He paused and then, as if he inwardly steeled himself, his expression changed, became less telling. It was as if a shutter had fallen. 'Miss Penrose,' he said, turning to Cathy.

'Yes, Kit?'

Was her response too eager, or had Roisin merely imagined it to be so because now she was watching for signs of affection between them?

'Would I be able to have a moment alone with Lady Roisin?' he asked simply. 'I have a matter I wish to discuss with her, if it will cause no offence.'

Cathy looked taken back. 'None at all,' she said, rising hastily. There was an edge to her voice that suggested—though her smile was intact as ever—that she felt slighted. 'I will catch up on some reading, I think.'

'Thank you.' He rose to his feet as she retired to the far end of the room rather more quickly than she would normally have done, and took up a book of poetry.

Roisin, who had been possibly more surprised than her cousin at his request, stayed in her seat, watching him. The room seemed to have shrunk now that

Cathy was out of earshot, making him seem closer. She had no idea what he could possibly want.

'Lady Roisin.' His voice was reflective. He perched himself on the edge of his chair and surveyed her. 'How are you after last Monday?'

'Shaken,' she replied honestly. There was no point in her not being truthful, she decided, looking at him. It seemed as if he knew what she was thinking.

He nodded.

'It is kind of you to enquire,' she began stiltedly, 'especially when your own sorrow must—'

'I wonder whether you would care to visit Oak-ridge,' he said abruptly.

Roisin fell silent, surprised. She just managed to stop herself saying 'why?' and instead managed a smile.

'I…would like that very much,' she said at last. 'I hear much about Richmond and I would like to see it.'

He nodded. 'I am close to the boundaries of Richmond Park. If it pleased you, we could drive through it and see the King's deer.'

She smiled again, even more bemused. 'That would…please me greatly, sir. Thank you.'

There was a slight pause, during which he sat like a statue in his chair. By the end of it she could no longer contain her curiosity.

'You should not trouble yourself with me,' she began hesitantly. 'You must have much on your mind.'

'It is no trouble.' For a moment their eyes met and

she saw all kinds of things in his gaze. She wondered what he was thinking. 'I had supposed you missed the country.'

'Yes.' Roisin smiled, and this time it was genuine. 'I do.'

'As do I when I am kept in town.'

Another silence. The air was thick between them—awkward, yet otherwise. She liked this man very much, all of a sudden, whatever it was he was up to. But she wished his eyes were not so sad.

'Right.' Abruptly, he rose. 'Does tomorrow suit you?'

'Oh—yes.' She found her feet and her tongue at the same time, delayed again due to surprise.

He nodded. 'I will send my carriage for you at eleven, if that is convenient.'

'Yes, very.'

She almost expected him to shake her hand, but he merely turned towards the door.

'Tomorrow, then.'

'Lord Westhaven,' she said, lowering her voice further. 'I take it my cousin is not included in this in-vitation?'

'You assume correctly.' His tone was not unkind. 'Goodnight, Lady Roisin.'

Looking up from her book and seeing that he was leaving, Cathy returned to them. 'Shall I see where that tea has got to? There is some lemon cake also—your favourite, I believe, Lord Westhaven!'

He shook his head. 'Thank you, Miss Penrose, but I must be going.'

'Oh.' The disappointment was plain on her face. 'Well, if you must.'

He nodded. 'I have taken up enough of your evening.'

'Then you must come again, soon, mustn't he, Roisin?'

'Thank you, I will.' He moved into the hall, where Simpson had materialised with his coat and fashionable tricorn hat. 'Goodnight.'

As the door shut behind him, Cathy frowned. 'Poor Kit. He seems much out of sorts. What did he say to you, Roisin? I tried and tried, but I couldn't hear a *thing!*'

She turned to her cousin with the look of one who expects to be filled in on every detail of an intimate conversation. Not that this was what her conversation with Lord Westhaven had been, Roisin thought grimly. He had seemed anything but intimate. She felt like she had been flattened by a carriage, so quick and unexpected had it been.

'He…invited me to his home,' she said, guilt rising as Cathy's frown deepened.

'To Oakridge? By yourself? Whatever for?'

'By myself, yes. He is sending a carriage for me.' Roisin lowered her gaze. 'He seems to think a little country air will do me good after Monday.'

Cathy's face suddenly cleared. She smiled. 'Trust

Kit. He thinks of others even at this trying time. He is indeed a good man.'

'Indeed.'

It *was* kind, she reflected. And she would very much like to breathe country air again, and to see Christopher Westhaven's home. It was a very thoughtful offer.

But something told Roisin there was more to it than that.

The carriage arrived exactly at eleven the next day, its driver giving Roisin a cheerful nod as she stepped through the front door. She was followed by Jane, Mrs Penrose's maid; a sweet-faced, middle-aged woman, who was to act as a chaperone. Cathy was close on their heels.

'You must make sure to tell me all about it,' she was saying eagerly. 'It has been ages since I was at Oakridge. And give Kit my best wishes.'

'I will, I will.' Roisin ran lightly down the steps and climbed into the carriage. Her cousin remained standing at the front door until Jane was inside, the driver clicked his tongue and they pulled away. Roisin gave her a wave, then leant back against the well-upholstered seats. She closed her eyes. It would be good to get away from the house for a while—Cathy did chatter so.

'Are you quite all right, miss?' Jane was examining her worriedly. Accompanying Mrs Penrose's young niece was by far the most exciting thing that had happened to her in a long time and she wished nothing to go wrong.

'Fine, thank you.' Roisin smiled at her. 'Just a little tired.'

'The country air'll do you a power of good. You look pale, if you don't mind me sayin'.'

'I hope so.' Another smile, and Roisin turned back to the window. A peaceful silence descended.

Outside the crowded streets of London fell away gradually, and countryside appeared. The fields were almost as green as those of Ireland, Roisin reflected. She could nearly believe she was home, about to saddle up her horse for a ride through the woods. A wave of homesickness rushed through her. There had been no time to think about Kinsale in recent days, but now she realised that she wished more than ever to go back there and leave the pettiness and gossip of society behind her once and for all.

There was small chance of that.

She looked up as the carriage passed through a pair of heavy wrought-iron gates, on to a long driveway. Before her loomed a huge white-stone house. It was all latticed windows and elegant columns, with or-namented chimneys and a low, sloping roof. It sat in grounds that stretched as far as she could see, and there was a lake and several clusters of trees. It was beautiful. Roisin could well imagine why Lord Westhaven wished to show off his home.

As they drew nearer she realised he was waiting for her on the steps that led up to the towering front doors. The carriage stopped and he opened the door, holding up a hand to help her out and nodding a greeting to Jane.

'Lady Roisin. I am glad you were able to come.'

He wore, as usual, a wig the same black as his hair, the curls that were tied at the nape of his neck falling forward as he bowed slightly. He did not look especially glad. They went up the steps together, Jane following at a discreet distance.

'Your house is magnificent,' Roisin said, not merely from politeness.

He gave a tight smile. 'Then I must show you around.'

He led her through more rooms than she could remember, in a house that seemed twice the size of her family home. There was a library stuffed full of books, several reception rooms that looked as though they were little used, a formal dining room with a table that seated fifty… And everywhere the ceilings were covered with exquisite paintings and plasterwork. Roisin took it all in, wondering all the while why he seemed so keen to show it to her. Every now and then, as he explained the heritage of a piece of armour, or gestured through a window, he would lay a hand on her arm or brush against her elbow. His closeness was not unpleasant. She watched his face as he looked upon the things he loved, and he seemed different, somehow. Glimpses of the vulnerability she had seen in him on Monday showed, every now and then, through his stiff, formal façade.

The house, though splendid, looked worn in places. Roisin spied a hole in more than one carpet, and there were gaps in rooms where furniture must once have stood. These were not the only things lacking. When he showed her the picture gallery, with its paintings of his ancestors and family, Lord Westhaven did not mention his brother. There were no paintings of James, though it seemed there must once have been. Spaces on the walls spoke volumes.

'You must love it here,' Roisin said, once they were seated in the cosiest of the receptions rooms, drinking tea.

'Yes.' His eyes did not quite meet hers. 'I do.'

'In some ways it reminds me of my home,' she told him. 'It feels lived in. So many people prefer to display their homes to their friends rather than live in them.'

He looked at her with interest. 'You have siblings?'

'Yes. Three brothers.' She smiled. 'My mother fought a losing battle to make me into a lady. Yourself?' Realising her slip at once, she dropped her eyes, feeling herself blush. 'I mean…apart from…'

'There is just me now.' His tone was level.

'I'm sorry,' she almost whispered.

He smiled. 'Lady Roisin, would you care to walk in the grounds?'

He led the way outside, down the steps and on to the immaculately tended lawn. In the distance the lake twinkled in the sun. Swans skimmed across the surface, feeding. Everything was calm, so different from the bustle of London. They made small talk for a time, but the beauty of their surroundings meant that any silences between them were not awkward ones. Roisin began to relax.

They had gone a little way when, abruptly, he stopped.

'I have not been honest with you.'

Roisin looked at him. She had known he was up to something. She was almost disappointed—things had been pleasant thus far. What he proceeded to say, however, defied her wildest expectations.

'Lady Roisin...' he began, then paused. 'May I speak frankly?'

She nodded, glancing over his shoulder to where Jane stood, just out of earshot, pretending not to watch them. 'Of course.'

'Thank you.' He did not seem to know where to begin. 'I was not going to burden you with this—I had, to tell the truth, intended to try to deceive you—but you are somewhat more perceptive than your twittering cousin.'

'Sir,' said Roisin, surprised, 'if you have some-thing to say, you start badly by insulting Cathy.'

His jaw tightened. 'Forgive me.' He stood over a head taller than her, and from her disadvantaged viewpoint it was hard to read his eyes. 'I do not quite know how to put this.'

They walked a little further. Roisin watched a squirrel, which sat at the base of a tree a few feet away from them.

He said, 'Lady Roisin—'

'You had better call me just Roisin,' she inter-rupted, 'or we shall be here for ever.'

He nodded. 'Roisin. I have a proposition for you.'

'Then tell me.'

'All right.' He shrugged. 'I want you to marry me.'

There was a pause. Somewhere a stag bellowed. Roisin looked at him.

'I beg your pardon?'

'I want you to become my wife.'

'I…' Roisin did not quite know how to reply. *Marry him?* She was sure most men waited longer before proposing to the lady of their choice. She gaped at him, wanting only to stop this madness before it went any further. 'I…sir…I… Please, do not continue. This is most inappropriate, without…'

'Without speaking to your uncle?'

Speechless, she nodded.

He gave a half-smile. 'Forgive me, I have already

done so. Yesterday, after I spoke to you, I took the liberty of visiting him at his club.'

Light-headed, Roisin could only look at him dumbly. 'Oh… And told him…what…?'

'That I had been struck immediately by you, and wished to make you an offer of marriage.'

'This is more than you have ever said to me, sir…'

Lord Westhaven looked back at her, serious. 'I was not, I admit, wholly honest with him. I do not mean to give you a false view of the situation.' He paused, as if appraising her. 'Roisin. When…when my father died he left us with many debts. He was not the upstanding Christian that everyone took him to be, and it fell to James and me to pay various monies to various…creditors.' He stopped again. 'I can only apologise if this sounds heartless. I am in danger of losing Oakridge, and my trust fund is unreachable until I pass my next two birthdays. As it is, I am forced to employ few staff and keep much of the house shut up—you will have noticed you saw nothing of the east wing, for example. I need money if I am not to be forced into a sale.'

'Money?' Debts, creditors; it was beginning to make sense. Money she had in abundance. Or, at least, her family did. 'I am fairly sure, Lord Westhaven, that it is not normal practice to make it so explicit to the lady of your choice that it is her money, not herself, that you desire.'

'I am aware of that.' His eyes searched hers. 'But, as I said, you deserve an explanation of my some-what…unorthodox behaviour. I am short of time, and to ask you to believe I fell in love with you within the space of a few days would be to insult your intelligence. It is, I repeat, more a proposition than a proposal.'

Roisin was amazed. So this was business, was it? 'And the benefits for me?'

'If you will marry me,' he continued, 'Oakridge will be your home. You will have the haven and the space that you desire.'

'How do you know,' she said quietly, 'what it is that I desire?'

He half-turned away. 'That was presumptuous of me. I apologise.'

'No,' she said. 'You are right. I do not want to live the life my cousin loves.'

'I will give you all you need,' he said. 'I will treat you with the utmost respect, and you would have all the benefits of being my wife. And I would ask for nothing in the way of wifely…duties from you. Only that you play your part to the world.'

Roisin's eyes widened. She could not quite believe this was happening to her. 'You do not, then, long for an heir?'

He looked away. 'Perhaps, in time, when you know me better, you would be prepared to… I realise at the moment it would be too much to ask.'

'I see.' Roisin sighed. It seemed that ever since she had reached these shores people had been seeing her as a walking purse. 'Perhaps it is my destiny always to fall in with highwaymen,' she murmured.

Beside her, his whole body stiffened. 'Highwaymen? What do you mean?'

'That's what you're saying, is it not? My money or my life? I must sacrifice one or the other—let you have my dowry, or end up like my Aunt Elizabeth?'

'I suppose it is.' He gave her a hard, almost suspicious, look.

There was a short silence. Roisin shifted her weight from one foot to the other, avoiding his dark eyes. Everything this man did or said to her left her at a loss to describe her feelings.

'I did not mean to insult you, my lord,' she said quietly, for his mood seemed to have taken a turn for the worse. 'It was not my intention to compare you with a criminal—I merely spoke without thinking.'

He seemed to relax a little, letting whatever affront she had caused him pass.

'Think about it,' he said. 'You may have all the time you need, and rest assured I will not kidnap and ransom you if you decline.'

Roisin realised that he was mocking her. She began to feel disorientated, barely knowing what it was he seemed to want her to say. This afternoon was fast becoming too much for her beleaguered senses.

She frowned. 'Why me, then, and not Cathy?'

A ghost of a smile from him now. 'I prefer you.'

'Based upon what? You assume that because I have a title I will be worth more than she?'

'I assume nothing.'

She surveyed him shrewdly as realisation—and irritation—dawned. 'No. Of course,' she said slowly, 'you have done your research, have you not, Lord Westhaven? How foolish of me to assume you had not thought this through. No one will pluck a fruit, after all, without testing if it is ripe!' Her eyes blazed up at him.

Abruptly, he turned and began to go back towards the house. 'Put it out of your mind,' he said flatly. 'It was an idiotic notion—I was foolish to speak of it to you.'

'What will you do now?' Roisin called after him, anger mounting. 'Lie to some poor brainless heiress?'

He rounded on her, dark eyes suddenly cold. 'That is none of your concern.'

'You would have lied to me!'

'I have no wish to lie to anyone.'

He stood, looking at her. The intensity of his gaze made her uncomfortable. He came closer.

'Roisin,' he said. 'I made a promise to my brother before…his accident. I ask you to think about my proposal. I wish my wife to be someone I could live with.'

'And you think you could live with me? Sir, we have met twice.'

It occurred to her that more had passed between them in that time than between most people in their first two meetings. She held her tongue, but, as usual, he seemed to have second-guessed her.

'Would I be such a burden?' As he looked down at her, a subtle change in his eyes made her catch her breath. His hand reached up to tuck a strand of hair behind her ear, the lace of his cuff brushing her cheek. His fingers touched her jawline before he let his hand fall. She knew suddenly that he wanted to kiss her.

Abruptly she turned away, eyes lowered, just as Jane came forward, puffed up and protective.

'My lady?'

'I'm all right,' Roisin told her, throwing her a tight smile. 'It was just…a misunderstanding. Thank you.'

The maid retreated a few paces, unhappy with the situation, but unsure what she should do.

Roisin raised her chin. 'I will need some time, Lord Westhaven,' she said, her voice as steady as she could make it. 'Allow me to walk by myself a little.'

He inclined his head. 'I will be waiting.'

She watched as he strode off towards the house, her heartbeat slowly returning to normal. She felt as if she had just awakened from the strangest dream.

He wanted to marry her.

Well, not her, she reminded herself. He wanted the substantial dowry that she knew her father had planned and left for her. That Lady Melville was now sitting on—ready for the news that her daughter, having now entered society, had done her duty and secured a match. Yet even her mother would be surprised at the speed of this proposal.

She turned towards the lake and put some distance between herself and the house, Jane hovering uncertainly behind. She had to admire Lord Westhaven for his honesty, belated as it had been. She knew she was a target for the less affluent men in London society, as were all wealthy debutantes. Should she consider his offer?

You are *considering it*, said a voice in her head. And, she had to admit, it spoke the truth. What was in store if she did not marry him? Balls, parties, meeting and flirting with many a young man—the uncertainty of courtship. Her heart sank in the same way it always did when she considered it.

And if she did? Her eyes roved over the countryside around her. Oakridge was beautiful. A place where she could pursue her own life. Where she could entertain her friends as and when the whim took her. No more forced laughter and simpering. No more boring gentlemen. No dreaded, stuffy town house in smoky London.

She could be happy here, she felt it.

So that only left the problem of Lord Westhaven himself.

Beyond the affairs of her brothers, Roisin had had

little interest in men before her encounter with Ewan Hamilton. Then he had kissed her and her world had tipped on its axis. She was not sure still what to call the feelings she had for him. But he was dead, and perhaps she would never feel such longing again, for any man.

She liked Christopher Westhaven. He would, as he said, be a kind, attentive husband. Her stomach fluttered once more as she thought of the way he had looked at her. She had almost wanted his lips on hers, for the moment before she remembered her dignity.

He said he asked nothing of her. A part of her knew that was not true. She was not prepared to admit to herself at this stage how that made her feel.

What are you saying? asked the voice in her head. *That you will marry him?*

It was a possibility. More than a possibility, perhaps. Why should she not accept, after all? Better a husband who did not lie to her than one who would.

Better a husband who offered her genuine respect than one who pretended love.

Who married for love, at any rate?

Roisin steeled herself and explored her feelings one more time, just to be sure. It was not ideal, but neither was it for him. They were two people who needed each other to escape their respective problems. It seemed, thinking of it like this, that fate had intended her to be his wife.

She would marry him. She could not afford to wait

and see what form her next offer took. She must take her chance for independence now.

Before she had time to change her mind, she started back towards the house.

He awaited her at the end of the stone veranda, hands in his pockets, facing away from her towards the unbroken green of the lawn. Roisin asked Jane to wait for her where they stood, then took a deep breath and went toward him. He did not turn as she approached.

She said, 'Will you not have Cathy? Her dowry would be adequate, and she cares for you, you know.'

His back looked tense. He said, 'She would not be happy with me.'

Roisin doubted that very much. 'She will be upset that I am chosen over her.'

'It was not my intention to hurt her.' His fingers tapped soundlessly against the stone balustrade. She sighed.

'You want me?'

'I want you.'

Roisin set her shoulders. 'Then I will marry you.'

Silence. He turned to face her.

'Why?'

Despite herself, she laughed aloud. 'You spend so long cajoling me and now you ask me why? I am sure you could have your pick of heiresses, sir, but I have met no man that did not bore me since—' She fell silent, cursing her impulsive tongue. 'Since I arrived on these shores,' she amended. 'It is better, I think, to know what I am getting into.'

Now that his plan had borne fruit, he did not seem to know what to say.

'Thank you,' was what he came up with at last.

The air between them was suddenly taken up with an awkward heaviness. Roisin looked at the man who was to be her husband and wondered what he thought of her. Enough, evidently, to marry her.

'Why do you want a wife you do not love?' she asked. 'Is the money worth that?'

'Yes,' he said simply. 'James and I swore a long time ago to keep Oakridge. Now that I have lost him, I will not lose our home as well. That is the promise I made to him, and to myself.'

She had not expected such a candid reply. His devotion touched her. Surely he was a man who would keep his promises. Who she could trust to behave rightly.

He mistook her silence. 'My father married a woman he did not love in a match arranged by their fathers. Yet he was happy with my mother.'

Roisin frowned. A man who had died with gambling debts large enough to cripple his sons did not sound as if his life had been particularly fulfilled. But Lord Westhaven, she could see, was trying to console her— he had evidently decided that she needed consoling.

'When do you wish to…' she still could not quite believe this was her, standing here, having this conversation '…have the ceremony?'

'As soon as possible,' he replied. 'I will not subject you to a vast public affair. There is a chapel here, beyond those trees.' He pointed towards a small wood, from which Roisin could see a steeple rising. 'My mother had it built. She liked to worship alone. We will marry there, with as little audience as we can invite without causing a social scandal. Does that suit you?'

'Um…yes.' Roisin was feeling a little dazed. He seemed to have given this considerable thought.

His eyes followed her face as she turned her head to gaze out once more out across the grounds. The place that was to be her home. 'What are you thinking?'

She sighed. 'I am wondering whether I am a fool.'

He smiled and said nothing.

She said, 'Please, call for your carriage. I wish to go home.'

He left then to do so, and walked with her to the front of the house once it had arrived. He did not speak, holding stiffly the arm he had offered to her, with her own arm through it.

'I will call on you in a few days to discuss practicalities,' he told her.

She nodded. 'Very well.'

Jane, tactful as always, entered the carriage first and they stood, not quite looking at each other, while she settled herself. Lord Westhaven took Roisin's hand and raised it to his lips.

'Until next week, then.'

'Yes.' She was just about to get into the carriage when he stepped forward, put one hand under her chin, tilted it towards his face, and kissed her.

It was a chaste kiss, his lips closed, lingering only for a second on hers. But Roisin felt the heat in his touch as his fingers sent shocks of awareness into her skin. She knew her lips parted under his of their own accord so that, when he pulled away instead of going further, she was somewhat disappointed—and not a little shocked by her own reaction. Colour suffused her cheeks and, unable to speak, she climbed into the carriage, face turned away from him. Her heart was beating very fast once more.

At a word from Lord Westhaven, the carriage started forward. Roisin looked out once they had moved a little away from the house. He was still standing there.

'It's all right,' she said, seeing the shock on the face of the maid. 'He was not behaving improperly.'

'Miss?' Jane looked unconvinced.

'We are going to be married.'

Saying it out loud made it real, suddenly. Roisin slumped against the seat, hands cooling her flaming cheeks, as the other woman expressed her surprise and delight. What had she done?

She had promised herself to a man she did not love, that was what. Who wanted her so he could renovate his home and secure his lifestyle. Who she barely knew.

And she still had to tell Cathy. That was not something to look forward to.

Her mother would be pleased. As would her Aunt Elizabeth, no doubt. She had done her duty and secured a more than adequate match. She would not mention his financial situation in her letter home. Best not to complicate things further.

She sat a while, avoiding Jane's gaze, and listened to the hooves of the horses. Would she regret her decision tomorrow? Only tomorrow would tell.

Roisin Westhaven. His name fitted with hers, at least.

She was to marry him. Sooner, it seemed, rather than later. And God forgive her if it was wrong, for she might not forgive herself.

Chapter Six

Having watched the carriage until it disappeared through the gates of Oakridge Park, Kit strode inside, wrenched off his wig, flung it at the wall, slumped into a chair and buried his head in his hands.

What had he done?

He was asking a woman to ruin her life and her chance of happiness for him.

Not just any woman—Roisin Melville was a sensible, beautiful woman with a wit as sharp as his own. And she had agreed to his ridiculous suggestion! He had planned it all so carefully, what he would say; he had ordered the paintings of James to be taken down so that she would suspect nothing—but he had not ever believed he would work up the damnable gall to actually ask her.

Until, that is, he had found himself blurting out the words like the lumbering idiot that he was.

And why? Why had he chosen her? he asked

himself, knowing well the answer. *Because* she was beautiful and sharp-witted. Because he desired her more than was proper for a man who was about to marry for convenience. He kept feeling her hand against his face at the hanging, the way her body pressed against his as he had carried her. That hurt look in her lovely eyes.

He was a damned fool, a selfish, stupid, *fool.* Perhaps he should have chosen Catherine Penrose after all. Her chatter would have been his penance. Not that she was likely ever to speak to him again, he mused, once she found out what he had asked of her cousin.

And he had kissed her! Kit clenched his jaw. He had told Roisin he would ask nothing from her one moment and kissed her the next! He could have sworn she responded at first, and it had taken all the self-control he had to pull away, so sweet had that first taste been. Yet afterwards she had clearly been mortified—that was not the expression of a woman who welcomed his advances, surely. So now he must drive himself mad with wanting her, for he could not allow himself to do so again. Well, so be it. He deserved each pang.

Kit leapt to his feet and paced about the drawing room. Surely she would find out the truth—and what then? If she did not, would his whole life become a web of lies, with himself, the spider, sitting in the centre?

He was angry at the very walls around him, their familiarity and their shabbiness. Why must he be tied to this house of ghosts? Jamie was dead. If he left Oakridge now, who would care? Who would know except the rats in the cellars and his dogs?

But he could not. Memories and phantoms kept him here. He respected the pull they had over him with a love that bordered on hate.

He cast his gaze about the room, as if noticing it for the first time. It did nothing to improve his rapidly worsening temper.

His mother's ridiculous ornaments were everywhere. Their china eyes looked at him, mocking him. They had seen what Oakridge used to be—and they saw what it now was. They saw him, and what he pretended to be.

Kit paused, his breathing erratic. Surely he would be driven mad with guilt if he stayed here? So much pain—so much history, clinging to his every move. How long must he bear this?

Lunging at the fireplace he swept it clean, porcelain deer and china dogs falling to the floor and smashing loudly.

He stood amid the mess, fists clenched. Inwardly he cursed his father for his weak will, his pathetic hope that he could gamble himself back out of the hole he had created. And Jamie, poor, *stupid* Jamie, for getting himself killed, for wanting always to be the gentleman, to do what was honourable.

And most of all himself, for letting it happen.

He must marry her. He had no other choice if he was not to break his word. What other woman could he ask, as he had asked her?

He went to the window and gazed out, anger draining. He would not be able to repay her for what she was going to do for him. But, in married life, he could try. He leant his forehead on the cool glass of the window and felt his strength seep out of him.

'Hello? Lord Westhaven, is that you?'

Kit swung around as the door opened behind him. Annette Farham stood there. She was looking at the smashed china with amusement, her polite demeanour having vanished as soon as she saw he was alone.

'Kit. I knew it. A small accident?'

He sighed. John's sister had come into his employ after he told Kit of her need for a position. He had done it as a favour to his manservant and friend, but when the girl had arrived he had been captivated by her. She was tiny, the top of her head level with his chest, her luxuriant dark hair and full red lips the dream of any man. She was not yet nineteen, but her figure spoke of a woman much older. Much more experienced. Dressed in the simple gown of a maid, yet with an air of riches long lost but never forgotten, she was a mix of contradictions the like of which he had never encountered. Hair braided and pinned to her head, eyes submissive, she had still managed to make him breathless as she leant over him each morning to hand him his breakfast tray. It had been to his cost, and his gain, both at once.

But he was not pleased to see her now.

'Leave me be, Annette.'

'I heard the crash. I thought you had leapt through the window in a fit of manliness.' She started to come into the room, broom in hand.

'I said *leave me*!'

The harshness in his voice halted her. 'It will need to be cleared up.'

He ran a hand through his hair, turning his back on her. 'I will do it.'

'You?' She gave a silvery laugh. 'Kit, when have you ever cleared up? You are out of sorts today.'

She crossed the room to where he stood and placed her small hands on his chest. She looked up at him. 'We shall have to see what we can do about that.'

'Annette.' He took one of her wrists in each hand and removed them. 'Not now.'

Her plump lips formed a perfect moue of disappointment. 'Have I fallen out of favour?' She moved closer, pressing her tight little body against his. Her dark eyes peered up at him through their lashes. The lace collar of her dress did not quite cover the deep shadow between her firm breasts.

Staring down at her, Kit surprised himself by feeling only a faint distaste. Where was the rush of desire he always felt up until now? Where was the urge to touch her soft skin? Gone, it seemed.

Gently but firmly, he pushed her away. 'Things are changed now, Annette. It was wrong of me to take advantage of you in the way I did. I was not myself… You know the pressure my father's death put on me, and…'

She frowned, the realisation that he was not toying with her dawning. 'Take advantage? What do you mean? Nothing is changed.'

He looked at her. 'No, nothing. Except that Jamie is dead.'

'And he would not want you to waste your life pining for his.'

He stared at her. 'He has not been in the grave eight days, Annette.'

'Then let me comfort you.' She crept close again. 'As I comforted you on Monday last.'

His stomach constricted as he remembered. He had returned from the hanging. John had helped him bury James's body. Then he had tried to drown his pain in his father's antique port collection.

She had found him in the cellar and given him the only comfort a man in his state had needed, up against the slimy stone wall. Usually her touch had the power to make him forget his troubles, but this time was different. Afterwards he had felt soiled, as if he had betrayed Jamie somehow. It was then, he thought, that his lust had died. There had never been anything but physical closeness between him and this woman.

'You remember, do you not?' she prompted. 'You were…a little drunk.'

He nodded. 'I am sorry to admit it, but, yes, I do.'

'Sorry?' She stepped back a little. 'You did not seem so at the time, Kit.'

Her use of his nickname jarred on him. 'Annette. There can be no more of this.'

'Fool,' she chided silkily. 'You are still a man, are you not?'

'I am to be married.'

For a moment naked surprise lay on her face. 'Married?' Then she laughed, genuinely amused. 'Kit, such ridiculousness! Who to? Who could you have found in the space of one day?'

'Lady Roisin Melville,' he said, without knowing why he told her.

Her eyebrows rose. 'You are serious?'

'Yes.'

She paused, mouth agape, digesting this. 'Lady? Landed gentry, I suppose? Rich?' Her voice was reproachful. 'So much for the man of ideals, the man who would not marry as his father did! Bravo, Kit!'

'I did not ask for your judgement,' he said coldly. 'I am master of my own conscience.'

She smiled. 'That must take some managing. But

surely, every man who marries for money must have a mistress?'

'Not me.' He looked at her, wondering all of a sudden why he had been so captivated.

Annette shook her head. 'What a waste of such…potential. Living a chaste life.'

Her words brought back his sense of frustration. He needed no reminding of his predicament. 'I intend to be faithful to my wife,' he said, his tone clipped.

Anger flared in her dark eyes. 'You really intend to do this thing?'

'I have asked her.'

'And she has agreed?' Annette gave a harsh laugh. 'She must be a bigger fool than you are!'

Kit advanced towards her. 'Watch your tongue, wench.'

'Or what?' Her chin tipped up defiantly. 'You will strike me?'

'Of course not.' He was suddenly weary. 'Annette. You must believe me when I tell you that it is over.'

'So you dispose of me? A few tumbles, then I am put out to pasture—like a horse that has served its purpose?'

'Your job is still secure.'

'Ha!' Eyes blazing, she tossed her dark head. 'So generous of you, Kit, when you led me to believe that—'

'To believe what?' He interrupted, genuinely surprised. 'I never promised you anything, Annette. You approached me, if I remember rightly.'

'Then I was a fool to grant you such favours!' Hands on hips, she surveyed him. 'What will you do with a wife you do not love, Kit? Keep her in a trophy case? I suppose she is a sickly, pathetic thing, likely to die of consumption in the country!'

'Far from it,' muttered Kit. 'Do you think so little of me?'

'Indeed I do!' She frowned. 'You clearly think far less of me!' She stood, fuming, then turned on her heel. 'Fine. If you say it is over, there is little I can do. But we will see whether you are so keen to have me as just a maid once your wife arrives. I wish you joy of her—and her money—*Lord Westhaven.*'

Kit breathed a sigh of relief as Annette flounced from the room. His past with her was only one more link in the chain that held his guilt to him. Not for a moment did he believe that she felt the slight as surely as she said she did. She knew, as he had, that their occasional afternoons of enjoyment meant little in the long term. He knew he hadn't been her first lover and—if he was honest—he was as glad to see the back of her now as once he had been to take her in his arms.

Which now only left him with his stack of other problems.

* * *

Annette felt less than relieved. She had enjoyed the security that bedding the lord of the manor brought her. They had enjoyed themselves. He was an excellent lover, and she had been fulfilled in his arms. And, she thought, he in hers. So much so that she was surprised not to be the one ending it. She thought he was building up a dependence on her.

This woman he was marrying must be a beauty, then—or so pious and suspicious that he lived in fear of being found out.

Alone in the kitchen, she paced up and down, hands balled into fists at her sides. He was a fool and an idiot! How dare he cast her aside? Anger mounted once more within her breast. She had hoped to have more time to make herself indispensable… She was well bred, after all—she had been used to the best of everything once and had promised herself that she would be again. To marry a woman of her calibre and background would be no bad thing for any gentleman!

Stamping her foot, Annette tried not to think of the hopes she had allowed to grow within her. It was not as if she cared two figs for Kit, or Oakridge, anyway. She could do better.

No, she did not care how he lived his life henceforth—but no one treated her as a commodity. She was a woman, and an attractive one at that. Had she been honest with herself, she would have realised that the slight lay not in his personal rejection of her—but that he had been the first not to want her.

But Annette did not stop to analyse her anger—she merely felt it growing.

She might have lost her chance, but she would have her revenge.

He could not treat her this way, no matter how much better than she he thought he was, merely because her family had lost its money and he was—barely—hanging on to his. She had a suspicion that there were more skeletons in Christopher Westhaven's closet. And if he was not careful she would ensure they saw the light of day.

The closer the carriage drew to home, the more apprehensive Roisin grew. All the way from Oakridge she had been practising her opening line, trying to make what she had done sound less like a betrayal.

It was no use. That was exactly how Cathy would see it.

All too soon they had arrived. Roisin, alighting from the carriage and thanking Lord Westhaven's driver, saw the curtains twitch in the parlour, and Cathy's face peer out. Then the door was opened and her cousin stood there. Simpson hovered behind her, looking slightly put out at having his job done for him.

'Come in, come in,' she said, gesturing wildly.

Roisin, wishing she could flee down the road after

the departing carriage, went instead up the steps and into the hall. She handed her outdoor clothes to Simpson, who disappeared. Cathy took Roisin's arm.

'I have the tea all ready,' she said eagerly. 'It's ages before dinner, and Cook has baked some of her scones—I know how you like them so.' She plumped herself down on the sofa, picked up the teapot and waited for Roisin to do the same. 'Well, do tell me, Roisin. I have been going mad with the suspense. How is Kit? Was it something to do with James? Has he confided in you—is he very upset? Did he give you a tour? Was—'

'Cathy.' Roisin held up a hand. Her head was beginning to ache. 'I have just taken tea with Lord Westhaven. But,' she added hastily, as her cousin was about to protest, 'I suppose I could have one cup. And perhaps a scone.'

Cathy handed her the tea. 'Of course you can—here. Now—'

'I will tell you all, if you allow me to speak,' Roisin interrupted gently.

Her cousin grinned. 'Forgive me. I have long been waiting for your news—and I've had such a tiresome day myself! Mother wanted me to come calling with her, but her friends are so dull, so in the end I ended up sitting home and—' She broke off. 'Why am I telling you my news? I wish to hear yours! Speak!'

'Lord Westhaven seems as well as can be expected,' began Roisin, wishing to ease herself gently into what she must say. 'He showed me around—Oakridge is lovely, as you have told me. From the upper stories you can see across into the King's park.'

'Yes, yes, I have been there.' Cathy was growing impatient. 'What did he want?'

'He said he thought the country would cheer me after Monday.'

Cathy nodded. 'You seem better. There is more colour in your cheeks. Did it lift your spirits?'

Roisin bit her lip . 'Er…not exceptionally.'

'What do you mean?'

Stalling her cousin was not working. Roisin realised that she was going to have to tell her, and that she owed her a full explanation. She took a deep breath and another sip of tea to calm her nerves.

'You must tell no one what I am about to say,' she began.

Cathy's eyes widened with excitement. 'A secret? How perfectly intriguing! I will keep it, of course—especially if it helps Kit.'

Roisin gave her a small smile. 'It was partly to do with James that I was invited,' she said. 'Lord West-haven has been experiencing…a few financial problems. He cannot cope alone now that his brother is not there to help, and it looks as if he may have to sell Oakridge.'

'No!' Cathy was aghast. 'His ancestral home? Oh,

it is too cruel! Can we help him in any way? Is that what he wished to discuss with you?'

Roisin realised that this would be harder than she had anticipated. 'He…has asked me to help him, yes,' she said slowly.

'And what must you do? Can I assist you?'

'Not really.' She steeled herself. 'He has asked me to marry him, Cathy.'

Immediately the effervescent society lady before her vanished. There was a pause, while every semblance of colour drained from the younger girl's face. Her eyes opened very wide and became very blue next to the ivory of her skin.

'Marry him?'

'Cathy?' Roisin leant forward in her chair and took the teacup, which had begun to spill into its saucer, from her cousin's limp grasp.

'I had no idea there was…feeling between you and Kit. I would never have said anything if—' She broke off, speechless for the first time since Roisin had known her. 'I have made a fool of myself.'

'It is not that simple.' Roisin knew she must be honest. 'It is not me he wants. It is my dowry.'

'And he…told you that?'

'Yes.'

'No.' Cathy was frowning. 'It cannot be true.'

'It is complicated, Cathy. If he had any other option—'

'He could have asked me.' It was almost a whisper.

'Believe me, I tried to tell him that you would be a better choice, but—'

'You *told* him?' Cathy rose to her feet. 'You told him how I feel, Roisin?'

'I thought he would prefer a wife who cares for him.' Dismayed, Roisin clasped her hands tightly in her lap. She was not easing the blow.

'And you do not?' Cathy's voice rose in pitch. 'And he did not want me?'

'I'm sorry, Cathy.'

'Oh, God.' Her hands pressed beneath her breasts, Cathy began to pace the room, skirts swinging wildly. 'I shall never be able to be in the same room with him again! Do you realise how you have disgraced me?'

'No!' Roisin too rose, watching helplessly. 'He is very fond of you, Cathy.'

'Fond?' A tone of hysteria was present now. 'Fond enough to marry a woman he barely knows over me, just because she has more money!' She stopped dead. 'What answer did you give?'

Roisin lowered her eyes. 'I have said yes.'

Shock filled her cousin's eyes. 'And you do not love him?'

She swallowed. 'I think very highly of him.' *He has kissed me. And I did not pull away...*

Cathy raised her voice. 'But you do not love him?'

'No.'

The younger girl covered her face with her hands. 'How could you? You know how I felt about him, and still you had to impress him with your fancy gowns and your curling hair and your...' she paused, lips trembling '...your compassion for highwaymen! I was his friend for years and years before you ever saw this country! There are so many men in London who would have made a fine husband for you, Roisin—men with money! Why could you not take one of them instead of mine?'

Roisin put her hands on her hips her mouth agape. 'You think this is my doing?'

'Yes, I do!'

'But how? Why? I was not trying to ensnare him— he asked me! I have done nothing untoward! I never wanted a husband at all—it was my mother's idea. He came to me with his offer—he says he will have no one else. How am I to know why? I think it is not me you should be angry at. Besides...' her tone softened '...I think you misread his friendship. He was not yours, Cathy.'

'Yet you still made a mockery of me by telling him I loved him!'

'I did not say any such thing! I said you were...' Roisin trailed off. 'What does it matter? He never wanted to hurt you—and neither did I!'

'Yet you did.' Cathy was crying. 'My parents have

taken you into their home, I have introduced you to my friends and into society—and I was going to try and help you secure a husband—and this is how you repay us?'

Roisin sighed. 'If your parents knew he was as poor as a clergyman, they would not allow you to marry him,' she pointed out.

'That is none of your business!'

'It is a fair point!'

Cathy's eyes narrowed. 'And what has your mother to say on the matter? Not to mention your brothers?'

'I have not yet written to them, as you well know, being that I just this moment returned,' said Roisin curtly. 'I intended to do so this afternoon.'

'They will be thrilled, I am sure. But you have no intention of telling them his circumstances, have you? I do not like to think of Aunt Camilla so deceived.' Cathy's tone was threatening.

'You would not!' Roisin went forward. 'Cathy, I have my reasons for doing what I am to do. You said you would tell no one! If you meddle in my affairs—'

'If *I* meddle?' Cathy shrieked. 'You have done nothing but interfere with mine!'

The door was flung open behind them. Mrs Penrose stood there, the ever-present Simpson lurking behind her. She took one look at the anger on both faces and the tears running down her daughter's cheeks.

'That will be all, thank you, Simpson,' she said hastily. Coming into the room, she shut the door on the curious butler. 'Girls!' Her tone was hushed but urgent, her smooth forehead creasing into a disapproving frown. 'What is all this? I can hear you screeching like fishwives from upstairs—goodness knows what the neighbourhood thinks of us! Catherine, why are you weeping? What has happened?'

Cathy turned, her face pale once more. Roisin noticed with a rush of foreboding that her cousin swayed on her feet.

'Mother,' she said quietly. 'Oh, Mother…'

Mrs Penrose gasped as her daughter collapsed in a faint at her feet. 'Cathy!'

Roisin gave a dismayed groan. Cathy must have had her corset tightened too much that morning, she thought caustically, despite herself.

'Roisin, what is going on?' Mrs Penrose was on her knees, her daughter's head in her hands. 'What have you done to her?'

Her niece lowered her gaze. 'Aunt Elizabeth…I am to marry Lord Westhaven.'

There was a pause. Her aunt gave a sigh that spoke volumes. 'Oh dear.' Then, shrugging, she said, 'My husband mentioned this might occur. Well, what passes between you and him is your own affair. It cannot be helped. But I fear Cathy has taken the news badly.'

'Indeed.' Roisin felt this to be a great understatement.

Mrs Penrose was stroking her daughter's hair. 'Roisin, bring my smelling salts from my dressing-room table, please.'

Roisin did so, and when she returned to the parlour Cathy was regaining consciousness. She sat on the floor, tears running down her cheeks, while her mother held her by the shoulders, half-supporting, half-embracing her.

Mrs Penrose held out her hand for the small glass bottle. 'Thank you. Now, leave us for a moment, please.'

Roisin left the room. Her cousin's sobs followed her into the hallway.

Once in her own room she threw herself face down on the bed, too exhausted to do any more crying. She had thought it would be hard to tell Cathy—but this? Her cousin had been all but hysterical. At least Aunt Elizabeth did not seem to blame her overmuch. That would change, she was sure, when she was told everything that had taken place.

Roisin sighed. It was, perhaps, too much to hope that Cathy would keep her promise and stay quiet. She thought of Lord Westhaven with envy. It was easy for him—he had no relatives to upset or make explanations to. He could behave how he pleased, within reason, and damn the consequences.

She dreaded telling her mother. Lady Melville

would more than likely insist on coming to this wedding. Roisin did not want her to meet her future husband, lest she suspect that all was not well. She was not really deceiving anyone, she told herself guiltily. He would be rich when his trust fund matured. Hopefully.

A knock on the door made her sit up, straightening her skirts. That would be Aunt Elizabeth, come to sort out this problem.

'Come in,' she said.

It was not. It was Cathy. She stood in the doorway, eyes red-rimmed. 'I have not told my mother why you do what you do,' she said quietly, 'because I gave you my word. I will keep quiet to everyone. But I will never forgive you, or Kit, for making such a fool of me.'

Roisin could not meet her eyes, all of a sudden more sorry than she could say. She wished she had never met Lord Westhaven. 'Cathy—'

But the door had already shut.

Roisin flung herself backwards across the bed this time, eyes on the ceiling.

Why could she have not stayed in Ireland? Why could nothing in life be simple? She had only just found a friend and confidante when circumstances conspired to drive a wedge between them. Perhaps her cousin would never forgive her. And circumstances were not entirely to blame, if she was honest with herself.

She sighed heavily. It seemed since arriving on English soil she had done nothing but spoil people's lives. Including, perhaps—now that she was betrothed to a man she did not love—her own.

Chapter Seven

Lord Westhaven visited in the days that followed, as he had said he would, to discuss arrangements with Roisin and her uncle. He was polite and courteous, while remaining distant. Roisin could not think that her uncle possibly believed they were marrying for love, yet neither he nor her aunt seemed to question matters. Their blessing was given again, and in due course—after some financial discussion in the study with Colonel Penrose—he took his leave. Roisin felt a little like a prize heifer at auction, but she told herself this was what she must expect. She had agreed to his terms, after all.

For her part, Cathy, who had been sitting in the drawing room with everyone before Lord Westhaven arrived, fled upstairs at the sound of his knock and did not come down until he was well clear of the house.

If he noticed her absence he did not comment upon it.

The date of the wedding was fixed for one month hence—a rider was dispatched by Lord Westhaven to personally convey the news to Ireland. Roisin could not believe her luck when a message returned not much more than a week later, saying that, due to the effects of a lingering cold, her mother was unable to attend. Lady Melville sent her blessing, however, having heard of Lord Westhaven's fine reputation; and her thanks to her brother for arranging matters. She also congratulated Roisin on doing herself proud. The letter was accompanied by the good wishes of Roisin's brothers, all too swept up in the business of their own wives and children to think of attending themselves. Although she would have liked to see them, Roisin could not believe her good fortune. By the time her family came to visit Oakridge, as they all promised to do in the future, she would be settled in and there would be nothing they could do to her if the truth was discovered.

Cathy continued to ignore her, leaving her mother to prepare Roisin for her wedding. There was much to be arranged, and little time to do it in. After much consideration—mostly by Aunt Elizabeth—a dress design was decided upon and Roisin spent many tiresome hours being measured and fitted. Food was organised for the privileged forty guests, about the maximum the chapel at Oakridge could hold. Roisin was glad Lord Westhaven had stuck to his word, and not forced her into a more public ceremony. As it was, so she heard, society was buzzing at the touching romance of the thing—a tiny wedding in a family chapel, a whirlwind courtship in the wake of Kit's family tragedy. It had all happened so quickly, it was said, because the young people concerned could not wait to set up home together.

Those who knew otherwise said nothing.

So it was that, before she had a chance to become frightened and flee, Roisin's wedding day was upon her.

She had not realised what day it was when she awoke, until her aunt had bustled into the room with two maids and started giving orders. It was then that the first twinges of nerves and anxiety as to her decision began.

The curling rags were untied from her hair, and one maid teased it up into coils on her head. Then she was helped into her dress, a beautiful white silk creation, all lace and panniers, with a small train that followed her as she walked. It was lovely, she had to admit, as Aunt Elizabeth cooed over her. There were new satin slippers, heeled at the back and pointed at the front, and flowers to wear in her hair. Standing in front of the mirror, Roisin barely recognised herself.

'You are beautiful,' said Mrs Penrose, pinching her niece's pale cheeks to bring some colour into them.

'So do not look as if you go to the gallows.' Realising her *faux pas,* she lowered her eyes, pinkening slightly. 'What I mean to say, Roisin, is that he will be good to you.'

'Thank you.' Roisin attempted a smile.

In truth, she had been looking forward to this day. She remembered well Lord Westhaven's promise to let her lead her own life, and she intended to hold him to it. Oakridge, with its many rooms and spacious grounds, would be a welcome relief from living with Cathy, whose frosty silences made Roisin increasingly uncomfortable.

It was time to go. Roisin, steeling herself, walked from her room and down the stairs with great care, trying not to trip over herself as she descended. The last thing she needed today on top of everything was a broken neck.

Her cousin was waiting with her father in the hall, ready to get into one of the two carriages that were to take them to Oakridge, a vision in pale blue damask the exact colour of her eyes.

'Cathy,' said Mrs Penrose, who had been eager since their argument to foster new relations between her daughter and her niece. 'Does not Roisin look lovely?'

Roisin met the eyes of the younger girl, wishing they could be friends once more. To her surprise, she found something similar staring back at her.

'Yes, you do look nice,' said Cathy quietly.

'Thank you.' Roisin smiled and was pleased to get a stilted smile back. Then Cathy turned away, going to the second carriage with her mother, and Roisin and Colonel Penrose entered the first.

Her uncle talked little on the way to Richmond, seeing that she was nervous. He did, however, tell her that Lord Westhaven was extremely well thought of in town.

'I had hoped he would make an offer to Cathy, but he never seemed interested,' he said, smiling. 'Giving him my niece will please me just as well. He will make a good husband to you, Roisin.'

Roisin hoped everyone who had told her this— and there were plenty of them—was right. She clenched her hands in her lap and fiddled with the lace around her throat. It was a fine May morning, perfect for the fairytale wedding everybody seemed to think they would be witnessing. She leant against the carriage window, the light spring breeze in her hair, and tried to brace herself against a drive that seemed to go on for ever. She just wanted to be there, to face her husband-to-be, and to get this thing done. She could begin the rest of her life—and not a moment too soon.

Without warning, yet after what seemed like days, they were at the gates at Oakridge. Suddenly her stomach felt like it was filled with butterflies and she was not so sure of anything any more.

Her uncle saw her face and threw her a smile. 'Good luck, child.'

She returned the smile with stiff lips and took herself firmly in hand. He would, as everyone said, be good to her. It was for the best. Then they were turning, starting on the long driveway and down towards the little road that led to Oakridge's chapel. Into her future, and she knew not what.

Kit had been unable to eat breakfast. Seated at the table, where he now ate in the mornings so Annette could not bring a tray up to him, he picked listlessly at the food in front of him, his mind sorting through the problems of the day.

Annette threw him a sultry look as she served him a fresh cup of tea and Kit, pretending not to notice, was suddenly anxious about his maid. Had he been foolish to keep her on, knowing she was so against his marriage? How would she behave towards Roisin? Would she be more trouble than all this was worth?

But he had employed her as a favour to John, and he had not behaved in a seemly way with his best friend's sister—how could he turn her out on top of it all? So perhaps he had no choice. Perhaps his fears were all for nothing and she had recovered from her fit of pique.

And so it went on, round and round inside his skull until at last, frustrated with his own dark mood, he had stormed from the room, overturning the water jug in the process. Annette, cleaning up, remarked to her brother that he did not behave like a man who was about to get married. John had only shaken his head at her and gone to find his master.

Kit was in his room, pulling on the splendid waistcoat that he had had made for the occasion. It was of blue silk, trimmed with gold braid. His wig was brushed and powdered, with a matching blue bow. His stockings were silk, and his shoe buckles freshly polished. His gaze lingered for a moment on the black armband that reminded him why he was here at all. Six weeks ago his brother had been alive and he would never have thought this possible.

He met John's eyes in the mirror. 'What am I doing?'

'The same thing your brother did. Giving all for Oakridge.'

Kit raised his eyebrows. 'Well, that makes me feel better. Thank you.'

John smiled. 'I say it only to remind you that you should be proud. You are living up to your word.' He added, 'And she is beautiful.'

'Indeed.' Kit adjusted his cuffs. 'Let us hope she comes.'

He was in only slightly better spirits as he stood before the altar in his mother's little chapel, filled with the correct people—none of whom he liked.

He had asked John to be his best man, but the younger man had only laughed, saying that he would cause a scandal.

So Kit had none, and stood at the altar alone. She would not come. Now he was almost certain of it. She had had four weeks to lament her decision. If he were she, he would have been back in Ireland by now.

The doors at the back of the church opened. Cathy entered. She met his eyes for a moment, and turned away hurriedly. Kit sighed. Another thing to regret.

She was followed by her mother and then, once they had taken their seats, the organ began to play. He could barely believe his ears. She was here. She had kept her promise. He did not know why the realisation surprised him so. He, after all, would go to any lengths to keep his word. Why should it be different for her? Yet he had feared it. He stood taller, head up, waiting—like the whole congregation—for a sight of her.

Roisin and her uncle entered the church and Kit's bad mood vanished. Dressed in her wedding gown she was exquisite, the sweep of her dress accentuating her small waist. Her hair fell in tendrils from the pile of curls on her head. As she came towards him she gave him a tentative smile. He smiled back.

John, seated to one side, thought that no one would know from seeing Kit's face that he was marrying this woman for her money.

She arrived by his side at last, her uncle stepping backwards. Kit reached out and took her hands in his, giving them a small, grateful squeeze. She smiled again, not quite meeting his eyes. She was nervous. The thought did not surprise him—so was he.

He did not remember much of the ceremony afterwards. He was regretting his words to her on the day of his proposal. He had said he would ask nothing from her until, if ever, she was ready. How could he stick to such a promise when she looked as she did this morning?

Her lips moved as she repeated the vows, her eyes only occasionally meeting his. Kit wondered what she was thinking. The priest—borrowed from the local parish church—finally drew to a close, after what seemed like an eternity. At his bidding, Kit leant forward to kiss her. Her lips were soft against his, and he had to fight the urge to pull her to him and kiss her properly, disregarding all the people watching.

He managed to control himself, pulling away after what was only slightly too long. The congregation took it as another sign of a budding love between the newlyweds.

Then it was over, the priest said a few last words, and they were walking down the aisle together, out into the early summer sun. Kit, taken aback at the swiftness of proceedings, realised he did not know what to say to her.

She glanced up at him, cheeks flushed. 'How do you feel?' she said.

He smiled. 'I was about to say the same to you.'

Neither of them had a chance to find out, for at that moment the chapel disgorged its occupants and they were surrounded by well-wishers and borne in opposite directions.

Kit lost sight of his bride as he conversed with various members of society, nodding and smiling in all the right places.

Dinner was served in his large formal banqueting hall, and Roisin's uncle made a speech about how pleased he was to be giving his niece to such a fine young man. Kit, sitting beside his new wife, wondered what he would say if he knew the business-like way the proposal and acceptance had been procured. She ate little, he noticed. He wondered if she was unhappy, despite the smile she wore.

There was dancing afterwards, and he took her by the hand and led her to the floor, beginning the dance before everyone else joined them. She had been unusually quiet during the whole affair, which did not seem to him a good sign. It was done now, though, for better or for worse, as the vows went—and there was little he could do to undo it. She would recover.

For, watching his wife in her finery, he could not imagine what he would do if she did not.

* * *

Dancing with her husband, Roisin found herself experiencing not wholly unfamiliar feelings. In his formal wear he was breathtaking, his face grave as he moved beside her in the dance. In the chapel she had seen the relief on his face when she had arrived, and had welcomed the pressure of his hands on hers. He had seemed genuinely glad she was there, although for the wrong reasons. Now he was polite but distant. Was he regretting what he had done?

She watched him as he danced and conversed with other women during the evening, how attentive he was to all. Despite herself, she felt a sinking inside. Did he feel nothing for her, then? Nothing more than he felt for any other pretty woman here?

Of course he does not, said the voice in her head. She had known why he married her, after all. She had as much to gain from this match as he. It mattered not what he did with his private time. She understood how things were.

Roisin bit her lip. Why, then, did she watch him dance with this strange feeling, almost like envy? Perhaps it was because he looked so very handsome.

'He is handsome, is he not?'

Roisin turned her head to discover who had read her mind. It was Cathy, of course.

'Cathy.' She smiled. 'It is good to see you.'

Her cousin reflected only a little of the smile back.

'I thought you said you and Kit felt nothing for each other?'

Roisin frowned. 'What do you mean?'

Cathy's head turned towards the dance. Lord Westhaven was smiling at the pretty creature who currently trod the floor nearest him.

'You do not look as unperturbed as a trophy bride should that your husband dances long with other women at his wedding feast.'

Roisin lowered her eyes, knowing not what to say. 'I am tired, perhaps.'

To her surprise, Cathy smiled. 'You should have told me the truth, Roisin. Whatever the reason you married him, that is not a man who feels nothing for you. Nor will I believe you feel nothing for him.' She paused. 'And that makes it easier to bear.'

Roisin frowned. 'Easier? How so?'

Cathy shrugged. 'There seems to be more than money between you. And I would want him to be happy with his wife.'

'I do not understand what you mean,' said Roisin. It was only a half-lie. 'But I am sorry for what we have done to you.'

'As am I,' said the younger girl. 'But I begin to believe that you were less to blame than I had at first thought.'

'I never meant to hurt you,' her cousin said, touching her hand briefly. 'And you must visit us whenever you can.'

'Perhaps I will, when I am ready,' said Cathy. Leaning forward, she gave Roisin a kiss on the cheek. 'Happy wedding day, cousin.'

Roisin watched her melt away into the crowded room, puzzled by what she had said. It must be the excitement of weddings that made people see what was not there. So many well-meaning ladies had told her how happy she appeared. With good reason, they said. Lord Westhaven seemed to have been sought after by many an eligible woman.

The evening drew on and, one by one, the guests took their leave, wishing the newlyweds good luck in married life. Eventually Roisin found herself by her husband's side, kissing her Aunt Elizabeth goodbye. Her family were the last to go. Oakridge was empty, except for its much depleted quota of servants, Roisin, and Lord Westhaven himself.

She stood alone in the drawing room as he saw them out to their carriage, her hands crossed beneath her breasts. The long wedding gown trailed behind her as she walked up and down the already worn carpet, awaiting her husband with trepidation.

Suddenly catching sight of her reflection in the window, she smiled. Look at her face. So many brides must wear this same expression. Nerves at the night to come—at the years to come. But did not many people marry for love? Yes, she supposed. About as many as who did not. She was not the first to go into marriage with her dowry held out before her.

He was only a man, she reminded herself. She had held her own against a highwayman; she could cope with whatever was to come. Roisin frowned. Talking to herself in this manner helped little to bolster her courage. She sighed aloud.

'You look unhappy.'

She spun around to see Lord Westhaven in the doorway. He gave her a half-smile, his boots sounding inordinately loud on the floorboards as he came towards her.

'Oh, no,' she said hastily. 'Just…overwhelmed, I think.'

She stood, watching him, wondering what happened now. It was, as usual, impossible to tell what he thought of the situation.

He said, 'Would you like a drink?'

Roisin did not have much experience of hard liquor. Yet something told her she would need it tonight. She nodded. 'Please.'

He crossed to where a decanter of whisky sat on a sideboard, not quite empty, and returned with two glasses. 'Here.' His fingers brushed hers as he handed it to her.

Roisin frowned.

'What is it?' he asked.

She shook her head. How could she explain this

sudden feeling of familiarity, watching his actions? Could their paths have crossed before she came to London, at a party or dinner? Surely his striking looks were not so easily forgotten—would she not have remembered him?

'Have you ever been to Kinsale, my lord?'

He sipped his drink. 'I don't believe so. Why do you ask?'

'Sometimes…I feel like I know you from before.'

'Before?' His tone was measured.

'Before London.' She smiled slightly. 'Sometimes it seems as though this is all a separate life. Parties, theatre…'

'Marriage?'

Feeling foolish, she nodded. 'It seems I have been away for ever. I can barely picture the people I knew there. It must be that you remind me of someone, but I cannot think who.' Aware that she was spilling her innermost thoughts to a virtual stranger, Roisin stopped. 'You must forgive me, I'm not sure what is the matter with me tonight.'

'You are homesick, perhaps?'

Touched at his perception, she nodded. 'It was strange, being married without my family present. My aunt and uncle were a comfort of course, and Cathy, but…'

'Well,' he said softly, 'in that at least I can understand how you feel.'

Roisin's mouth fell open in horror, hers eyes going to the black armband that stood out against his formal wear. She had done it *again*—remembered nothing of his own, much more deep and recent, pain in the face of her own discomfort.

'My lord…I'm so sorry… You must think me—'

'Do not distress yourself,' he replied, drawing himself up a little.

'Forgive me,' she all but whispered, touching his arm without thinking.

He stepped away from her then, turning his back and replenishing his glass as she stood very still and cursed her own thoughtlessness. He drained his whisky in silence and Roisin, realising her own glass was still in her hand, sipped gingerly, nose wrinkling at the unfamiliar taste. She looked up to find him facing her once more, and coughed slightly.

'You are not a whisky drinker, then?'

She realised he was teasing her, trying to lighten the mood. 'No.'

Awkwardness crackled in the air between them, coupled with something else. The weight of Lord Westhaven's gaze began to unsettle Roisin. She swilled the amber liquid around in her glass, wishing she could think of some way to redeem herself.

He cleared his throat. 'Should I go out and come in again, d'you think?'

A laugh rose in her throat as she saw the sparkle

in his eyes. She felt suddenly like bursting into tears, oddly reassured that he did not think less of her for her ramblings.

He came forward a little, lessening the chasm between them. 'Roisin. Are you so ill at ease with me?'

She forced herself to look at him, surprised at her own reticence. Such behaviour was so unlike her usual confidence—but something about him completely unseated her… And she knew it had to do with that dark hunger in his eyes.

'This is all very new to me,' she said shortly.

'You think I have been married before?'

'No…' She smiled, despite herself. 'You know what I mean.'

'Ah, that I do. And did you enjoy your wedding day?'

How was she to answer that? 'It went very well,' she said at last.

He inclined his head. Then, after a pause, he said, 'You looked lovely. I lost count of the number of people who told me how lucky I was.'

She dropped her gaze to her drink once more, yet through her lashes she saw that he was still watching her. 'Thank you,' she murmured uncomfortably.

Silence. Roisin wished she could think of something to say. She took another sip of her drink, grimaced, then held out her glass to him.

'Here, you have it.'

He took it, drinking with his eyes still on her face,

as if trying hard to fathom her thoughts. She wondered why he did not just ask—then realised she would not be able to tell him, even if he did. Her brain was concentrating on the way his jaw set when he gave her that look. It did strange things to her.

'Well. If we are done with conversation, we had best to bed,' he said after a time.

She nodded, nerves bunching in the pit of her stomach. A woman's wedding night should be a time of excitement, should it not? Why then did she feel such foreboding? She took a deep, unsteady breath.

'It has been a tiring day,' she said, in order to say something, then realised how foolish this sounded. From what she had heard it was not sleep that he had in mind.

His expression gave nothing away. 'Follow me.'

He led the way down corridors which she was sure she would never remember, his way lit by an oil lamp. The house seemed larger by night, the windows blank as she passed them. Roisin shivered a little, running her hand along one wall.

'This is your room,' he said at last, stopping so abruptly that she almost walked into him. He hung the lamp from a hook on the wall and pushed open a door to reveal a large, richly furnished room, with huge latticed windows. Lights were already lit within, as was a fire. The marble fireplace was ex-quisitely carved—two lions standing on their hind legs, with the mantel shelf balanced on their heads. A rug lay before it, on which stood a bath with carved feet. It had been recently filled by some unseen hand, Roisin saw, and the scented water was steaming.

Puzzled, she turned to Lord Westhaven. What had he planned?

He smiled a little stiltedly. 'I thought you might like a bath. If not, just let it go cold. Annette will empty it in the morning.'

'Thank you,' she said softly.

His smile faded. 'Is something wrong? You do not like the room?'

'Oh, no.' She smiled. 'I like it very much.'

'Good.' He nodded.

It suddenly struck her. This was her room. He had said so. He was not going to share it with her. She was glad the light of the lamp was not sufficient to show up the deep flush that suffused her face. What had she been thinking? He did not want her for a wife—not in any respect. He had told her that.

'Thank you, Lord Westhaven,' she said automatically.

He seemed amused. 'There are very few people who call me Lord Westhaven,' he told her. 'It would be most odd for my wife to be one of them. In polite society I am rarely even Christopher—though you may call me that if you prefer. But usually, as you know, I am just Kit.'

Just Kit. Whatever this man was, towering over her, his shoulder leaning against the doorframe, he was not *just* anything. Nevertheless, she nodded.

'Thank you. Goodnight.'

'Still no Kit. Never mind, there is time.' His smile came easier now. 'Goodnight.' He bent his head and kissed her lightly on the cheek. Roisin closed her eyes as his lips made contact. Shyness was not a trait she would usually admit to—but she felt it now. His touch burned her skin and made her stomach lurch. She heard him exhale close to her ear and, opening her eyes, saw that his face was still very near hers.

She lifted her chin and looked into his face, breathing shallow. Then, before she knew what was happening, she was flat against the wall and his lips were on hers. His kiss was not gentle—far from it. His mouth pressed against hers, urging a response from it, as his hands took her by the shoulders. Roisin's brain exploded into shards of sensation, the feeling in her stomach spreading out and downwards. Her mouth knew what to do, although she did not. Her hands, not daring to touch the body that was so close to hers, found the wall behind her and she braced herself for dear life.

His hands moved from her shoulders, one cradling the back of her head, in her hair, his fingers thrusting themselves into the mass of curls and dislodging them. The other went behind her waist and flattened itself against the wall. His body pressed against hers, awakening all sorts of very pleasant feelings as he moved. Roisin gave a little gasp between kisses, her body beginning to tingle with awareness. Her hands gripped the wall, wanting to let go and not daring to do so. At last, she lifted one hand and placed it upon his chest, his shirt rumpling between her fingers. His heartbeat, beneath her fingers, added to her sense of timelessness. It seemed as though they had been there for ever, and for no time at all. She desired him as he did her—she wanted him to show her what happened next. He tasted of whisky, but it was not unpleasant. Far from it, in fact. Her eyes closed.

Then, just as she was finding the courage to begin to touch him as he was touching her, he gave a strangled moan and pushed himself away from her.

Roisin fell back against the wall.

They stood, both breathing heavily, her hair falling down, his eyes wide open in an expression that she would have best described as horror, had anyone asked her. She frowned at him, confusion breaking through the cloud of desire that still filled her head. This was not how a man looked at his wife, surely.

'My God,' he said, his voice rough. 'I'm…' He swallowed hard. 'Forgive me, Roisin.'

Her lips formed words that would not come.

Lord Westhaven dropped his eyes from hers. 'Goodnight.'

He strode away down the corridor, leaving her gasping. One hand to her lips, she stood, back still to the wall, confusion and hurt filling her.

Why did she elicit such a response from men? Her mind flew back to the last time she had been kissed like that, and abandoned in a similar manner. But Ewan Hamilton had been gentler, and he had not seemed sorry, though he too had asked her forgiveness… And *he* had not been married to her.

The way Lord Westhaven—who *was* her husband—framed the words made her believe them.

Tears trembling on her lashes, she went into her room and closed the door. *You knew why he married you,* said her common sense, for the hundredth time that day. It was no less right than it had been every other time. But now she felt different. His kiss awakened sensations in her that she had felt only once before, with another man entirely.

'May I undress you, Lady Roisin?' said a voice, making her jump. It was Jane, standing discreetly to one side, awaiting her. Aunt Elizabeth had insisted that she accompany her niece until a suitable maid of her own could be appointed. Roisin had quite forgotten this, but suddenly it was a comfort to see a familiar face.

'Yes.' Roisin pulled herself together. 'Thank you.'

Jane's hands were deft but gentle, and Roisin barely felt them unlacing and unbuttoning her, so confused was she by the day's events. Her mind wandered, restless, as her body stood still. She dismissed her aunt's maid as soon as her clothing was removed and put away, at a loss suddenly. What to do now? Go to bed, where sleep would surely evade her?

She examined the bath. It smelled comforting, the warm water rippling against the high sides. Stripping off her white underthings and flinging them to the ground, she stepped into it, then lay down, knees bent, with the water up to her chin. Warmth spread through her, soothing her, in body at least.

She wrapped her arms about her knees, thoughts still locked on to her husband, the kiss, and the horror on his face when he realised what he had done. She closed her eyes. Was she so unattractive? If so, why had he kissed her in the first place? He had said he would not ask her to fulfill the duties of a wife—and that could only mean he did not wish her to, even if she was willing. Had she done something to make him kiss her against his will? She did not understand the etiquette of the bedroom—surely he knew that.

For the first time in her life, Roisin wished her father had been a poor man. Such a situation would never have arisen for his daughter if he had been— and Lord Westhaven would be in bed with Cathy even now. She hated the helplessness he made her feel—as if she had no control over anything. Not even her own body obeyed her now.

She stayed in the bath for a long while, and lay in bed for even longer before she was able to sleep.

Kit ran through the darkened corridors until he reached his own room, cold and dark, the dying fire he had ordered lit casting the only light. He flung open the door, slammed it behind him and leant against it, as if preventing himself from going back down the corridor, wrenching her out of that bath and—

He stopped the thought with an effort. He was no gentleman. She was vastly inexperienced, that much was obvious. He had taken advantage of her in the most disgusting way, as the look on her face told him. Sliding down the door, he buried his head in his hands. *He had promised her.* It was no use. Her presence would torment him, as he had feared. She probably thought he was some sort of animal—unable to control his urges, unable to behave in a decent manner. She had said she was tired, made it clear that she wished to sleep, rather than anything else he might plan—and he had leapt on her, before he could stop himself. He was a fool.

Indeed, the force of his reaction surprised even Kit. She was desirable, yes, but he did not wish merely to bed her as he had done with other women. He wished her to be more than that. Which was a pity, for in marrying her under such circumstances he had waived his right to anything at all. The irony was not lost on him.

There could be no more kisses. Not unless she asked him.

Which was unlikely now. She was probably confused beyond measure at his behaviour, upset at his assault. Anger suffused him. He had offered her his home, his name—and his protection. What good was that if she needed protecting from *him?*

He *would not* allow it to happen again. He would be the kind, attentive husband he had promised her he would be. In name only. She had upheld her end of the bargain—was not her substantial dowry now in his possession? He would keep his, though it might well lead to nights of torment.

Kit sat, the cold from the floor seeping into his buttocks. This was not how he had imagined spending his wedding night. But he supposed she had not intended hers to be this way, either. He sighed. He wanted her to trust him—he wanted to please her. He would have to do something to make amends. But what?

After a time, an idea came to him, and he smiled. It was just the thing to show her that he respected her, and acknowledged her right to her own lifestyle.

He would set off first thing in the morning.

Chapter Eight

Roisin awoke late the next morning, opening her eyes and sitting bolt upright once she realised where she was. She looked at the clock on her mantel. It was eleven o'clock—no one had called her for breakfast.

There was a dull ache in her head, which made itself known to her gradually. Roisin frowned. She had not slept much, or well. There was too much to think about. She wanted to lie back and sleep for the rest of the day, but knew she must face her husband at one time or another. Best get it over with.

Scrambling out of bed, she saw that clothes had been laid out for her—so Jane had been in. She frowned. No doubt Lord Westhaven would complain at her lack of punctuality. Or perhaps he had welcomed the opportunity to breakfast alone.

Roisin rang for Jane and made sure she was dressed as quickly as possible. She waited impatiently while her hair was pinned up and twisted

round in front of the mirror to inspect it, uncharac-
teristically critical of her appearance. Then, when she
was finally satisfied, she went to explore the house.

She met no one, but the fact did not surprise her,
for the house was run solely by John and his sister
Annette, and the cook. Kit had explained that, with
the exception of those needed to run the estate and
its surrounding farms, he had been forced to let most
of his servants go. Now, perhaps, she thought with a
wry smile, he could afford more.

Walking along corridors as the whim took her,
Roisin eventually found the main staircase. It was in
fact two, twisting around from opposite ends of the
large hall in almost a heart shape, to become one,
wider staircase. She descended, eyes roving over the
mounted stags' heads and portraiture. Kit's house
was indeed packed with memorabilia—perhaps even
more so than her home at Kinsale. Her mother's
home, she reminded herself. *This* was her home now.

At the bottom of the stairs she met Annette, on her
knees polishing the brass carpet rails on each stair.
'Have you seen Lord Westhaven?' she asked, as the
girl got to her feet.

The maid's dark eyes studied her new mistress
with a little more familiarity than was appropriate.
'He left early this morning,' was all she said. 'I don't
know where he went.'

Roisin nodded. 'Thank you.' She carried on

walking, across the freshly polished hall floor, and out on to the terrace. It afforded a lovely view of the grounds, including the chapel where just yesterday she had been a bride.

It did not seem possible that she was married. Had she chosen rightly? As she looked at her predicament now it did not seem so. Not even twenty-four hours a wife and already rejected on her wedding night—and abandoned the morning after. Roisin sighed. She did not want to see him. Things were bound to be awkward. She had imagined none of this when he had proposed. She had thought only of the green beauty of Oakridge—and the escape it promised from everything she hated about society and feared about impending marriage. Of course, she had not expected that Kit and herself would fall in love and live happily ever after, but she had imagined they would at least share the same bed!

Roisin glanced up as hooves on the drive caught her attention. Two men were riding towards the house on seemingly identical dark brown mounts, with a third, white, horse on a leading rein behind one of them. As they drew closer she recognised her husband, with John slightly behind. Kit waved at her as they approached, just as she was wondering whether she should go inside before he noticed her.

'Good morrow, Roisin!' His tone was genial, to her surprise.

She did not wave back. Her headache was still present, his healthy aura making her feel worse. She wondered irritably whether the events of yesterday had affected him at all. He certainly seemed happy to pretend nothing had happened.

He dismounted, untying the white horse and keeping hold of its bridle, while John led the others away, around the side of the house.

He beckoned. 'Come down here, wife!'

Needled by his address, Roisin went slowly down the steps. He seemed pleased with himself. She did not return his wide smile.

'What is it?'

He gestured to the horse. 'Do you like her?'

She was a fine beast indeed, well bred, with flowing mane and tail. Dark eyes looked at Roisin placidly. She stroked the velvety nose that was pushed into her hand. 'Very much,' she said, despite her ill mood.

'Good.' His pride increased. 'Her name is Belle. She is my wedding gift to you.'

Roisin looked at him evenly.

He stared back. 'What is wrong? You do not like her?'

'I have told you I do,' she said shortly. 'I thought only that perhaps a man with debts such as yours should spend my father's money more wisely.'

She regretted the words as soon as they were out

of her mouth. That increasingly familiar invisible shutter fell over his face.

'My finances are my own business,' he said quietly.

'Indeed?' So now he was not even willing to discuss money with her? 'That was not what you said when you asked me to save your home.'

'You agreed—'

'I agreed to be your wife,' she said. 'You have secured me now, Lord Westhaven, you do not have to sweeten me with fancy presents. If I wanted my family's money to buy me a horse, I could have asked them directly.'

His lips pressed tightly together, he surveyed her. 'It seems I have misjudged your needs. I thought only that you would want sometimes to go riding in the grounds. Take her back if you wish. I care not.' With that he was off, striding across the lawn to the house, pulling off his wig as he went in that way he had that told her he was genuinely riled.

Roisin gazed after him. Perhaps she should not have been so harsh… Yet he did not need to buy her a horse of her own—she could have borrowed one. She shrugged, defensive of her thoughts. It was true, after all. Her dowry was supposed to help him mend his affairs, not be squandered on foolish things to please a wife he did not love.

Perhaps she had phrased it badly.

She stroked Belle's neck, deep in thought. It was a

practical gift—and he had seemed eager to give it. Yet, people should not buy things they could not afford!

Take her back, he had said. Roisin knew she should. Such a fine beast would not have been cheap. But she had already insulted him…and the horse was beautiful. Perhaps it would not hurt to try her out before making a decision.

Roisin led the horse to the front steps and, with their aid, pulled herself up on to Belle's back. She had learned when young to ride bareback, to the chagrin of her mother. It felt good to be on a horse again—it had been too long.

Digging her heels into Belle's flanks, she urged her forwards. They started slowly, then Roisin took her into a canter, circling around the lake and beyond. The horse responded well, her powerful muscles bunching and lengthening under her rider, carrying her effortlessly. Roisin curled her fingers deeper into Belle's mane, holding on as they flew across her husband's land. Her skirts flared up around her knees, and she did not care. There was no one to see her—and even if there was, it was none of their concern.

Presently, the wind in her hair began to cool her head. *This* was what she had imagined when she had thought of Oakridge in the last two weeks—plenty of land and a horse to ride over it. She slowed, hands caressing the silky flanks beneath her. He had known that. So why had she been so rude to him? Because he had not wanted to bed her?

Of course not, she told herself hurriedly. There were a thousand other reasons. It was just that, sitting here on the hill overlooking his home on the horse he had given her, none of them came immediately to mind.

She awoke the next morning to find a cart full of slate parked in front of the house. Above her there were noises on the roof, as if men worked there, while below her husband was deep in conversation with a beefy man holding a sheaf of paper.

As she stood at her window, hair falling over her shoulder in a thick plait, he looked up, as if he felt himself watched. For a moment their eyes met and she felt a flush growing in her cheeks, for no reason she could think of. Then he turned back at the man and whatever he was explaining, his expression altering not at all.

Roisin sighed, drawing away from the window. He was still displeased, then. Dinner last night had been an awkward affair. He had spoken little to her, restricting his remarks to comments on the weather and eating hurriedly. She had remained in the dining room alone after he had excused himself—perfectly politely, as one would to someone one barely knew.

He had not mentioned work was to begin on

Oakridge today. Perhaps he had not thought her important enough to tell.

These thoughts did her little good, she told herself. If she was unhappy with the way things were with her husband, she had only herself to blame. She must attempt to make amends, if only for the sake of civility.

She dressed and went down to him.

He stood alone now, before the house, eyes shaded with one hand against the morning sunshine, watching the men at work above.

'You're having the roof fixed?' As an opening line it was not one of her most inspired. Roisin grimaced inwardly.

He looked round. 'It would seem so.'

Well, she had laid herself wide open to that. Taking a deep breath, she tried to take on Cathy's soothing approach.

'What are your plans for today?' she asked brightly.

'Why do you ask?'

'I had considered a ride around the grounds. I thought you might like to come with me.'

'A ride?' His eyes were cool, questioning. 'So my gift has not yet been made into dogmeat?'

Again, she felt a tide of colour rise in her face. 'No. In fact, I—'

'Thank you for the offer,' he cut in. 'But I am needed here. Perhaps another time.'

His tone belied his polite words. It was clear he did not wish to discuss the subject of riding.

'Then perhaps a short walk?'

'Please, Roisin. I am busy.'

He addressed this last to the chimney pots at which he gazed. Roisin gritted her teeth, no longer able to hold her annoyance at bay. She crossed her arms firmly, trying to quell the wish to strike him across the back of his stupid head. How dare he speak to her as if she was some numb-witted trophy wife? Her money was paying for all of this!

'Fine,' she said tightly. 'I was merely trying to be civil. Good day, Lord Westhaven.'

She could feel his eyes on her at last as she stalked off, making her way back indoors. She did not care what he did, she told herself. He was none of her concern now—it was not as if she was truly his wife. It was not her responsibility to coax him out of his—

She cried out as she was grabbed from behind and pulled backwards, the breath knocked out of her against her husband's chest as something fell past them and exploded on the stone at their feet.

It was a large slate tile, and it had almost fallen squarely on her head. Roisin found herself frozen to the spot, heart pumping furiously. Her eyes fixed themselves on the remains of the slate and the spot where she had been standing seconds ago. Lord Westhaven's hands were on her shoulders.

Shouts from the roof made her look up, dazed. The three men working there had come to the edge and were calling down. One of them, the one who appeared to have dropped the slate, was apologising profusely. He looked worried, probably fearing for his job as much as for her well-being. Roisin swallowed hard.

'It's all right!' her husband was calling up to them. 'No one is hurt!'

He led her a little way away as they returned to work.

'You're *not* hurt, are you?'

She shook her head, not knowing what to say. Her heart was still pounding uncomfortably, and she knew from his expression that her face must be pale. Inside, however, she was flushing beetroot. She had tried to assert herself and ended up making an idiot of herself all over again.

His hands supported her gently as he tried to steer her towards the house.

'Come inside, sit down.'

'No.' Pride won over shock. Roisin disentangled herself from his grasp. It seemed she was nothing but in the way here. She felt foolish. 'Thank you. I'm fine. Go back to your work—I will not disturb you again.'

He reached for her arm once more. 'I think you should—'

'I don't need your help!' Hearing the peevish note in her voice and hating it, Roisin batted his hand away.

She was humiliated, and wanted to be out of sight of those piercing eyes. Why could he not leave her be?

As if hearing her thoughts, he stepped back. 'Very well.'

With that he turned away, and she watched his broad back retreat towards the scene of the accident.

Suddenly Roisin wanted to weep. Anger and humiliation fused with guilt and shame at her behaviour. How dare he be so kind and make her feel like such an ingrate? He probably did it on purpose.

She turned in a swirl of skirts and retreated back to her bedroom, vowing that she *would not* shed tears over the wretched man. He was nothing to her, after all, and she was nothing to him.

For some reason this thought made her feel only worse, if possible. Reaching her room, she flung herself upon the bed, head buried in her pillows. She wondered if she could scream out her frustration without bringing the whole household running.

Probably not. Tears it would have to be then, she resolved, as the first few began to roll down her cheeks. Although he was not worth them.

She lay there until, exhausted by all this unladylike emotion, she fell asleep.

Kit strode away from the house on legs that were still not quite steady after the shock of his wife's near-accident. He saw again the expression on her face as she had looked at the fallen slate, and the re-vulsion that had followed as she pushed him away from her.

She still felt violated, he told himself. He had failed to be a gentleman. How else did he expect her to behave after he had forced himself upon her? But how could she speak to him so, when he had pulled her back from injury, perhaps even death? Anger coursed through him, speeding his retreat.

He would never understand women. She seemed to find him entirely to blame in all this. Why could the stubborn wench not see that he was trying to help her?

And this horse—he wished he had never bought the wretched animal. It was half in his mind to go up to the stable and shoot the beast here and now. Perhaps that would please her, as nothing else seemed to. All her accusations about her dowry… It set his teeth on edge to contemplate it.

He closed his eyes. The same thoughts rattled through his brain, over and over again. He would give anything to stop them.

He was grateful, of course, that he had pulled her away in time. He was sure she would feel the same, once she was over the shock of it all. He had wanted to buy her a present, and he had. But why could she not thank him? Why could she not attempt to see him as a human being, instead of her owner?

He stopped, abruptly registering where he was—

where his body had brought him while his mind was elsewhere. Jamie's grave. The very sight calmed him.

It stood silent beneath the towering oaks in which they had climbed as boys: a forlorn mound of earth with a makeshift cross at one end. John had knotted two branches together to make it. Just a temporary measure, he had said, until a fitting headstone could be erected. They had felt there should be something.

Kit felt his anger drain. It was nothing, he knew, compared to this.

What would Jamie do? he asked himself. Probably pick himself up, dust off his clothes and find another woman. He would not have placed himself in such a situation in the first place. But he would have also told her the truth.

Kit frowned. The truth was not a road he was willing to take at this point. Not, perhaps, at any point. His marriage—if it could be called that—was volatile enough already.

He clenched his jaw, remembering her look of scorn as he had touched her. Was he so repulsive to her? There was many a woman in town who would not say so. Jamie would tell him she was not worth the indigestion, he thought with a half-smile. Perhaps he would have been right.

For now, he would keep well clear. He did not want to say something he would regret.

Eyes fixed again on his brother's grave, he suddenly

wished more than anything to have Jamie back with him. He would give Oakridge, he would give all, for these thoughts that haunted him to be gone.

He turned and went back to the house.

As Jane dressed her for dinner in her room that evening, Roisin determined to be more civil to her husband. Her embarrassment at walking under a falling slate had abated, to be replaced by an equally burning humiliation for her rudeness towards her rescuer. It was true, she hated to think of him as such because of her own foolish pride—but he *had* saved her skull from being cleaved in two.

As for Belle… Meeting her own eyes in the mirror, Roisin examined her conscience. His intentions had been good, she knew, although he had obviously not thought the purchase through. She knew she had spoiled his pleasure in giving her his gift.

It was time to put a stop to this quarrelling—she had not planned her married life to be lived on a battlefield. Dinner this evening *would* be pleasant, she vowed, even if every minute of it pained them both.

She had chosen a light green gown for this evening, the bodice embroidered with flowers. Her hair she pinned up simply, because she was too tired to worry about it. Meeting her own eyes in the mirror, she knew she would prefer not to dine with Lord Westhaven again, in the stiff surroundings of the dining room. She would much rather have supper here, before the fire. She sighed. There would be time for such things when she was more settled. For now she must put in an appearance, as a new wife should.

Steeling herself and reminding herself once more to be pleasant, she headed for the dining room. She was late—the gong had been rung. He would be waiting.

To her surprise, the room was empty save for John, standing against one wall. He bowed as she entered, pulling out her chair and tucking it in again after her. She thanked him, then noticed that there was only one place setting.

'Is Lord Westhaven dining out?' she asked, trying to keep her tone conversational. She could not blame him if he was—now he knew he had a shrew for a wife.

John seemed just a little uncomfortable. 'He wished to take supper alone in the library,' he told her.

'Oh.' Roisin lowered her eyes. 'I see.'

'I think, perhaps, he feels unwell,' offered his manservant.

'Perhaps.' She sighed. The first week of her wedded life was continuing on no more pleasant a vein than it had started.

She ate little, for which she felt guilty, because Cook had provided a fine meal. There was wine to accompany it, and she drank a glass in an effort to cheer herself. It did not work. She was unaccustomed to dining alone, and disquieted by John and Annette appearing every now and then to see to her needs.

At last, when she felt she had pretended to eat for long enough, she rose, laying her napkin on the table beside her still mostly full plate.

'Thank Cook for me,' she told John. 'And apologise to her. I ate too much at luncheon.'

It was a foolish thing to say. He knew she had eaten nothing earlier, had been closeted in her room all day. He merely nodded, however, and took his leave.

Roisin stood for a moment, wondering what she should do. Go to bed? Read? She wished she had brought one of the interminable samplers that her Aunt Elizabeth loved so. Perhaps it would have served to take her mind from the increasing feeling of rejection.

She went listlessly into the hall, where she almost collided with John, carrying a tray that Roisin could not help notice held the half-eaten remains of someone else's supper. She did not have to think hard about whose.

'Lord Westhaven had no appetite?' she asked before she could stop herself.

'Perhaps he too had a large luncheon,' said John.

Despite herself, she smiled. 'Perhaps.'

He went to move away, then stopped, uncertain.

She waited, knowing instinctively that her husband confided in this man. 'Yes, John? Is there something you wish to tell me?'

He looked down at her, only slightly shorter than her husband. 'Forgive my impertinence, Lady West-haven, but…'

'Please, go on.' She tried to ignore the strange feeling it gave her to hear herself addressed so. 'I would be glad to hear anything you have to say, I am sure.'

He nodded. 'Ki— Lord Westhaven… He mentioned the conversation…the *discussion* he had with you yesterday, about the horse that he gave you…'

'Yes?' He was so wretched that Roisin smiled despite herself. 'Friends talk to each other of such things. What about her?'

'I went with him yesterday to buy her…' He paused, and she nodded encouragingly. 'His brother had a pocket watch that he carried with him always. It was very valuable.'

A sinking feeling took hold of Roisin. 'Go on.'

'Lord Westhaven took it with him. Before we went to buy the horse we stopped at a jeweller's shop. I do not think he got what it was worth, but…'

She stood, staring at him, dismay filling her. 'Why are you telling me this?'

John shrugged his huge shoulders. 'You should not judge him too harshly.'

'And you think that is what I have done?'

He would not meet her eyes. 'It is not for me to say.'

'That means yes.' She gave him a small smile. 'I hope I may make amends. Thank you, John.'

He nodded. 'Only, do not mention me. He would not take kindly to the idea of me meddling in his private affairs.'

Roisin put a hand on his arm. 'I think he is lucky to have such a friend. But fear not. I will say nothing.'

She stood quite still until he had left her. Then, she cursed herself roundly for her own stupidity. *Why* did she go rushing into confrontations without finding out what was really going on? No wonder he had seemed so put out. She clasped her hands together, thinking of the lost pocket watch. What should she do now?

The answer, really, was clear. She should find her husband and apologise for her behaviour. Offer to make amends, if she could. Although it was a wrench, she would offer to take Belle back, and buy back the watch.

She headed in the direction of the library, remembering vaguely where it was. The corridors were growing dark as the evening drew in, and Roisin shivered as she walked along. He must have been lonely living in this huge place by himself. Probably he still was. She knew she did nothing to ease his mind, as he did nothing to ease hers. Still, perhaps it was not too late to make amends.

She rounded a corner and there, at last, was the library door, shut firmly, no sound issuing from within. Steeling herself, she knocked.

No answer. Yet, without knowing how, she knew he was there. So she turned the knob and went in. It was a large room, walls covered almost entirely in full bookshelves that reached right up to the ceiling. There was a ladder mounted on castors for access to the higher books, and a desk, covered in papers, with a battered but cosy-looking chair before it. It was a comfortable, lived-in room. Roisin could see why Kit made it his refuge.

As for her husband, he was slumped in another chair before the fire, back to her, face hidden by the hand in which his chin rested. His wig was nowhere to be seen, his hair mussed, as always. He did not turn as she entered.

'I told you I did not want to be disturbed again, John.' His voice was tired.

She shut the door behind her. 'It is not John. It is I. The shrew you married.'

The hand moved from his face. He half-turned his head towards her. 'The same applies.' This time the tone was colder.

'You were not at dinner,' she said.

'I am aware of that.'

'You did not wish to eat with me?'

'I had no appetite.'

He had not yet turned around to face her. It was tempting to slip out of the room and hope things appeared better in the light of a new day. But the niggling feeling of shame at her actions would not allow her to leave. Roisin stood her ground.

'I wanted to thank you for today.'

'Which part of it?'

She sighed inwardly. *You know very well which part.* 'The accident.'

'Oh.'

'I was rude to you, I am sorry.'

'Yes, you were.'

A glass of amber liquid, warmed by the light of the fire behind it, stood by his chair. He had been here all evening, by the look of him.

She was not going to leave, although he clearly wished her to. Nothing was said. At last, she gave an impatient sigh. Enough procrastinating—she would just have to say it, she decided.

'You did not buy Belle with my dowry, did you?'

There was a silence. The fire crackled in the hearth, shadows moved across his face.

'Please,' she said. 'Tell me.'

He did not move. 'I don't wish to discuss it.'

She frowned. 'Why?'

He erupted from his chair, an anger she had never seen before in his eyes. 'Why must you question everything? Because it matters not—it is done now!' As his voice echoed around the high-ceilinged room, filled with shelf after shelf of books, he closed his eyes. 'I am so tired of talk. If you want her, keep her. If not, send her to the knacker's yard. Only do not bother me!'

His words were swallowed up by the silence. He stood, just for a moment, watching her. Then he turned his back once more, standing at the window, his tall frame silhouetted in the fading light from outside.

'You wanted the chance to live your own life,' he said quietly. 'You have it. You need not seek me out for pleasantries that neither of us want.'

Roisin swallowed. He was not merely brooding. Something deeper was at stake.

'I only…wanted to say I am sorry for my ingratitude,' she said again. 'I had no right to be so callous when you were thinking of my needs.'

His shoulders were set. 'Please. I have not the stomach for this tonight.'

'I will get the watch back for you—' began Roisin, then, realising what she had done as he faced her, she clapped a hand to her mouth.

His eyes were like lit coals in his face. 'John had no right to tell you. I will teach him to interfere between myself and my wife!' He started forward, past Roisin.

'Wait!' She placed her hands on his chest to restrain him. 'Please!' It was like trying to hold back a brick wall. He stopped, though, at her voice, eyes boring into hers. She sighed. 'John was trying to help. He thinks I have behaved badly.'

'So now he insults my wife as well?'

'No! He did not have to say so.' Roisin cast about

for the right thing to say. 'Forgive me for judging you so harshly. I had no right.'

He gave a sigh that seemed to come from the very depths of him. 'Fine. I accept your apology. Thank you. Let that be an end to it.'

She frowned. 'But—'

'Please, I am tired.'

His back was to her again. He looked out of the window, seemingly intent on something. Roisin went forward slowly. There was nothing there. She stared at his broad back for a moment, recouping for another attempt.

'You should not have bought Belle for me,' she told him. 'She is lovely, but at such a price…'

'What does it matter?' Her husband put up a hand to massage his temples. 'He is dead. What use are his things to me now?'

Frowning, she drew closer. His breathing was strange. 'Are you ill?'

He gave a short half-laugh, a sound of pure bitterness. 'Not ill. Sick at heart, perhaps.'

As he spoke he turned his head a little, his profile sharp in the dying light. With a jolt like a hand tightening round her heart, she saw that there were tears on his face.

'Kit…' Roisin's eyes widened.

'Get *out*,' he said, quietly, but with fervour.

'I will do no such thing.'

She drew closer, placing one hand on his arm. He did not move. Without really thinking about it, she put her arms around him, pressing her body against his, as if trying to take his pain into herself.

There was a pause, while he held himself stiffly in her embrace, as if unsure what to do. Then, with a muttered oath, his arms were around her, his face in her hair, his chest heaving.

She clung to him as he wept, her heart contracting with a painful sympathy than bordered on fear. This was a man who, up until now, had kept a tight reign on his emotions. It had been weeks since his brother's death—yet he had not allowed himself proper time to mourn. There was such strength in his arms, such misery in his eyes.

Kit was desperately grateful for the physical closeness of another as his grief overwhelmed him. He wept like the child he had been when his mother died, throat sore, breath coming in gasps. All the while she made comforting noises in her throat, beside his ear. Her hands were on his back, stroking him, soothing him like a wounded animal. It had been so long since someone had held him like this. It was as if she absorbed the pain and grief that overflowed from him after so long contained. He no longer felt a fool in her embrace for allowing such emotion to break free. Something in the way she held him made him feel that she understood.

After a time, exhausted, he grew quieter, still

holding his wife tight to him, her breasts pressed against his chest. He marvelled at how good the pressure of her arms about him felt. Such closeness of being—it was almost better than kissing her.

But he should not be having such thoughts.

He pulled away enough to meet her eyes. 'Forgive me.'

She gave him a sad smile, one hand touching his cheek, her curled fingers on his stubble-roughened skin. 'It is you who should forgive me.'

They stood, looking at each other, bodies touching. It occurred to Roisin that he wanted to kiss her, yet he did not. He was holding himself back. Perhaps it was her imagination, she told herself. Yet there he was, staring at her, lips parted, his thumb massaging her shoulder. He did. He wanted to kiss her.

'Is something wrong?' she asked.

He seemed to shake himself awake. 'No.' He pulled gently out of her embrace and dropped on to the window seat with a sigh. 'I should not have let myself…'

'You are human, are you not?' she asked, smiling. She joined him, skirts resting against his thigh. 'A man, not a block of marble?'

Kit managed a smile in reply. 'Yes. It seems so. Still…'

'Still nothing. To try and forget your brother is to dishonour him,' she said softly.

He nodded. 'You are right.' They sat, side by side, the silence between them now a natural one. 'So you do like Belle?' he asked at last.

'Very much,' she said. 'It's wonderful to be able to ride again. You should join me one morning.'

'Perhaps.'

She studied his profile as he stared into the middle distance.

'Kit?'

'Mmm?'

'Is marriage as you had thought?' she asked.

His smile was genuine this time. 'Much different.'

'Do you regret it?'

There was a pause. She watched as the pain came back into his eyes. He looked long at her.

'Roisin, there are many things I regret about my life, short as it has yet been. Strangely, this marriage is not one of them. At least my wife has stopped calling me by my title.'

Despite herself, she smiled. 'I see.'

'Although,' he added, 'two days of marriage do not tell the full story. We must wait and see in the fullness of time.'

She nodded. 'Indeed.'

Then, because it felt like the right thing to do, she lifted her head and kissed him lightly on the mouth.

To say he was surprised seemed an understatement. He started back, a frown crossing his face.

'Roisin…' He seemed lost for words.

She gave him a level stare. 'Am I not to kiss you? If you do not wish it…'

Something changed in his face as his eyes moved over her. 'If I did not wish it I would be a fool. But—' He stopped, turning to face her. 'I don't expect you to—'

'I would not do as you expected for that reason alone,' she assured him.

His face was very close to hers. Again, she kissed him, her lips brushing his, lingering dizzyingly.

He frowned, whole body tense. 'Roisin. Do not play with me.'

'I am nothing but serious,' she told him, eyes dimming, hurt by his tone. She withdrew from him. 'Yesterday you seemed to want me, then did not. Now you stop yourself. I am your wife, yet I am not. Perhaps *you* are playing with *me*.'

He stood up, frustrated. 'I was trying to be a gentleman!'

She too rose. 'Well, perhaps you should not. Perhaps you should ask me what I want!'

There was a silence. He moved closer to her, and she felt her breathing quicken. Her physical response to him overwhelmed her thoughts. His eyes flicked over her face. Then he took her hands in his and, slowly, kissed them. Roisin breathed out slowly, light-headed as he caressed her.

'I swore I would make it up to you for marrying me,' he said softly. 'And that was only the day before yesterday.'

She smiled and saw its languid reflection in his eyes, liking the way his fingers lingered on her hand. He turned it over and kissed the palm.

'Do you regret marrying me?' he asked gently.

Roisin looked at him. This morning she would have said yes. Yet already she was beginning to feel that she knew this man. He was letting her see him unmasked.

'No,' she said slowly. 'But then, compared to my behaviour, yours has been faultless.'

He kissed her then, softly, teasing her lips with his, still holding back, she sensed. Yet the feel of him ignited a fire within her that warmed her whole body and showed in her eyes when he pulled back and looked at her once more.

He enclosed her in his arms, and held her to his chest. She rested her cheek against him, desire suddenly swamped in a much stronger emotion as she closed her eyes and felt her husband's heart beating beneath his shirt.

'Thank you,' he said, 'for tonight. It has done me more good than you realise.' Then, smiling, he kissed the top of her head. 'As for making it up to you, it is time society saw Lord and Lady Westhaven together in public.'

Chapter Nine

He took her to the theatre the very next evening—where it had all started. Roisin wore the new burgundy evening gown that her aunt had given to her before she left, and had her hair put up elaborately. She did not want to disgrace Kit, she decided, so she made herself as lovely as she could.

'You are beautiful, my lady,' said Jane from behind her, as Roisin fiddled with a stray curl.

Roisin shook her head at her own foolishness and turned to her maid. 'Thank you, Jane. You must be exhausted with my fussing.'

'It was worth it though, was it not?' The older woman looked fondly at her temporary mistress.

Roisin smiled. 'Thank you,' she said again. 'No need to wait up for me tonight, you have worked hard enough today. One of us should get some sleep.'

With a grateful nod, Jane withdrew and left Roisin to her own thoughts.

The only thing that made her sad, as she examined herself in the mirror, was her lack of jewellery. She was lamenting her lost pearl necklace in front of the glass when Kit knocked at her door.

She turned as he came in. 'I'm almost ready,' she said.

He was very handsome, different in a powdered wig and a waistcoat that matched her dress. He smiled, seeing her eyes on it. 'I asked Jane what you were wearing. I hope you do not mind.'

She shook her head. 'Not at all. We will make a fine pair.'

'Indeed.' His eyes swept hers. 'My wife will be the envy of Drury Lane.'

Roisin sighed, biting her lip. 'Not without jewellery, she won't, and I have none. It was all stolen when…' She shrugged, looking back into the mirror at her bare neck. 'Well. There is no use in worrying about it now, I suppose. At least I have this left.' She indicated her emerald ring, glistening on her finger next to her simple wedding band.

'What is this?' Kit took her hand.

'My father gave it to me before he died. It is the only thing I managed to keep when I was robbed.'

'Ah, I see.' He ran his finger over the gold with its bright stone, a strange expression on his face. 'You hid it from him?'

'Yes.'

His eyes moved briefly, involuntarily, to the low neckline of her gown, then back to the ring.

Frowning, Roisin looked up into his face. 'How did you know?'

His face was expressionless 'Know what?'

'About my ring.' She coloured slightly. 'That I hid it…there?'

He smiled, slowly. 'It seems like the perfect hiding place.'

'Does it indeed?' Amused and not a little flustered by the look in his eyes, Roisin found herself shyly returning his smile. 'Well…'

'I was intending that to be a compliment,' he said, very softly, raising her hand to his lips and kissing the ring.

'Then I thank you for it.' Taking a deep breath, Roisin turned her back on him and returned to perusing herself in the mirror. 'As to the rest of my jewels, I suppose they are scattered far and wide by now. There is no use in mourning them, don't you th—'

She turned to face him once more and he was gone. She leant back against her dressing table and made a face. Men were not concerned with such things, she supposed. Strange, though, when he had been listening intently but a moment ago. Still, she had better stir herself—the carriage would be waiting.

She was just heading for the door when he reappeared in the doorway, almost knocking her over and making her cry out with surprise.

'Here.'

She frowned at the polished mahogany box he held out. 'What is this, Kit?'

'Something for you.' He saw her questioning glance and added, 'It was my mother's.'

Taking the box, she went to her dressing table and set it down. He followed her, watched her open the lid. Inside the box was lined with velvet in which several very fine pieces of jewellery nestled. Roisin's mouth fell open.

'There used to be much more. It has mostly been sold,' he said, at her shoulder. 'But what is left is yours. They were her favourites.'

She raised her eyes to his face. 'Are you sure that—'

He stopped her with a hand. 'I am sure that my mother would want someone...close to her son to wear them again. It has been too long. She died when I was nine.'

Roisin smiled. 'Thank you.' She raised herself up and planted a kiss on his cheek. 'Which one shall I wear tonight?'

He considered, then plucked a necklace from the glittering nest. It was gold, a delicate line of garnets and diamonds, with a larger diamond in the centre. It went perfectly with her dress. Roisin stood while

Kit fastened it around her neck. His lips touched the lobe of her right ear as he breathed in the scent of her hair. Roisin watched him in the mirror, her ear and senses tingling.

He met her eyes over her shoulder. 'There were earrings. I remember her wearing them.'

He searched again in the jewellery case. Matching drop earrings emerged. Kit watched as Roisin put them on, a wistful expression on his face. She knew what he was thinking, and it squeezed her heart. She took his hand.

'Do I look like the wife of a lord?'

'Very much.'

'Then shall we go? Or the play will start without us.'

The carriage was waiting. They did not speak much on the way to the theatre, but Roisin could feel her husband's eyes on her. She had been in London only two months—and only that short time ago she had first visited Drury Lane. Yet so much had come to pass between visits. Despite herself, she was nervous. Her first time in society as Lady Westhaven…

The carriage drew up outside Drury Lane, and her husband alighted, holding out a hand to help her down. Bending her head so as not to brush her hair against the top of the carriage, she stepped on to the street. Kit kept hold of her hand, tucking it through his arm. They went up the steps and into the theatre together.

'Roisin!'

It was Cathy. She was waving at them from across the foyer, where she stood with her father and a young man. Roisin smiled at Kit as her cousin weaved through the crowd towards them. She looked like her old self again.

'How lovely to see you!' She kissed her cousin on the cheek and smiled up at her newest relation. 'Hello, Lord Westhaven.'

He took her hand and kissed it. 'Miss Penrose. I trust you have forgiven me.'

She dropped her eyes, blushing furiously. 'Let us not speak of such silliness.'

Roisin was surprised. Something had happened to cheer Cathy up. Perhaps it had something to do with whoever that was with Colonel Penrose. He was watching them. She smiled at him and blew a kiss to her uncle across the room. She must talk to him later, but for now there was digging to be done.

'Cathy,' she said taking her cousin's arm and drawing her aside, 'who is that gentleman with your father?'

Kit took his cue and moved off into the crowd, leaving her alone to question her cousin.

Cathy gave a barely suppressed—and very unlady-like—grin. 'Phineas Jonstone. He is an American—the son of my father's oldest friend. His father wanted him to see London society.' She smiled. 'He is very charming. I was going to bring him over to

Oakridge and introduce him to you and Kit, but I have not yet had the chance.'

Roisin suppressed a grin of her own. 'Indeed. I must be sure to make his acquaintance later in the evening.'

'Why, you must do so now!' Cathy took her arm. 'There is still plenty of time before the performance starts, and Kit will not begrudge you talking to us for a little while. He has you all to himself at home, after all!'

As she was propelled across the foyer, Roisin met Kit's eyes and, in response to the question in his eyes, gave him a wide smile. Her cousin was back to her usual bubbly self—it seemed she was forgiven.

'She has forgotten that she was ever enamoured of you,' Roisin told her husband, as they travelled home that evening. 'This Phineas Jonstone fascinates her. I think it is the accent.'

'He seems a decent fellow,' said Kit, seated across from her, his long legs stretched out and crossed at the ankle. 'Though he is an American.'

'Really, Kit,' she admonished, smiling at his wicked grin. 'We are back in favour with Cathy, at any rate. She says she will visit us at Oakridge within a fortnight.'

Kit nodded. 'Pity. I had anticipated having my wife to myself.'

Roisin's smile dimmed a little, her pulse quickening at the look he gave her. With a swift movement, he was beside her, taking her chin in his hand and bringing her lips to meet his. Her senses leapt to life. Unconsciously she moistened her lips, and saw in his gaze, clouded with desire, how the small gesture affected him.

'Did you see how every man followed you with his eyes tonight?'

She turned her head away, teasing him. 'You flatter me, sir.'

'Indeed,' he said, one hand creeping behind her head, 'I do not.'

Their lips met once more, Roisin burying her fingers in the lace of his shirt, the sweetest sensations curling deep within her as he explored her mouth gently with his tongue. Pulling back for air, she gave a gasp as she saw where they were and protested as he began to kiss her more ardently. With effort, she pushed him off. 'Kit! We are home!'

The carriage had just turned through the gates of Oakridge and was drawing closer to the house. She could see John waiting for them at the top of the steps.

He grinned at her. 'It is only John.'

She gave him a warning frown. 'Shh.'

Kit leapt out of the carriage and Roisin waited for him to offer her his hand. Instead he reached in, picked her up bodily, and carried her up the steps.

She was a deep red that almost matched her gown when he set her down.

'Kit!'

He only smiled at her.

'Good evening,' said John, as if nothing had happened. 'I trust you had a pleasant time.'

'We did indeed.' Kit placed a hand on his manservant's shoulder as he passed into the house. Roisin thought that he winked at the younger man, but was not sure. She followed him.

'John—I quite forgot—I gave Jane the evening off. Please ask Annette to come and help me out of my dress.'

He nodded. 'At once, Lady Westhaven.'

He retreated, and Roisin caught up with her husband at the foot of the stairs.

'You are in a good mood tonight,' she told him, as he turned to her, his arms wrapping around her. He did not speak, merely pulled her closer.

He kissed her until she was breathless and unfocused, then stood back, pulling off his wig.

'Roisin?'

'Yes?'

'I'm going to bed.'

She knew there was something else behind those words and suddenly, regretted letting him kiss her all the way home. Some things she was not ready for. She gave him a small smile. 'Kit…'

He put up a hand to stroke her hair. 'My wife is a very beautiful woman. And whether she sees fit to join me or not tonight, I am a very happy man.'

'Thank you,' was all she said, but her eyes showed him the gratitude she felt for allowing her time. He bowed low and, turning, strode up the stairs and away.

She followed, more slowly, heading for her own room. There was a fire lit for her, and Annette was already there, waiting.

'Good evening, ma'am,' she said, inclining her head. 'How was the play?'

Roisin smiled at her. 'Very good, thank you.'

'My brother said you both seemed happy when you returned.'

Roisin frowned slightly. 'Yes.' She always thought Annette a little more friendly than befitted their relationship. Still, perhaps the girl was just chatty.

She stood, thoughts far away, as the maid helped her out of her dress and brought her nightgown. Then, pulling on her robe, she sat at the dressing table so that Annette could dismantle the elaborate hairstyle Jane had created earlier.

'Ma'am? May I ask you a question?'

Roisin glanced up and met Annette's eyes in the mirror. 'Of course.'

'Will there be more staff again, now?'

'What do you mean?'

The maid's wide eyes were quite innocent. 'Lord Westhaven had to let a lot of the staff go, as you know, ma'am. There is a lot of work for just the three of us. Now that he has married you, perhaps there will be more of us again.'

Roisin looked long at her. 'What do you suppose I have to do with it, Annette? You think I should talk to my husband about this?'

'No,' said the maid. 'I just meant, now that Oakridge has money again.'

There was a long silence.

'What do you mean, money again?' asked Roisin, unsure how to handle this.

A stricken expression crossed across the maid's face as her mistress turned to face her.

'Forgive me, ma'am—I had no idea—'

Roisin rose. 'No idea about what, Annette?'

'That…I mean, that you did not know he was poor—the master. That Oakridge was near-bankrupt. That he married you because…'

Roisin watched her as she faltered. The girl was a good actress. But something was going on.

'I am well aware why Lord Westhaven married me,' she said quietly. 'And of his circumstances beforehand.'

Annette froze. 'What?'

'You thought he lied to me?' Roisin's eyes narrowed. 'What are you up to, Annette?'

The girl had gone pale. 'Nothing, ma'am, I was only—'

'Why would you want to cause trouble between my husband and I?'

'I do not—'

'Wait.' Roisin held up a hand as a terrible thought occurred to her. 'How long have you been working here?'

'A year, ma'am.'

'How old are you?'

'Nineteen.'

Nineteen. The same age as herself…yet this girl was so confident. Roisin leant against the dressing table. Could it be true, what she suspected? This girl, like Cathy, could be enamoured of Kit, without feeling in return… Yet Cathy had stepped back once he was married to Roisin. Could that mean…?

Looking into the girl's eyes, she knew, suddenly, that it was true. Something about the way she stood, staring brazenly back, told Roisin that she had been—still could be—Kit's lover.

'Get out,' she said quietly. 'You have accomplished your aim.'

'I beg your pardon?' Annette was taken aback.

Roisin took a step forward. 'Get out!'

The young woman needed no second bidding. She fled, slamming the door behind her. Roisin stood, her mind racing. Why had he said nothing? But then, she supposed it was foolish to expect that he would. Why would a man tell his wife about his mistress?

Pushing herself away from the dressing table, she flung her bedroom door open and headed for Kit's room. Anger mounted in her as she walked. He had not been honest with her! If he needed a wife for money that was one thing—but if he already had a mistress, then why was he playing with her as well?

She knocked firmly on Kit's closed door and, when he called her to come in, strode inside. He turned from the window, an expression of surprise and pleasure on his face.

'Roisin.'

He came forward to meet her, stopping as she slapped him, hard, across the face.

His look changed to one of confused anger. 'What are you about, woman? What was that in aid of?'

His wife squared up to him. 'She is your *servant*, Kit!'

'Who…?' She watched as he registered what she was talking about. 'Annette.'

'Yes, Annette.' Roisin glared at him. 'She paid me a visit and went out of her way to ensure that I knew exactly why you married me.'

He froze. 'Why?'

'How do I know why? All I know is that you do not need two lovers if you already have one!'

Having said what she had come to say, she turned on her heel to leave.

Kit grabbed her. 'Roisin. I do not have two lovers. I have one wife. And one maid.'

'Then why does she come to me with all this now?'

He sighed. 'She is jealous, I suppose. She was not best pleased when I informed her of my approaching marriage. But I wished to be true to you. She has not come to my bed these six weeks.'

Roisin lowered her eyes. She did not like the thought of Annette in his bed at all.

'She has not come?'

'I told her that she could not.'

Jealousy, unwanted and unexpected, had taken hold of her. She wished to go down to the kitchen and slap Annette as she had slapped her husband. Why had Kit wanted that slip of a girl, at any rate? What had he thought she could offer him?

'Roisin.' He seemed to read her mind. 'My life before our marriage was my own, to do with as I pleased. As was yours. I do not apologise for anything. But since you have been my wife, believe me, she has only been our maid.'

She believed him. His gaze hid nothing. 'Why did you keep her in the house?'

He shrugged. 'She is John's sister, I wished to keep her in work. That was why he asked me to employ her in the first place. Things…became out of hand. She has behaved herself up to now.'

She did not know what to think. 'Is your whole household aware of your marriage of convenience? What must they all think of me? Am I to be the laughing-stock of my own servants?'

'John knows because he is my friend,' he told her. 'And I had to tell Annette so she would understand why I no longer welcomed her attentions.'

There was a short silence.

'Although,' he said quietly, 'since I met you I have not wanted her, anyway.'

She crossed her arms. 'Is that true?'

'Yes.' He came closer, disentangling her and taking her hands. 'I last bedded Annette on the day my brother died, because I was in no state to stop myself. But every day since then I have wished it had not been so. I do not want her.'

Roisin sighed. 'I hope you are being truthful with me, Kit.' Stepping away from him, she went to the window. 'Sometimes I wonder.'

'What do you mean?' The look he threw her was guarded.

She shrugged. 'There is so much about you that I do not know. I cannot help but feel there are things you do not tell me, even now.'

He crossed to her, taking her by the shoulders. 'She has upset you.'

'I do not want her in this house!'

He nodded. 'I will tell her she can stay for the rest of the week.'

'No.' Roisin's voice was firm. 'I will tell her. Now.'

She broke away from her husband and went into the corridor. Then she stopped.

'Kit.'

'Yes?' He seemed drawn.

'You have my money. You do not need me.'

He came towards her. 'You are wrong.'

They looked at each other for a long moment. She nodded, giving him a small smile. Then she turned her back on him and walked away, down to the kitchen.

Annette was still there, sweeping out the huge stove. Apart from her the room was empty. Roisin stood, waiting until she noticed her. At length she did, with a start.

'Lady Westhaven!'

'Stand up, Annette.'

She waited until the woman girl did so. Then, drawing her robe further around her, she went closer.

'I am not pleased with your conduct in my house,' she said quietly, but firmly. 'I have consulted with Lord Westhaven and he agrees with my decision. We are asking you to leave. You may stay for the rest of the week.'

'Leave?' Annette's eyes flamed. 'I have done nothing! It was a slip of the tongue!'

'You are lying,' said Roisin. 'I know what happened between you and my husband.'

The girl gave a sardonic smile. 'And you wish to rid yourself of your competition.'

Roisin paused, mouth open, genuinely surprised at this remark. She drew herself up, trying to retain her dignity.

'I beg your pardon?'

'He was mine until you came,' she said, her face flushed with anger. 'He would not have wanted you if it hadn't been for the money! You think your wealth makes you better than me? This isn't *your* house— you were just a way for him to keep Oakridge! And he would have come back to me in time, once he realised who the better woman was!'

'How *dare* you!' Roisin restrained the urge to go forward and strike the girl, pressing her hands against the oak table behind her. 'Watch your tongue when you talk to me!'

'Why?' Annette was livid. 'Who do you think you are? We're of a similar age—and you've half the character! Kit needs a proper woman, not a simpering lady!'

Roisin was barely holding her temper. 'You will find it very difficult to find alternative employment with that attitude, young woman!'

She turned to sweep out of the room as her mother always did after upbraiding servants, just as

Annette gave a strangled scream of fury and launched herself forward.

Both women fell to the floor with the force of her impact, rolling on the cold stone. For a moment there was nothing but confusion, skirts and limbs everywhere in a flailing mass. Roisin was trying to disentangle Annette's claws from her hair, but Annette was stronger than she appeared. They struggled, rolling beneath the table, Roisin with Annette's wrists in her hands, trying to free herself, and her maid kicking her—spitting words that Roisin had never heard a woman use.

Roisin resisted wildly, yelling at her to let go; her mother's voice in her head telling her sternly that a lady was never violent to servants. This only further enraged the girl, however, and the struggle grew fiercer. She was wondering whether she would have any hair left—and whether she should start knocking Annette's head against the underside of the table—when there was a shout from the doorway and they were wrenched apart, with what seemed like several male arms coming between them, holding them fast.

Roisin let out a cry of pain as she was dragged out from under the table—Annette had managed to administer one last scratch to her arm.

Kit's arms held her, her back to his chest. They faced Annette, still flailing in the firm embrace of her brother, across the room. She was protesting at the top of her voice, kicking John in the ankles and attempting to make him let her go.

'Silence!'

Kit's voice cut through her wails, and there was suddenly no noise but the dripping of the kitchen tap. Dazedly, Roisin noticed a few of her red-brown hairs in Annette's fist.

'What have you to say for yourselves?'

She realised that the question was not only addressed to the maid. She rounded on her husband, who would not let her go. 'I will not make an account of myself to you before this…ill bred…slattern!' she said, furious.

Annette raised her eyebrows. 'Perhaps I was wrong about half the character,' she said, her smile mocking.

'Quiet,' Kit ordered. 'Annette, do not expect to remain in this house for the night unless you apologise to my wife for your behaviour.'

'Apologise?' Annette curled her lip. 'John!'

'Shh, Annette,' said John gently, his arms holding hers down.

Kit looked at him. 'She is safe in your hands. Come, Roisin.'

Roisin, with a last, haughty glare at Annette, allowed herself to be led away. She followed Kit into the library, where he shut the door firmly before he turned to her.

'What do you mean by brawling in my house like a common—?'

'Brawling?' Roisin drew herself up. 'I did nothing! She flung herself upon me! She is a—'

'And you are a lady,' he interrupted. 'You should not lower yourself so, Roisin.'

'I see!' Tears of injustice came into her eyes. Her head ached and she felt covered in bruises. 'Well, I am sorry to have so shamed you, Kit! When next your mistress sees fit to assault me I shall lie without struggling and let her claw me to death!'

'Roisin.' He came towards her. 'You are overreacting. Sit down.'

'No!' Tears ran down her face. Never had she been so ashamed. He thought she would behave so? True, she had wanted to, yet she had held herself back! 'I am leaving this house! I have never been so *insulted*!'

She was halfway to the door when a wave of dizziness assailed her and she stumbled sideways. Kit came forward to stop her hitting a bookshelf, and instead she ran into his chest. His arms closed around her.

'Come. Sit down a while.'

She allowed him to lead her to his winged chair before the fire. The dizziness was past. She had hit her head, she remembered, on the table leg as they rolled. Kit squatted beside her.

'Are you all right?' he asked gently.

Roisin nodded, leaning her head against the side of the chair. 'I'm sorry,' she said. 'I thought I knew how to handle such things. My mother would have a fit.'

He smiled. 'This is why I chose you, Roisin. Not merely for your money. You have more fire in you than most of your peers.'

'Apart from Annette.'

'She may have met her match tonight. But from her I searched for something different, at a time in my life when I was very hurt. My father, then my brother—in the space of a year… Do you understand?'

'Yes.'

'I should have asked her to leave before you came.'

She made a sound in her throat. 'Because then I would never have found out.'

'No. Because then this would not have happened. And I would not have a scratched street urchin instead of a wife.' As she sat forward, indignant, he smiled. 'I jest, Roisin.'

She looked at him. 'Is my hair pulled out?'

He examined her head. 'No. Just tangled.'

She sat as, gently, he smoothed it out between his fingers, and laid it across one shoulder. Then he kissed the long scratch on her arm.

There was a knock on the door.

'Sit there,' he told her, getting to his feet and crossing to it.

It was John. Roisin could not hear what they said as they conversed in hushed tones, over by the door. She heard Kit thank him though, before he returned to her.

'Annette is willing to apologise.'

She frowned. 'Why?'

He smiled. 'I think her brother had a hand in it. Still, do you wish to hear what she has to say?'

Her wish never to see the girl again was overcome by curiosity. 'Yes.'

She sat up straighter in the chair, pulling her robe around herself, smoothing a hand over her hair. The door opened again and Annette entered. Roisin stood up, turning from the fire to face her. Kit, leaning against a bookshelf in the corner of the room, watched.

'I have come to apologise,' said Annette stiltedly.

Roisin nodded. 'Go on.'

Annette cleared her throat. Her eyes widened into the innocent little-girl act that she had given Roisin upstairs. This was obviously for Kit's benefit.

'I am sorry for the way I behaved,' the maid was saying, hands folded demurely in front of her. 'I was wrong to speak to you the way I did—and I should never have assaulted you in such a way. I will behave with nothing but respect in the future if you will accept my humblest apology.'

Roisin met her eyes. Annette did not seem sorry. But then, neither was she. The girl arched her eyebrows just enough for Roisin to see, daring her to protest. She would not give her the satisfaction.

'I accept your apology,' she lied sweetly. 'You may go.'

'Annette,' Kit said as the maid was leaving. 'You

may stay until the end of the week if I see no evidence of this behaviour again. Otherwise both you and your things will be flung out.'

The maid nodded, docile as a lamb, and closed the door behind her.

'Still until the end of the week?' Roisin looked up at him.

He perched on the arm of her chair. 'John has long been with me, Roisin. I do this as a favour to him so his sister is not disgraced. At least now she will have a chance to find herself somewhere to go.'

She gave a heavy sigh. 'She had better not cross me,' was all she said.

He smiled. 'From what I have seen no one should.'

Roisin put a hand to her head. 'I am going to bed,' she said softly.

'Let me walk with you.'

She sighed, eyes closed. 'Kit, I—'

He was on his feet. 'I will come no further than your door.'

'All right.'

He took her arm and they walked together, not speaking. Every now and then his shoulder brushed against the top of her arm, and she took comfort in his presence. He did not seem to blame her for what had happened. But, said a niggling voice, he had not told Annette to leave, either.

It mattered not, she decided. The wretched girl

would be gone in three days, and she would not have to worry about her ever again.

Kit stopped outside her room. 'Straight to bed, now,' he said, opening the door for her. She put a hand on his cheek, feeling the day-old growth of stubbly bristle.

'Thank you for taking me to the theatre,' she said.

He smiled. 'I almost forgot we had been.'

'It was lovely,' she told him.

'Then we shall go every week.'

He took her head in his hands and kissed her gently on the lips, just for a second, as he had at the altar on their wedding day. Then he pushed her into her room.

'Go.' He stood, watching her.

'Goodnight, Kit.'

'Goodnight.'

As she shut the door, she listened to his footsteps receding down the corridor. She was exhausted. Walking to the bed, she lay down, pulled the covers over herself, blew out the light and closed her eyes.

Not even the thought of the day's events kept her awake that night.

In her small room at the top of the house, Annette sat on her bed, her hands clenched so tightly together that her knuckles were white. On the outside she appeared calm, yet she was fuming, her mind picking over all she knew about Kit and his new wife. There had to be something she could find—some secret she could unearth to spoil their perfect love-nest. Even if her brother did not see why she felt so slighted.

She had put a few scratches on the bitch he had married—that much pleased her. She wished she had had the opportunity to try again. The thought of Roisin's haughty tone made her blood boil!

There *must* be something. She had three days until the end of the week. She would keep her eyes and ears open, and she *would* find it. Kit had sided with his wife—she should have known he would. There was a time when he would have brooked no insult to her, but now all he could think of was his trophy bride. More than ever she wanted to make him pay. But now it was not only him.

When she was finished, Annette vowed, Roisin was going to wish she had never met Lord West-haven, or laid eyes on Oakridge Park.

Chapter Ten

Roisin stood by the window, looking out into the night and fashioning her long hair into a plait. It seemed odd that she had been Lady Westhaven for only four days—so much had happened in that time. Already it was like she had always been here. Her days were filled with a peace that came from the ability to make her own decisions. She missed her family, of course—but it was nice to have a place of her own at last. She had never thought she would enjoy marriage.

Of course, there were other benefits than the freedom to ride and read as she wished, she thought, meeting her own eyes in the mirror before which she stood. Kit was proving to be the husband everyone had said he would be—and more. She tied her plait with a ribbon, combing the end of it absently with her fingers.

She was already enjoying life at Oakridge, that was true. And there was no denying the way she responded to her husband. Yet she could not give him all. Still at night the red hair and dark eyes of another haunted her dreams. Sometimes she awoke crying, her own, loose hair tangled around her throat.

It was foolish, she knew. He was dead. She was married. What she felt for Kit went beyond fondness— even, perhaps, into love. Which was remarkable, given that she had been marrying for convenience.

She did not know what she felt, in truth. But she hoped that time would tell her.

There was a gentle knock at her door. Roisin set down her brush.

'Come in.'

There was only one person it could be. He pushed open the door and stood in the doorway, wearing only his breeches and white ruffled shirt. She met his eyes in the mirror, feeling suddenly naked in her long nightgown, though it reached nearly to the floor. She had barely seen him all day, for the work on the house kept him enthralled. Now, it seemed, he had come seeking her.

'I thought you were in bed,' she said softly.

'I was.' He looked restless. 'I could not sleep.'

'Would you like me to ask Cook to make you a hot drink?'

He echoed the teasing smile she gave him. 'That will not be necessary.' He leant one shoulder against the doorframe. 'May I come in?'

She nodded. 'I was just preparing for bed.'

Kit came up behind her and put his hands on her waist, eyes meeting hers in the glass, seeking her permission. She smiled. His lips brushed her throat and Roisin, powerless to do anything but drift in the tide of longing that suddenly overtook her, dropped her head back against him as fire licked at her. She leant into her husband as his arms snaked around her, pulling her to him. He let out a long sigh. 'I couldn't sleep,' he said again, 'for thinking of you.'

His body pressed hers from behind. Through the thin fabric of her nightgown she felt his growing awareness of her. One hand kept her trapped against him, while the other reached for her plait, pulled out the ribbon and shook her hair loose.

'Kit,' she protested, smiling. 'I've only just—'

She was quieted by his mouth covering hers, as he pulled her round to face him. They kissed long and deeply, her mind dissolving, her lips seeking his with a passion that matched his own. Though almost faint with desire, Roisin sensed that something was different now. He wanted more from her than she had given so far. A sweet ache began somewhere deep inside her. Kit trailed kisses down her neck and lower. Holding her away from him, he studied the way the nightgown clung to her breasts, hands on her shoulders now. 'You're beautiful,' he said quietly.

She met his eyes, her hair everywhere, mussed

from his touch. His jaw was lined with stubble, as usual. He nibbled her fingers as she traced it, taking them into his mouth one by one. The world lost focus as lovely sensations ran from her fingertips through her entire body. Abruptly, she took hold of his shirt and pulled him to her, fingers splayed against his chest as they kissed once more.

She became aware, through the familiar haze of need, that he was walking her towards the bed. Then the backs of her knees came into contact with the feather mattress and she fell backwards, hair pooling around her head. He stood for a moment, looking at her. Then he joined her, laying his body alongside hers.

She responded to his kiss, trapped beneath him. He ran his mouth along her jawline, kissing her neck once more. Then his fingers reached for the laced-up top of her nightgown.

And everything swung abruptly back into focus.

With a small cry, Roisin pulled her mouth away from his as she felt his fingers on the bare flesh between her breasts. She felt suddenly strange, as if a bucket of cold water had been flung over her.

'Kit.' She sat up, the nightgown loose.

He stopped, desire clouding his gaze. 'What is it?'

'I…' She trailed off, both hands holding the unlaced sections closed, ashamed at her abrupt about-face, yet unable to move.

There was a pause. He sat back on the bed, frustration flashing across his face for the slightest instant before he suppressed it. 'You don't want this.'

She dropped her gaze, drawing her legs under her. 'I don't know.'

'Forgive me,' he muttered. 'You are not ready for—'

'No.' She held out a hand. 'You have done nothing wrong. I thought I wanted to… But I cannot. You must forgive me.'

She, too, felt frustrated with her own emotions. One moment she had wanted him every bit as much as he seemed to want her and the next… She sighed aloud, not realising that she did so.

Kit was watching her closely. 'Roisin?'

'Yes?'

He reached out and took a strand of her hair, curling it around his finger. 'Am I the only man you have ever kissed?'

She had not expected that. She felt a deep blush rise through her. She could not raise her eyes for fear of what he must think of her. 'No,' she said. She owed him the truth—he was her husband. And he had been honest with her. She was not ashamed of what she had shared so briefly with Ewan, was she? She raised her chin, meeting his eyes.

He watched at her, expressionless. 'Who?'

She swallowed, unable all of a sudden to find any words.

'Hamilton,' he said flatly.

Closing her eyes, she nodded. Was she that obvious, that he had known so instantly? Had he heard her dreams, on those restless nights? When she opened them there was still no clue to his reaction in the eyes that watched her.

He cleared his throat. 'Did he assault you?'

She frowned. 'No! He was never anything but a gentleman!'

Kit looked dubious. 'Yet he kissed you?'

Roisin nodded. 'It just…happened. I don't know why.'

'Did you feel anything for him?'

Tears came to Roisin's eyes, though for which reason exactly she could not say. Fear of hurting her husband, grief for her companion of that night; perhaps both combined. She did not want to talk about Ewan Hamilton. But Kit had no secrets from her. He had told the tale of himself and Annette.

'I…don't know,' she said truthfully. 'I knew him for so little time…'

'Enough time to alter your feelings for me?'

She met those dark eyes and her heart hurt physically. 'Kit. You are two different men. But I cannot…'

'You cannot forget him?'

She shook her head. 'But he is dead. It doesn't alter what I feel for you.'

'Which is?'

Roisin wished she knew what he was thinking. 'I don't…' She trailed off.

He nodded, then stood up. 'I understand.'

'No, Kit—' Scrambling off the bed, Roisin caught her husband by the arm as he was about to leave. 'I'm sorry. I should have told you before now. Please, don't leave.'

'What was he like?' he asked.

'Why?' Roisin looked up at him, searching for a sign.

'Curiosity.'

She considered. 'He was…wild. Daring, I suppose. But kind. A gentleman, though perhaps not at the start. Scottish, I think.' She lowered her eyes. 'He did not deserve what they did to him, Kit. Do you remember how the crowd cheered for him at Tyburn? It seems so long ago.'

An odd look crossed her husband's face. He nodded.

There was a silence, in which he brushed her hair back from her temples on each side. He said, 'Am I like him?'

Roisin looked into his face, thinking. 'No,' she said at last, then grimaced. 'In some ways, I suppose. I think he was well bred, despite how he ended up. In kindness, you are like him.'

His smile was a ghost of what it usually was. 'Kindness?'

She took his hand. 'Of course.'

Kit sighed, withdrawing it gently. 'I think I should not be here. Goodnight, Roisin.'

She watched him retreat, her eyes wide. He seemed strange—not hurt, exactly, more… She could not put her finger on it. He was not happy, that was for sure. She sank on to the bed, no longer tired. Why did he want to know about Ewan? Could it be that he felt more for her than she had thought?

Taking her wayward hair in her hands, she re-plaited it, her mind replaying the conversation, reviewing the expression on his face. It was not the way she had expected such an evening to end—for she had anticipated his coming to her for the last couple of days now.

She climbed into bed, turning out the lights and sliding down under the coverlet. The dark surrounded her, comforting her. Kit said the house was full of ghosts, but she felt nothing but at home here. Usually she slept quickly; but not tonight.

Roisin closed her eyes. She tried to clear her mind of everything swirling through it—concentrating on something simple. Belle. She imagined riding her horse, the wind in her hair and in Belle's mane, free for an afternoon to go where they pleased. It was a nice image. A gift from her husband, who seemed to think he was not a kind man.

He had sold his brother's watch for Belle.

She remembered his face on the day she had held him, days ago, though it seemed like weeks. Still no pictures of Jamie had appeared. She supposed it was natural. Give him time. Guilt assailed her as the expression in his eyes tonight resurfaced.

Roisin opened her eyes.

This was not working.

She sat up, sighing. Perhaps some food would help—she had eaten little at dinner and was beginning to feel hungry. Slipping out of bed, she headed for the door. It was a balmy June night, the heat of the day not quite gone from the night air. Wearing nothing but her nightgown, Roisin went swiftly along corridors and downstairs. The draughts about her bare feet were deliciously cold, making her feel more awake than ever. Her plait was beginning to unwind—she had lost the ribbon after Kit had taken it out. Pushing her hair behind her ears, she reached the heavy kitchen door and pushed it open gently.

There was no one there. The room stood quiet, so unlike during the day. Roisin loved to sit there, at the huge and much-scrubbed oak table, consulting with Cook about meals. Even with only Cook, Annette—and often John—it seemed always to be busy. Now it stood, stove cold, waiting for the morning.

Roisin stood just inside the doorway. Moonlight made a faint pattern on the floor, filtering softly through the large window at one end of the long room. She went across to stand by it, gazing out, her snack forgotten.

It was a lovely night.

Suddenly wishing to go outside, she made for the door that led into the kitchen garden. It was securely locked, but she managed to slide the huge metal bolt and let herself out. The rows of vegetables were different by night—etched in moonlight—as were the privet hedges surrounding the little garden.

She ventured out on to the lawn. The grass tickled her bare feet, not yet damp with the dew that would come later. She stood, facing down towards the lake. The moon was in its last quarter, casting its silvery rays on to the water, which stood like a mirror, unrippling, reflecting back the light. There was no activity nearby—no night birds swimming on the water, no fish breaking the surface. Roisin went closer.

The night was warm, and the still water looked inviting.

She ran lightly to the edge of the lake and dipped in a toe. It was deliciously cold. She swirled her foot around, disrupting the mud and sand in the shallows. She had longed to swim in the lake since her arrival at Oakridge, but it had seemed impossible before now. She had swum many times with her brothers in a pool near their home when they were children—whipping off their clothes in the bushes nearby, they had run whooping into the cold water. Until, that was, her father caught them, drawn by their cries, and dragged them home. Such outings had nearly always ended in such a way.

Not so this one. This was her home. If she wanted to swim in the lake, then surely she could without recriminations. But she was no longer a child. She was a grown woman who should know better, even after dark.

Roisin was sorely tempted. Did she dare?

She glanced around at the house. No one in sight… They must all be fast asleep by now. Surely a quick dip would harm no one? She stood at the waters edge, undecided. Then, in a moment of impetuousness, she pulled down her drawers, flung her nightgown over her head, let both fall in a heap on the floor—and propelled herself into the water. At first it only reached her calves, then the tops of her thighs, and was merely refreshing. It was only when the level rose to her waist that she began to grit her teeth. It was *cold*! She jigged up and down on the spot, gathering the courage to plunge in. The longer she waited, she knew, the harder it would get. So, screwing up her courage, she closed her eyes, tensed her calves, and jumped.

As her legs went out from under her, her body pitched forward into the water, her skin tingling, aching from the cold. Her head broke the surface, and she gasped aloud, mouth open in shock, unable to take a breath at first. Then her breath came in short gasps as she began to move, swimming to and fro in order to warm herself. Towards the centre of the lake the water was deep enough to do so—but even colder. Roisin kicked her legs, water splashing over her hair, slicked to her head like the fur of an otter.

It was wonderful.

She floated upright for a while, adjusting to the temperature a little, feeling every inch of skin on her body as it tingled, every pore. Her hair, completely loose now, floated around her like seaweed, swishing to and fro as she moved.

She pushed herself on to her back. The sky above her was clear—she could see several stars. It was beautiful. She began to relax, legs and arms working to stave off the cold, her body adapting to it, her eyes sweeping the sky.

Wisps of mist lay across the lake now, forming slowly as the night cooled. Roisin swam through them, forgetting the events of the evening as she went. She dipped under the surface and came up, water streaming off her hair, a smile on her face. Why had she left it this long to do this?

She grinned, thinking of her mother's face if she could see her only daughter now. *Have you no modesty, Roisin?* That had always been the question when she was young. She smiled, remembering. One did not need to worry about modesty in nature, she had always said. *The fish are just as naked as I am.* Her mother had never accepted that point.

Roisin flipped on to her back again, so she could identify constellations as she swam. She had known one day her education would come in useful.

Kit did not go to his own room once he had left his wife's. His restlessness, far from being cured by his visit, had been increased a thousand-fold. He went to the library, which, since his youth, had been his favourite room. In the days before his marriage he had found himself spending more and more time there, trying to read, or balance the wildly spiralling accounts for Oakridge—or just staring into the fire, thinking.

His fire was still burning down, its last embers glowing red. Kit stood by the fireplace, watching the hands on his father's clock move, little by little, and thinking about Roisin. He had gone to her room tonight driven by his need for her, although he had argued long and hard with himself. He had not expected her lack of surprise at his visit. And he could have sworn that she wished the same as him.

Apparently not. He thought of her in her nightgown, hair loose about her shoulders, and it was all he could do not to rush back up to her chamber. However, she felt differently, that much was obvious. Did her feelings for him go beyond the physical?

It was hard to know what to make of her confession. All he knew was that his wife appeared to be in love with Ewan Hamilton, a character created by his brother. Jamie would be amused, he felt sure, if he were here.

Crossing to the bureau that sat in the corner almost physically groaning under the weight of his papers, Kit took a tiny key from his pocket and unlocked a drawer. From it he drew the only picture of his brother that he kept in the house. It was a miniature, done when Jamie was about eighteen, but it captured all of his brother's spirit. Kit, eyes resting on it, felt the sting of recent grief that he carried with him increase. Wild. Daring. Such characteristics were Jamie, that was certain. Much more the younger brother than the elder.

But Scottish… A smile curved Kit's lips. As for that, Jamie had spent hours perfecting the accent. Ideal for his red hair, he said. A good disguise when all his victims had to go on was the way he sounded. Other highwaymen, Kit knew, carried pebbles in their mouths for just such a reason—the voice is what you notice first. Certainly, it had been that way with Roisin.

Gentlemen they both were. It was in their upbringing. But kind. That was the difficulty. He found it difficult to believe that Roisin could call a man who had abducted her 'kind'. Yet it had brought her into their lives. And ended Jamie's.

His brother stared at him from the portrait. Wherever he was, did he know that the roof was almost intact again, and work was to begin shortly on the rest of Oakridge to renovate the more worn-down parts of the house? That rooms that stood, dirty and neglected, their furniture covered with dust sheets, would soon be restored to their former glory? That their father's debts were almost paid? Kit doubted it. He had stopped finally believing in God and in heaven when his father's body had been discovered hanging in one of the outhouses. An easy way out of his debts, leaving the problems to his sons.

What would Jamie say to his brother if he knew the web of deceit in which Roisin was caught? It had seemed the easiest way, those weeks ago when Kit had proposed to her. The best way to avoid all sorts of chaos.

But now… Kit felt that familiar twinge of guilt. He had to tell her. Surely, he did, before things became so out of hand that there was no going back. Lying to her made him feel increasingly uncomfortable, especially now she was truly his wife, no longer playing the role he had handed her. He had not known where to look when she spoke to him so honestly of her feelings for Hamilton. This was a man she admired, perhaps indeed loved. A man who, for the most part, did not exist. He must be honest with her if there was any chance of the stolen happiness he was beginning to find with her crystallising. It made him physically nauseous to think what would happen if she found out.

Could he tell her? Perhaps he had no other choice.

This was not helping his peace of mind. With a swift movement, Kit put the portrait away, locked the drawer, and left the library. The restlessness had not left him. He must think longer on this tonight. Then, tomorrow he would seek her out…

He was passing through a corridor, idly glancing out of the window, when something caught his eye. He froze, moving nearer the window, from which he could see across the lake.

A figure was visible there, waist deep in the water, surrounded by mist. Fear gripped him. Was the house filled with real ghosts, after all, not only those in his mind?

His common sense followed close behind. It was probably nothing—a trick of the light. He would investigate. He went back to the library and, opening another drawer, drew out the pistol left to him by his father. He always kept it loaded, in case he had need of it. Perhaps he would tonight.

Steeling himself, he made for the front door, swept up a lantern and some matches from the table there, and went out into the night.

The mist touched his face as he walked across the grass, droplets of moisture clinging to his clothes and skin. Whatever was out there—if anything—must be soaked. Kit held the lantern out in front of him and walked with long strides, heading for the lake.

* * *

Roisin was getting colder. The mist had come down over the lake now and, atmospheric as it was, she was starting to think of a warm fire and a comfortable bed.

She located the patch of grass on which she had left her clothes, and began to move nearer it, her body gradually rising above the water as she walked. She crossed her arms over her breasts, shivering deliciously. Her swim had relaxed and calmed her—she felt sure she would be able to sleep now.

She was just about to leave the lake when she heard a sound nearby. Footsteps, and the creak of a lantern. Her eyes widening in panic, she was momentarily frozen. Who was that? John? Kit?

Whichever, she was not keen to parade her nakedness before one or both men. With a splash, she was back in the water, moving out until only her head was visible, mist swirling round her. The footsteps became quicker as the water became still once more, and a figure became visible at the edge of the lake.

'Who is there?'

It was Kit. Wincing, Roisin tried to remain still.

'I can see you!' She squinted through the dark, trying to see what he was doing. 'Show yourself this instant!'

Go away, she willed him, teeth chattering so loud now that she was sure he must hear them. *Please*! He did not. In fact, he seemed to be coming closer, so that his boots touched the water.

'Show yourself!' he called again. 'Or I shall shoot!'

Shoot? He wouldn't! Yet she could see him better now, and he did indeed appear to be holding a pistol, aimed at arm's length. What should she do?

'I won't warn you again,' came her husband's voice. There was the sound of a pistol being readied. He was actually considering it!

'It is I!' called Roisin, raising herself a little from the water. 'Hold your fire!'

There was a silence. She heard him exhale sharply. 'Roisin?'

'Yes!' She was shivering.

'God's teeth, woman!' She had never heard him use such language. 'I thought you were my mother, returned from the grave! What are you doing?'

'Freezing to death,' she replied through gritted teeth.

'Then come out here!'

'I c-can't!'

Kit sounded exasperated. 'Why?'

'Because…I don't have any clothes on!'

Another silence. This time broken by his deep chuckle. 'I don't mind.'

'Well, I do, I assure you! Now, please!'

'Shall I turn my back?'

'No!' Roisin was jigging up and down once more. 'Go away!'

'As you wish.'

The outline of Kit disappeared. Roisin waited a few moments to ensure that he had gone, then ran from the lake, water dripping from her. For a moment she was unable to move, so stiff were her limbs after her attempt at hiding. She rubbed the tops of her arms with hands that were so cold she could barely feel them. Why did he have to come and interfere? She could have been back inside now, with no one any the wiser! Instead she must make a fool of herself in front of him! Again.

Her clothes were gone.

Shivering uncontrollably, Roisin searched the grass on either side of her. They had been here—she had seen them! Panic seized her. What was she to do? She could see little in the dark, not to mention this mist!

'Here.'

Roisin let out a shriek as Kit came up behind her. He was holding a blanket.

'Kit!' She grabbed it, pulling it around herself. It smelled of horse. 'I told you to leave me!'

He grinned. 'It was a good thing for you I did not. I went to the stables to get this for you instead. I thought you would have need of it.'

She did not answer, too busy wrapping herself in blanket. Kit put out a hand and touched her shoulder, exposed to the night air.

'You're freezing.'

'I'm fine, thank you,' she told him, pulling away, irritated by his interference. She had just been relaxing, forgetting her inner turmoil, when here was the cause of it, large as life. The night air was still quite warm, now that she was beginning to dry, and her shivering was growing less. She could feel his eyes on her, though, and that made her just as uncomfortable. She pulled her wet hair over her shoulders, covering her breasts under the blanket, for further decency.

'Come with me.' Kit took her by the arm and pulled her in the direction of the house. 'I'll see if I can get the stove lit and we'll make a pot of tea.'

'No!' Shaking herself free, Roisin gripped the blanket firmly. 'Thank you for your assistance. I can make my way back alone.'

He grinned. 'Indeed? And what would you be doing if I had not come along? Trying to creep naked back into the house?'

'I have a feeling you know who stole my clothes,' she snapped back.

'So now what am I to do?'

'Leave me!'

'Leave you?' He crossed his arms, and something wicked lit in his eyes. 'What sort of a man would that make me? Surely the least I could do with my catch is to throw her back.'

'What?' Her eyes widened as he began to advance on her. 'No, KIT!'

He was upon her before she had even begun to run, sweeping her up into his arms and carrying her with long strides to the water.

'Kit!' Roisin's screams echoed off the surrounding trees. She thrashed in his arms until, to her horror, the blanket slipped from her grasp, falling first away from her and exposing half of her body, then slipping away altogether, on to the grass. Roisin, mortified, crossed one arm over her breasts as best she could, while the other clung to him. Kit's hands on her bare flesh were warm. His eyes glinted at her in the dark.

Water swirled around his boots as he entered the lake, walking deeper until it must be filling them, for he was up to his thighs.

'Now,' he said, 'to return you to the wild from whence you came.'

'NO!' Roisin clung to him, half-laughing, half-horrified. 'Kit, ple—'

She got no further, for at that moment he let go and she fell back into the cold water, her mouth filling as she plunged. Her head broke the surface at last and she emerged up to her waist, coughing. 'You son of a—'

'Now, now,' he interrupted, looking thoroughly pleased with himself. 'Remember you are a lady, even if you are not dressed as one.'

She gasped, feeling his eyes on her bare breasts. Her hands flew to cover them, even as she drew closer to him.

He stood, water surrounding him, watching her with a strange look on his face. A mixture of amusement and desire and…something else, again.

'Kit,' she said softly, her breath visible in the cooling air.

'Yes?' He reached out for her.

Swiftly she moved her right foot beneath the water, hooking it behind his calf and pulling hard. Her strength was not as great as his, but surprise gave her the advantage. With a cry, he pitched backwards, a great splash wetting her as he disappeared.

He resurfaced, and Roisin found herself laughing as she had not laughed since she had come to Oakridge. His expression was a mixture of surprise, indignation and shock at the chilled water. For a moment he could not speak, just watched her, standing laughing at him. She was almost doubled up, forgetting the cold and even her modesty, her hair falling over her breasts. Kit smiled, finding his feet beneath the surface. His dark hair was plastered to his head.

'I suppose I deserved that.' Now he was shivering. She nodded, helpless.

He did not join her in laughter. Instead he waded towards her, took her by the waist, and began to kiss her. Roisin's hands went to his shoulders, mirth forgotten, her insides lurching as his lips met hers. His shirt was stuck to him, transparent with water, his body and broad shoulders clearly defined through it.

Her hands slipped down, over his chest, crushed to him as he pulled her closer. She could feel every inch of him pressing against her nakedness, and his arousal sent ripples up through her body. Only a thin layer of fabric separated them. The thought was an exciting one.

Reverently, Kit touched her, his fingers trailing heat over her body, offset by the cold of the water. Her head fell back as he kissed her breasts, and she found herself arching against him. She felt as if she would die, so strong were the sensations he created in her. Unbelievably, it seemed she did the same to him. He held her as if she was precious, his hands exploring her as his lips did, until it seemed the only way she could remain upright was due to the pressure of the water around them.

She found herself saying his name softly into his neck, almost without realising she did so.

He tore himself away from her immediately, water running down his face, his eyes like those of an animal. 'You want to stop?'

She looked at him, eyes half-closed, her body in a state of almost painful awareness of him. 'No. No—please, do not—'

'Roisin.' His voice was harsh. 'Are you—'

She nodded. 'Yes, Kit.'

With a sigh of relief and pleasure, he pulled her back to him, and away from the centre of the lake. Together they moved through the water, her body held close to him, pulled along in his wake, her feet not touching the lake-bed, her arms around his neck. She felt so close to him she wanted to cry. But more than that, she wanted him to show her the act that would make them truly married. She was not afraid any more.

He laid her down at the edge of the lake, water lapping around her buttocks. His body covered hers, soaked and cold, yet alight with his passion for her. Roisin arched against him, her hands in his hair, pulling his head down towards hers.

There, surrounded by water, earth and mist, he showed her, as she had wished. He was gentle with her at first, until they were both lost in the moment and carried with a current that had nothing to do with the lake beneath them. Roisin clung to him, pulled, it seemed, out of her body and into another world, of shadows and sensation, nuances of feeling rather than words. His touch told her that she was beautiful, that he wanted her above all others and, surely, that he loved her. How could such a thing happen in such a way if he did not?

They moved together, falling through nothing, until, at last, they came to rest with one final explosion of pleasure, her arms around him, holding him to her, his face buried in her hair.

She lay beneath him, his warm weight sheltering her from the elements.

'Kit?'

He glanced up, breathing heavily, arms encircling her. 'Yes, love?'

She did not miss the endearment, and it sent a wave of warmth through her. 'Can we go inside?'

He rose off her a little. 'Are you cold?'

She shook her head. 'No. But I want to do that again.'

Chapter Eleven

When Roisin awoke the sun was streaming through the open-curtained window, falling upon her naked form, covered only by rumpled bedclothes. She stretched, enjoying the blissful feeling of awakening beside the man she loved. She turned to look upon her husband.

Kit lay on his back, chest uncovered, exposed to the world. He breathed steadily, like one who still sleeps deeply. Roisin put a hand on his chest and, suddenly overtaken with a bout of childish wickedness, slowly slid it down until it rested where the sheet covered his waist. She wanted to see all of him. She slid the sheet down carefully, exposing inch after inch of flesh until he lay like Adam before her, unclothed and perfect.

In all but one respect. There was a scar just below his right shoulder, on his upper arm. It was barely healed, the skin red and puckered, only beginning to form scar tissue. What had he been up to, she wondered, idly tracing it with a finger, to have been hurt so? It appeared to be only a few weeks old—it must have happened just before he met her. He had mentioned nothing about an accident.

Sleepily, she laid her head on his chest, hand covering the hurt. He stirred slightly beneath her. Her fingers traced the scar. As he moved she saw that there was a corresponding mark on the other side of his arm, as if something had passed right through. Not such a small injury, it seemed. In fact, it looked almost like a gunshot wound.

Roisin sat up, suddenly alert. *It looked like a gunshot wound.*

She frowned, leaning forward to get a better view. Her mind pulled her back to another wound of this sort: the blood-soaked right shoulder of another man, lying under a leaking roof in a hovel in the woods. The shape, the size, the location—all were identical, familiar to her. Was she mad, or had she dressed this very wound less than a month ago? Had she not caused it herself? She could not have, of course— that man was long dead. But how else could such a coincidence be possible?

Suddenly her head was swimming. She found herself backing away from the sleeping form of her husband as if he were a danger to her. It could not be, she told herself more firmly. Unless…

She crept out of bed, her knees barely holding her up, pulled on a dress and shoes, and slipped outside. Once in the corridor she steadied herself, leaning against a wall. Her mind fed her snippets of information—things she should have pieced together weeks ago. His eyes were so familiar. His kiss was so familiar. The feel of his hands on her skin…

She closed her eyes, her breathing irregular. She was finding it hard to think beyond the rising panic in her mind.

What was she to do?

The nameless suspicion growing within her—she did not dare name it—held her very world in jeopardy. Suddenly she knew what action she must take.

On legs that did not seem her own, she flew down the stairs and along the wide passage that led to the breakfast room, where she knew John and Annette would be laying out the morning meal. They were there, sure enough. He was building a fire to take the early morning chill from the room; she put out cutlery.

They turned to greet her. She ignored their smiles.

'Why are there no pictures of James in this house?' Her voice was not her own. They did not speak. She saw the alarm on John's face before he could hide it. Annette merely feigned puzzlement.

'Kit…Lord Westhaven…' John rose to his feet, coming towards her. 'Your ladyship, his lordship is still overcome with grief after—'

'No!' Her tone was shrill, filling the room. 'The truth.' Had she not been in such a panic she would have felt sorry for Kit's manservant. He knew not where to look, obviously wishing to protect his master and not lie at the same time.

'I do not know—'

'You know, John.' She faced him, tears brimming in her eyes. 'I can see you do. Do not lie to me, please!'

He dropped his gaze. 'It is not my place to—'

'Then tell me where they are, at least,' she blurted. He could not face her. 'I...don't—'

'They're in the chapel,' said Annette calmly. 'Behind the altar screen, covered in dust sheets. He ordered us to put them there. I don't know why.'

Roisin looked at her. The woman wore an expression in her eyes that was almost like triumph. It was clear that she spoke the truth. John's face was a study in surprise and horror as he looked at his sister.

'Thank you.' Roisin turned and walked from the room as calmly as her expression showed she was not. When she was alone she began to run.

The grass was damp beneath her shoes as her feet pounded across the lawn. The grove of trees that held the chapel had never been so far away as it was now. She could barely see for the pressure in her brain—questions pressing up against each other, jostling for room. She did not know what to feel.

The chapel was silent, the sound of the door being

wrenched open echoing about it. The sun pouring through the simple stained glass spilled a coloured pattern on to the flagstones. The cold came up through them, passing through Roisin's feet and into her soul. She was, for a moment, rooted to the spot, afraid of what she might find, and of what it could mean.

Then, slowly, she made her way down the narrow aisle, past the few pews, to the painted screen that stood behind the simple altar. The dying eyes of Christ looked down at her from it, and they seemed to mock her with a knowledge that she did not possess.

Behind the screen a number of flat shapes stood against the wall, covered in a white sheet. The paintings. There seemed to be around four of them. Steadying her breath, Roisin went forward. Then, kneeling before the first painting, she pulled on the cloth. It slid down, revealing a portrait—the head and shoulders of a young man. His tawny red hair was tied back from his face, and his dark eyes sparkled. His mouth was curved upwards in a wild, wicked grin.

Roisin found herself staring into the face of Ewan Hamilton.

Kit woke to find his wife gone. He rolled over, yawning, and buried his head in her pillow. The smell of her still lingered there, the scent of warm hair, of smooth woman.

He smiled. She had been all he imagined.

Last night had banished the ghosts that stalked his mind to its furthest recesses. She had shown that she loved him in every movement, every sensuous, languid motion.

And now she left him, steeped in contentment, unable to reclaim some of the ardour he had given her last night.

Kit sat up. He was naked, he realised with a smile. He hoped that she had put some clothes on before going down to breakfast.

He padded barefoot down to the breakfast room. The smell of something cooking reminded him how hungry he was. What an appetite he had worked up!

He went to the table that ran along the side of the room, picked up the teapot and poured himself a cup of strong tea. Sipping appreciatively, he wandered to the window. Perhaps she had gone for a walk before breakfast. There was no sign of her outside, though. A thought crossed his mind—perhaps she was hiding to drive him to distraction. It was somewhere he would not mind going, he told himself with a smile.

Annette entered the room, a covered platter in her hands. A wholesome food smell came with her. Kit gave her a cheerful smile.

'Good morning.'

'Indeed it is,' she said, dark eyes brighter than usual. She was not usually so positive with him these days.

'Have you any idea where Lady Westhaven is?' he asked, taking another sip of tea.

'She's gone to confession,' said the girl. Something in her face made Kit stop. 'But I think, somehow, that it shall not be hers.'

'What do you mean?'

'I mean she was curious to know what your brother looked like. So I sent her to the chapel.'

She smiled.

The teacup smashed at Kit's feet before he realised he had dropped it. He stared at her as the full meaning of her words hit him. She met his gaze with a level one of her own.

'Do you know what you have done?' he asked.

'I have a fair idea,' she told him sweetly. 'There is something about your dear departed brother that you don't want anyone to know.'

'Oh, Jesus,' muttered Kit. Why had he allowed her to stay in his house? His legs uprooted themselves from the tea-soaked rug and he fled, running outside, throwing open the door of the chapel and standing there, with the sun streaming in behind him, out of breath and out of time.

So it was that he discovered his wife, kneeling on the floor before a painting of James Westhaven—Kit's favourite, the one he had commissioned for his brother's twenty-first birthday. She was very still, not even turning her head as he came in. He went forward, walking around her, eyes fixed on her motionless form as her face became visible.

Tears were running down her cheeks, slowly. Silently. He stood before her, unable to speak, until at last she turned her face to him.

'Who *are* you?'

Her tone was like a whip across his face. He withstood it. 'I am your husband.'

'That is not what I asked.' She closed her eyes momentarily, gesturing to the painting. 'This is your brother.'

'Yes.'

'There was no hunting accident.'

'No.'

'Ewan Hamilton was James Westhaven.'

'Yes,' he began. 'But—'

His voice was cut off as her calm exploded into the furthest corners of the chapel. Rising to her feet, she surveyed him with an anger that burnt him where he stood.

'Then who are *you*? And why do *you* have a scar where I shot *him*? Tell me, Kit, before I am driven mad! What is going on, and why have you lied to me when I trusted you?'

'I was coming to tell you,' was all he could think of to say. 'Last night, when—'

'Liar!' Her face was almost unrecognisable. 'Every word you have ever spoken to me is a lie, Kit! Do yourself the favour of telling the truth for once, before I leave you in whatever swamp of deceit you have created!'

He sighed. 'Roisin. My brother was a highwayman by night, and a gentleman by day. We were desperate to save Oakridge when my father died. There was no money left, and one evening he came home with a bag of gold and told me he had held up a stage-coach. He always loved to take risks.' Kit started forward. 'Please—'

She held out a hand, and he saw that she was shaking. Not trembling, but shaking bodily, as he was beginning to himself. 'Don't come near me. Just speak.'

'It is not unknown for the sons of gentlemen to earn money in such ways,' he began again. 'And I…I would—*could* not allow him to take all the risk, though the rewards were great. So I joined him.'

'Joined him?' Her eyes were vacant. 'I don't understand.'

Wordlessly, he crossed to the paintings and from behind them pulled out a bundle of muslin. He unwrapped the thing within and held it out to her.

A wig. Red gold, so familiar. She took if from him with fingers that did not seem her own, moving independently from her. It was *his* hair.

'I had that made so I could look like him,' said Kit softly. 'He hated wigs more than I do. He would never wear one. He grew his own hair long and tied it back. So I had this made to look real.' He paused in front of her, watching her expressionless face. 'And I wore it when I robbed you.'

Her eyes focused. 'You.'

'Yes.'

'But, James—'

'You never met Jamie,' he said. 'It was me, that night. But they arrested *him* the next day, in a tavern outside the city.'

Tears spilled from Roisin's eyes. She felt as if she had been picked up and shaken, so that all the compartments of her life spilled their contents into each other. Nothing she had known to be true was true anymore. 'I grieved for you,' she whispered. 'The man who—Ewan Hamilton—the one who took me—I thought he was dead.'

'I know.'

'The hanging—why then did he look at me so?'

'He asked me to bring you.' Kit closed his eyes. 'He could see even then that I was taken with you. And he wished to see the woman who had bested his brother.'

'And then…' She shook her head a little, to clear it. 'He winked at me, but then he was looking at you, when he seemed so sad. You were just behind me, and I never thought…'

'Yes.' His voice was barely audible, even to his own ears. The memory of his brother's last glance was not one he liked to linger on. 'I promised him I would attend.'

She gazed at him, and he did not want to put a name to the expression in her eyes. 'You let your own brother die for something you did.'

Kit felt sick. An invisible hand gripped his guts and twisted them. It was as if the angel of vengeance had alighted before him, in the form of his wife. 'Rois-in—you were not there. Once he was arrested in my place I tried to save him, with no effect, and it haunts me every day. He made me promise I would not die as he had.'

'Could you not have saved him?'

'I tried,' he said softly. 'Do you remember that first evening at the theatre? I was going to Newgate to be with Jamie when you saw me outside, then I returned to plead with Justice Webbe. He would not listen to me.' He raked a hand through his hair 'Do you think I did not try? Do you know me so little that you would think that of me?'

She shook her head. 'I don't know you at all.'

'You do not know how many times I have wished it was I swinging from that—' He stopped, bile rising in his throat. 'It should have been me, I am well aware of that.'

She watched him, silently. 'I loved you,' she said. 'I did not know how I could feel the same thing for two different men. You were so kind to me that day when I shot you. You made sure I was safe. But everything was a fiction. You were playing a role.'

'No.' His voice was firm.

'Forgive me.' Her anger was rising again, outstripping the confusion. 'I have been such a fool. I felt so sorry for you because your brother was dead. And so sorry for myself, because…' Her voice gave out and she pressed a hand against her mouth.

'Roisin.' Kit moved forward.

'Leave me,' she said.

'What?'

'Leave Oakridge. Take yourself away somewhere until I have gathered my things together. I never want to see you again.'

His jaw was set. 'You are my wife.'

'And I cannot believe that you thought I would not find out.' Roisin's strength ebbed. 'Did you think I would never ask what your brother looked like? Or wonder why you did not wish to have his paintings around you?'

'I could think of no alternative.'

'You used me,' she said quietly. 'You knew I hated the idea of being stifled. Yet if it had not been for you I would be home by now, in Ireland! You ruined my plan.'

His jaw tightened. 'Plan? You could have been killed if I had not found you.'

'I could have—but at least I would have been

minding my own business!' Roisin turned away, trying to stop her tears. 'You took everything I had—including my dignity!'

He sighed. Then, as if something had just occurred to him, he pulled out another bundle from behind the painting. 'You had better have these back.'

She took the pouch he offered her, her hands recognising the feel of it before her brain registered what it was. Her money. Her jewellery. Voice dull, she raised her eyes to his face. 'And my dignity?'

'I have never had anything but respect for you,' he said quietly.

'Respect?' Blindly she threw the purse at him. It struck him in the chest and fell to the ground between them. 'Here, then, take it back! You took it from me fairly, now—'

He crossed the space between them and grabbed her wrists, pulling her close to him. By the look in his eyes she could see he was barely keeping his temper. 'You gave me little choice that day,' he said quietly. 'We could both have gone about our business and then you would never have found yourself here.'

'Do you think I have not told myself that a hundred times?' she shrieked. 'Do you think I do not wish I had let you go?'

'You *shot* me,' he said, giving her a little shake. 'Do not think you are without blame in this!'

She was outraged, struggling against his grip. 'Was

I the one committing a crime? Was it me robbing young women on a darkened road? I think not! You laid yourself open to assault, Kit, you brought us here—and God knows you have paid the price!'

He was silent for a long moment. 'God knows I have.'

Roisin let out a little sob as her knees finally gave way. She knelt on the floor with the red wig in her lap, her fingers stroking it gently.

Kit squatted beside her, calmer now, head angled to see her face under the curtain of hair that fell over it. 'I behaved badly that night,' he told her. 'I should never have taken you with me. And I should not have kissed you. But there was something about you that I have never seen before.'

'Stupidity?' she asked softly.

He shook his head. 'I had to marry you for the money, I cannot deny that. But I chose you because of that night.'

Their eyes met. 'I cannot believe I didn't see it before,' she said, seeing now the line of Ewan Hamilton's jaw in the man before her. 'But you were so different. The way you rode with me, when those men were following us…'

The ghost of a smile crossed his face. 'You have seen me as few have, Roisin.'

Her mind recalled the dash to safety, the firm control with which he had handled the situation. Seeing Kit you would assume he was another rich country lord with no idea of what happened on the other side of the law. Anger forgotten momentarily, she tipped her head to one side.

'Where did you learn such things?'

'On the road. Out of necessity.'

'Why, Kit?'

He shrugged. 'Jamie was so caught up in it. We had never led such a life before.'

'You were fools to play with fate so,' she told him.

'Perhaps.' His eyes were distant. 'But my brother was happier in those roadside inns than he had ever been at our father's dinner parties in our youth. It was not pretence for him, I think.' He smiled. 'We knew Dick Turpin, you know. I could tell you some tales…'

His tone brought Roisin back to reality. She stared at him. 'Tales? Of how he was killed for what you describe as if it was a hobby? Of how I could have killed you when I shot you?'

Kit grew grim. 'We did not go into this lightly, Roisin. And you would not have killed me.'

'Why? Because a woman could not be an accurate shot?'

'Because you were not aiming for my head or my heart! I have no doubt you would have hit me if you had been!'

'And you trust to that?' She rose, eyes flaming. 'So I am either a bad shot or a coward, is that it?' Hands on hips, she faced him. 'Let me tell you, Kit, what I did took more bravery than your efforts that night. Is it brave to hold up a carriage with a pistol and a mask between you and your victim? I was an unarmed woman! Is such a deed manly?'

'Do not question my manhood!' On his feet once more, he caught her wrists in an iron grip. 'When you have been driven to the lengths I was, Roisin—when you can see nothing between you and losing every-thing, then you may judge me.'

Face flaming, she fixed him a with a glance that neared hatred. 'Let me go.'

Eyes locked with hers, he let go. For a moment they regarded each other, neither backing down. Then he said, 'Besides, you were very well armed.'

'You were not to know it!' she flared back instantly.

'Roisin—'

'And then to woo me—as if you had not already ruined my life enough!'

'You were happy, were you not?'

She stopped. His words hung in the air between them as they eyed each other.

'What does that matter now?' She stared at him. 'You lied to me.' Tears sprang to her eyes. 'I told you things I have told no one—about Ewan and what he—what *you* did! I thought you understood and that is why when you came to me…' She stopped, humil-iated and miserable. 'Last night…I trusted you. And you *betrayed* me. And I cannot live here any more.'

He looked at her, stony faced. He was very still. 'What do you mean?'

'I am leaving. You are right—it was wrong of me to ask you to leave your home—after all you have done to save it!'

'Roisin—' He caught her arm as she wheeled about. 'You are my wife—you stay here with me.'

'Can you live like this?' she shouted at him. Then a bitter laugh escaped her. 'How foolish of me—of course you can. Your whole life has been a fantasy.'

'Roisin—'

He held on as she tried to leave, and for a moment they were in the hut in the woods again, and he was a faceless highwayman.

'Is this the only way you can keep your wife?' she yelled. 'Let me go, Kit!'

Finally he did so, and she stumbled back, steadying herself against a pew.

'I admit my fault,' he said softly. 'You do me wrong to suggest I would hurt you.'

She stared at him. 'Yet you have.'

With that she fled, throwing open the chapel door and running as fast as her shoes and her skirt would allow her, up the hill towards the house. She would leave now while she still had the strength.

He was following her, she knew, as she ran, but he did not catch up by the time she was in the house, slamming the huge front door and taking the stairs two at a time. Near the top her shoe gave way, the heel snapping away from the rest. Roisin pitched forward. Her shins hit the tops of the stairs beneath her and she ended up on all fours, legs bruised. Cursing the shoe aloud, she yanked it off and flung it at the wall, where it made a satisfying dent in the plasterwork and fell into the hall below.

She carried on. She hoped Kit tripped over it on his way in and dashed his brains out on the marble floor. She hoped the dent grew into a crack and the house fell down upon him, burying him in the rubble of his own lies. She wished she could stop crying—it would give him the idea that she cared.

Her room had never seemed so far away.

Once there, she grabbed a small case from under her bed and flung the first clothes that came to hand into it. From downstairs came raised voices—it sounded like Kit railing at John. So like him, she thought, to take out his anger on the one person who would never criticise. John must be trying to calm him down.

Roisin slammed her case shut, narrowly missing trapping her fingers. She must leave this place, now, before she was driven mad by her own thoughts. Her happiness of a little over an hour ago had gone completely. She felt naked.

A thought struck her on her way to the door. Where would she go? She dropped her case, a wave of hopelessness washing over her. She could not go back to her aunt and uncle: the shame would be too great. People would notice that she had moved back in, gossip would ignite—and her mother would get to hear of it sooner rather than later. She knew no one else in London that was not merely a casual acquaintance…

She must find a hotel, then. If she sold the contents of the purse Kit had returned to her, she had enough money to survive on her own for a little while. Her shoulders slumped as she realised it was still in the chapel, on the floor, where she had flung it. She would have to go and get it before she left. It was either that or remain here. Or ask her husband for money—and that she would never do. She put on her outdoor things, picked up her travelling bag, and took one last look at the room that was no longer hers. Then, swallowing her nerves, she opened the door.

She made sure the corridor was clear and crept out, hastening to the main staircase and peering over into the hall below. There was no sign of Kit or John. She descended, making her way outside and over to the chapel. No one was inside, to her great relief— and her familiar old purse lay on the floor where they had left it.

So he had not been back. She wondered what he was doing now, and decided he had probably holed himself up in the library with a bottle of scotch.

Slowly, she went forward and picked up the money pouch. Several painted eyes watched her from where portraits of Jamie lay uncovered. Roisin paused. She wondered what Kit's beloved brother had been like, really. From what she had seen he was everything his elder sibling was. Would he have abducted her? Somehow, she doubted it, although she did not know why. Too professional, perhaps? Kit had said it was no pretence to him.

It did not matter, she told herself firmly. She would be away from here in no time, and then she would never have to think about Jamie, or Kit or Ewan Hamilton, ever again. Her lip curled at the thought. As if she would ever be able to do anything else.

She was almost surprised to see the bright sunlight outside the chapel. It seemed like the whole day had passed in just a few hours. Or that it should be raining. A greater surprise, however, was the person waiting for her.

Annette was there, holding Belle lightly by the bridle. 'I thought you would need your horse,' she said.

Roisin looked at her. 'How kind,' she said, voice cold. She took Belle's reins from the woman, who regarded her levelly, her face totally devoid of feeling.

'Where will you go?'

'Do you care?'

Annette shrugged. 'It does not matter to me.'

Roisin snapped. 'Then do not ask me questions, girl.'

As she fondled Belle's muzzle, gazing into the large brown eyes of her horse, a thought came over her. She handed the horse back to Annette, who started in surprise. 'I will not need her,' she said.

'Why?' Annette frowned. 'Have you decided to stay?'

'No.' Roisin drew herself up. 'But I will not leave by the back way, as if I am ashamed. I have done nothing wrong.' She turned away. 'See that she is taken care of.'

Annette made a noise in the back of her throat. 'And what of your husband?'

Roisin shrugged. 'Keep him.'

Head high, Roisin walked away from the chapel and Kit's erstwhile lover, her heart numb. She did not care how the girl took her words, she told herself, even as her mind ran through the possibilities. Would she try to ensnare Kit once more now there was no obstacle? In his pain, would he let her? The thought was too much to bear after the day she had had.

Roisin closed her eyes for a moment in an effort to compose herself. *She did not care.* It was none of her business what went on at Oakridge now—she was no longer mistress here. She would take the carriage into town like the dignified lady she was supposed to be, find a place to live, sort her thoughts back into the proper compartments of her mind, and seal off those involving Oakridge, Annette and Kit. She would not allow this to ruin her life. She *could* not, or it would drive her mad.

Chapter Twelve

Flattened against the wall outside the chapel, Annette had listened to the words ricocheting off the walls within. Whatever he had done, it was serious. She had known from the moment her shoes had been covered with spatters of dropped tea that she had struck gold. Something was rotten at the core of this outwardly perfect marriage, and now the world would know it.

It was only as she listened further that she had realised just how serious this was. She could not hear everything of what passed between them, but it became apparent, from what she could catch, that Jamie Westhaven—impulsive, headstrong, Jamie Westhaven—had been Ewan Hamilton. And so had his brother. Her eyes grew wide with horror. Kit had never told her, and look at what she had shared with him. He had been living a double life all this time. Now she understood the hours the brothers had kept—the time they spent closeted alone in the library. She had wondered how, given their evident financial difficulties, they had managed to stay afloat.

Now she knew—it had been from a life of crime. It was more perfect than she had ever imagined. She drew back further as footsteps, loud on the marble floor, approached the door of the chapel.

It was flung open and Lady Westhaven flashed past Annette, skirts flying as she ran towards the house. She appeared to be crying, and did not even notice the maid standing there, staring after her.

Kit followed a moment later, long legs carrying him up the hill after his wife at an impressive rate. She watched his firm backside disappear. It was a shame, in a way, that she must do what she must do. But she had promised herself she would make them both pay.

Quietly, Annette stole towards the chapel door, poking her head around it at first to assure herself that she was alone. She went inside, light from the stained-glass windows falling on to her. It was peaceful here, as if the argument of moments ago had never happened. She went forward.

There, in a pool of light, lay a most interesting object. A discarded wig, tawny red in colour, tied with a black ribbon. Bending, Annette swept it up, examining it. She had never seen it before. It was very good quality—human hair—and it looked natural, unlike the wigs that were fashionable for men to wear these days. They had waves and curls built in. This merely looked like a long head of hair. More than that, she realised, it looked like James Westhaven's head of hair. And there, in the portrait that lay on its side before her, was the proof. Wearing this, it would be difficult to tell Kit from his brother—especially after dark.

She shook her head in amazement. So this is how two men had played one part. She had not imagined Kit had it in him to hold up coaches and steal from people.

Smiling, she tucked the wig inside a pocket of her dress. Now she was stealing from him—and he would soon find out how it felt. She knew several people who would be very interested to hear a tale such as this one—but had one in particular in mind. Especially now she had evidence.

Annette left the chapel. She had business to attend to in town.

But before she went, it would be nice if she saw her mistress off, would it not?

Having taken Belle to Roisin and been refused, Annette set off on her task. She returned from London some hours later, with a full purse in her pocket and a feeling of gratification in her heart. Had it been a play that she had written, the events of the day could not have gone more in her favour. She would have preferred it if Roisin had taken the horse into town, granted, for a lady arriving on horseback and alone would have attracted more attention than a faceless carriage. Still, it was enough that she was out of the way. The town would find out that Lady Westhaven had left her husband once the gossips got to work, she was sure.

Things would start to happen very soon now, Annette told herself, making for the kitchen below stairs. She could not wait to see the expression on her brother's face when she told him what his precious master was.

John was helping Cook. Now that there were only three of them, domestic tasks took more effort. That was something else Kit should have remedied long ago.

'May I have a moment of your time, John?' she asked sweetly, leaning in the doorway.

He looked up from the pots he was scrubbing. 'Why?'

'Must there be a reason for me to talk to my brother?'

His eyes were wary as he excused himself, wiping his hands on his sackcloth apron as he followed her from the room. She led him down to the cellar, despite his protests that he had work to do, shut the door, and turned to face him.

'I have such news, John, you'll not believe it.'

'You have been up to something,' he said. It was

not a question. She knew her eyes were sparkling, face alight with her triumph.

She smiled. 'Not I, brother. It is your beloved Kit that has been playing us all for fools.'

'*My* beloved Kit?' He crossed his arms. 'What about—'

'He means nothing to me,' she said impatiently, waving him away. 'And your loyalties too are about to be sorely tested.'

There was something odd in his face. 'By what?'

She wanted to draw out the moment, to savour his reaction. 'Remember how he made such a fuss about having to go to that hanging? The highwayman, Ewan Hamilton?'

'Yes.' His eyes were guarded.

'Have you never wondered why a man who never took any pleasure in such things before suddenly wished to attend the public execution of a stranger?'

'No,' said John firmly. 'I have not.'

'What a good thing one of us is more concerned about what happens beneath our noses,' said his sister. 'I wondered, even then. He gave me the day off, a thing he rarely does for no reason. Now I know why.' She paused, frustrated by his seeming lack of curiosity. 'It was no stranger that was hanged, John— it was James Westhaven! His brother was a common criminal!' Shaking her head, she failed to notice her brother's reaction. 'Now I understand why by the time I came home everyone was talking of a hunting accident that no one seemed to have witnessed—and how the burial had already taken place! But Kit was not too overcome by grief to have a public funeral— he was salvaging his reputation! He took the hanged body of his brother and buried him here because he was out of harm's way.'

There was a brief silence. She watched John eagerly. He did not seem as shocked as she had anticipated. In fact, there was little shock there at all.

'Well?' she cried. 'Have you nothing to say?'

'I was there,' John said softly. 'I helped him conceal it. We buried Jamie's body together.'

Annette's mouth sagged. 'What?'

'He gave you the day off, but I went with him.'

Fury lit within her, turning her face scarlet. 'And you did not think to tell me that I had been working for such a man? How could you keep this from me?'

'He asked me to tell no one.'

'Even your own sister?' She was astounded.

'It was the master's business.'

'Oh!' Sarcasm dripped from her voice. 'Then you were right to help him conceal this shame.' She regarded him, disgusted. 'Do you think yourself so high and mighty? Do you suppose you mean anything to him? Would he keep a secret for you? We may have been his equals once, but now he sees us as mere servants, John—see how he disposed of me! Think, man!'

'You may say what you like,' he said calmly. 'I did what I thought best.'

'Oh, you did more than that,' hissed Annette. 'You are accessory to his crime. Wait until I tell you something else about this great man who you hold in such regard—he is no better than his brother!'

Now he did turn pale. 'What do you mean?'

Triumphant, she tossed her head. 'Ewan Hamilton was two men, not one. All the nights James was at home before the fire Kit was out in his place. He is a highwayman himself, nothing but a thief in the night. And he had the gall to speak to me as he did! He lied to us, and he lied to that brainless wife of his.'

John stared at her. 'How do you know this, Annette?'

'I was outside the chapel this morning,' she said, unashamed. 'It did not please her, let me tell you, when his lies saw the light. We shall not be seeing her around Oakridge again, I'll warrant.'

His face was a study in amazed horror. 'How could you? We may be merely servants now—as you put it—but we were brought up better than to sneak around the private business of—'

'It is no longer his private business,' she interrupted. 'Now that we know we can do something about this.'

'There is no proof,' muttered John, his face still

white with shock. As he looked at her, Annette realised with a start that it was not the right shock. Her eyes narrowed.

'You knew.'

'What?'

'You knew!' It was a shriek this time, and she stood, legs braced, glaring at him. 'I don't believe it, John! You knew the whole story, the whole time?'

His eyes met hers. 'Yes, I did.'

'You *fool* of a man!'

'Don't speak to me that way,' he said, voice low but firm. 'Kit is my friend and my master, and whatever he has done he thought was for the best.'

'And you believe this idiocy?' Her eyes were ablaze.

'Yes, I do. And it would serve you well not to spread rumours, Annette.'

'Hah!' She almost walked away then and there, so great was her disgust. But she wanted to tell him all she had come to impart. 'Rumours? There is proof, John! I had his red wig and that was more than the proof they needed. I suppose you knew about that, too?'

'They?' He approached her. 'Who are "they", Annette?'

'Why, the authorities, of course!'

He stared at her as if he had never seen her before. 'You must tell no one of this.'

'And why not?'

'You would betray him? When he did whatever

was in his power to help me? When he gave you a job for the asking?'

'He is a thief and a liar!' she yelled. 'I do what I can for justice!'

'You do what you can for your own wounded pride!'

That stopped her. She stood, body rigid, head up. 'You think so?'

'I know it.'

Annette tossed her head. 'Whatever my reason, it is done now. Let him weasel his way out of it if he can.'

If she had not thought he could turn more white, he confounded her. 'What do you mean, done?'

'Remember father's friend, Mr Forbes? He was always very fond of me. I used to sit on his lap when a young child. That was, of course, before he came to his present occupation.'

John's lips were stiff. 'Which is?'

'He is a Parish Constable now. He was pleased to discover the daughter of an old friend—I think he thought we were all emigrated with Father. He sympathised with my...reduced circumstances and we had a very nice tea.'

Her brother was staring at her as if he had never seen her before. 'Annette—for God's sake—what have you done?'

'I have been to see the magistrate,' she told him. 'Mr Forbes and I, that is. He thought my information should be passed on.'

'They would not believe you!' he stammered.

'Yet they did. The word of a lady counts for something, still, it seems. Plus they were very interested in this…' Again, she waved the wig. 'Unusual, isn't it? More for disguise than decoration, wouldn't you say? Yes, we had a very profitable talk. Profitable on both sides. They were both very grateful.' She pulled out the bag of coins to show him.

John took a step back, steadying himself against the wall. 'Oh, God.'

'No need to blaspheme, brother,' she said calmly, putting the bag away.

'You enjoyed yourself,' he said, almost inaudibly. 'What have you become?'

'I have become someone who will not be used!' she snapped. 'I will not take the crumbs he throws us and be grateful any more—crumbs bought with ill-gotten gains, John! He deserves whatever he gets, when they investigate this affair!' Annette nodded decisively. 'That is what I mean by done, John. So I think, on reflection, that we will not be seeing Kit around Oakridge for some time, either.'

There was a pause, while it seemed all he could do was stare at her. His eyes on her face were not the most comfortable feeling, but she stood her ground.

Then, 'I have to warn him,' muttered her brother.

'Warn him?' Annette laughed harshly. 'You still keep up this foolish loyalty? I am your blood, John!

Can you not support me against the man who has you polish his boots? You will have no master within a few hours—he will be in Newgate with his fellow criminals! Where will you be then, when—?'

She stopped short as, face unrecognisable, he stepped forward and slapped her.

Her mouth fell open, her hand going to one cheek.

'You stupid, selfish, ungrateful girl,' he said, his voice warped with emotion. 'You ruin a man's life because he didn't want you? He is more than a way to regain your lost status, Annette—he is my friend! I am sorry I ever brought you to work here—and more than ashamed that it was at my request. You are not my sister.'

She gasped, outraged. 'How dare—?'

'Silence!'

She jumped as the shout issued from him. Staring at him, cheeks flushed, she curled her lip. 'Still trying to be Kit, brother? You'll never be like him.' Her eyes swept up and down his body, and her glare grew even more contemptuous. 'Not in any respect.'

His lips were the only colour in his face as he came up very close. 'Annette. Hear what I say. Leave Oakridge now. I do not want to see you here when I return—or ever again, for that matter. I only hope to God that the evil you have done today can be undone.'

Her jaw was slack as he mounted the cellar stairs at speed.

'I am your blood!' she repeated, impotent rage thrashing within her.

He was gone. Annette ground her teeth. It did not matter—if he wished to be a blind fool that was up to him. As for her, she would leave Oakridge. Not because he had commanded her to—but because she had done what she had vowed she would do. There was nothing here for her now.

Marching up the stairs and out of the cellar, Annette went to pack her things.

Kit was in the library, standing before the fire, trying to take the chill from his bones. His wife had departed in his carriage, taking only a tiny case of clothes with her, bound for he knew not where. He was the biggest fool on the planet.

Why had he allowed himself to be distracted last night? One sight of her naked, dripping form in the lake, and any thoughts of his confession had been driven from his mind. He sighed, forehead rested on the high marble mantelpiece. Last night had been like heaven—this morning, a form of hell.

Would she have taken it any easier if he had told her? He suspected it would not have been such a blow. The memory of her face, of the way she had looked at him, froze him every time he thought of it.

He would have given almost anything not to have her look at him like that.

He turned, heart pounding, as the door was shoved open behind him. It was John, and by the expression on his face something was very wrong.

'Kit.' He stood, catching his breath.

'What is it?' Kit went forward. Had his wife met with some accident in her haste to get away from him? He pictured her carriage crushed, her body flung into the road, before he could stop himself. The thought made him go cold all over. 'Is it Roisin?'

John shook his head. 'I have grave news. My sister has told your story to the authorities,' he said, breathing heavy, as if he had run through the whole house. 'You have to leave before they get here.'

'What do you mean?' Kit stared at him, feeling the colour drain from his face.

'I mean she has betrayed you!' John's eyes were urgent. 'She knows everything—she hid outside the chapel.'

Kit sighed, dropping his eyes from those of his friend. 'I see.'

John frowned, confused. He had obviously expected anger. 'Kit,' he said gently. 'They will send riders to bring you in. You cannot tarry here.'

'I know.' Kit leant against a bookshelf. 'I know. But as I feel now, John, I wonder if it would be such a bad thing. She no longer wants to be my wife.'

'I have our horses ready. This is not the time to think foolish thoughts—we must leave.' John's voice was gentle. 'Kit. Think of Jamie.'

Jamie. Kit's head lifted. John was right, of course. All he could do now was leave. But how would fleeing from the law help Oakridge? More, he supposed, than if he languished in a cell at Newgate. He had promised he would not end his days at Tyburn.

'Your sister is a force to be reckoned with,' was all he said.

John nodded, recent anger still in his face. 'And I am more sorry than I can say.'

'Perhaps I should have treated her with the respect her birth afforded her.'

'And perhaps she should have behaved like the lady she is so desperate to be! Do not allow yourself to think that she is the one who was taken advantage of!' John sighed impatiently. 'Kit, *please*, make haste. There will be time for this later. For now—'

Kit pushed himself upright. 'Let us go, then. '

They hurried through corridors, wordless, making for the stables, stopping only to pull on cloaks and boots for riding. Two horses waited outside, saddled and bridled. Kit stopped, forehead creasing into a frown.

'Wait. John, you cannot come with me.'

'What?' His friend turned to him. 'I must, Kit. You will need—'

'I need someone to stay here, to keep an eye on

Oakridge. And I cannot risk taking you down with me. Please.'

The younger man considered a moment, face set. By the time he nodded, Kit was already on his horse. 'Very well.'

'I will wait for you in the hut in the woods a few miles from here. Remember, where we used to hide from my father when he was in one of his rages?'

John nodded, a small smile on his lips. 'I remember. I will come as soon as they are gone. If I cannot I will send word somehow. Be careful.'

'I will. Thank you, John.'

'Thank me when you are away from here,' was the grim reply.

Kit nodded, and spurred his horse on, down the long drive, keeping under the trees that were planted along it. He pulled the hood of his cloak over his face, head low. The road was empty.

It was only as he rode through the gates of Oakridge, the hooves of his horse throwing up stones, that he became aware of three riders coming the other way. They were armed, and rode with a purpose. When they saw him they began to shout, as the thief-takers had on that fateful night. Cursing, Kit drew his horse up sharply and turned her in the opposite direction, away from the woods and towards he knew not what. He had underestimated the efficiency of the magistrate.

His horse was swift, but his pursuers were determined. Within very little time he looked over his shoulder and saw that they were gaining on him. It seemed he would be unable to outrun the law this time. Teeth gritted, Kit leant forward in the saddle, urging the horse on.

It was to no avail. The first of the riders drew level, shouting something at him, just as another appeared on his other side. A gloved hand reached for his bridle and pulled on it. Kit's horse slowed, panic in her eyes. Surrounded by her fellow animals, she lost her footing. Kit felt the road slip out from under him and they fell, his body flung to the ground with a jolt, his horse on her side, struggling up again even before the riders had turned around and were upon them. Kit lay, breath knocked out of him, watching his horse disappear down the road, back the way they had come, towards Oakridge.

John would know soon enough that he was not coming back.

He turned his head upwards as the three riders dismounted around him, boots throwing up dirt in his face. They had thin, mean faces, and his jolted brain could not distinguish one from the other.

'Somewhere urgent to go, Lord Westhaven?' asked the tallest.

Kit clenched his jaw. 'No. Just out for a ride.' He stood, brushing the dirt from his clothes, relieved to find himself unharmed. Where he was going there would be no medical attention. He faced them. 'Is there something I can do for you gentlemen?'

'Yes, as you ask, there is.' The man smiled, teeth crooked. His companions closed in beside him. There was no escape. 'You can come with us.'

Chapter Thirteen

Roisin stood at the window of her hastily found hotel room, staring out at the passing traffic. Her heart lay like a dead thing in her chest. Her whole body was numb as she rocked gently from side to side, her mind far away.

How could she not have known? The whole time she had been married to her highwayman and she had been too dense to see it. She remembered the talk she had had with Ewan about being far from home, missing the wide-open spaces of Kinsale. She had never spoken to anyone about such things before, and Kit had taken that knowledge and used it against her—manipulated her into marrying him with it. Had he ever cared about her personally? She had been sure Ewan had. He had been nothing but a gentlemen. Though neither had Kit.

She clenched her fists. She must stop thinking about them as if they were two different men! Yet they might as well be. Ewan was as dead to her as he had ever been. And she could never see her husband again.

A knock at the door interrupted her milling thoughts. She frowned. She had asked not to be disturbed. Plus no one knew she was here.

'Come in,' she said, wearily.

The door opened and John entered. Of course, she thought bitterly. He would not come himself, not when he could send his shadow to grovel for him.

'My lady,' he said, bowing slightly.

'I gave orders that I was to see no one, John,' she told him.

He inclined his head. 'I know. But I would not let them stop me.'

'How did you find me?'

'I have…contacts that help me in such situations.'

She sighed. Evidently there was more to Kit's manservant than she had previously known. 'I see. And what do you want of me?'

'I bring grave news of your husband. When I told them so downstairs they allowed me up.'

'Grave news?' Despite herself, a cold hand gripped Roisin's heart. 'What has happened?'

In the slight pause before he began to speak, he threw her a shamefaced glance. 'My wretched sister took the wig to the authorities,' he said quietly. 'Along with an account of what she heard between you and Lord Westhaven.'

Roisin felt herself growing pale. 'What does this mean, John?'

'He has been arrested. He is held now at Newgate, awaiting trial.'

'Oh, my God.' She gripped the windowsill behind her, supporting herself. His sins had come back to haunt him—and her. 'How could Annette—?'

'I blame myself,' he said swiftly. 'I should have known what she planned to do and—'

'No.' Roisin shook her head at him. 'You are not at fault here, John. But, Heaven help me, if I ever see that hellcat again—'

'Please,' he interjected. 'There is no time for this. Lord Westhaven bids you go to him at once, ma'am.'

'Go to him?' Suspicious, she frowned at John. It did not seem like Kit to beg help from the wife he had alienated. 'Did he say that?'

John seemed uncomfortable. 'Not precisely.' He looked at her imploringly. 'But if you cannot help him, Lady Westhaven, who will? He will hang for sure, as his brother did before him.'

A flash of Tyburn came to Roisin. The crowds, the screams… She could not let that happen again. Not after seeing it, and knowing that he, standing beside her, had seen it too. Not to her husband, the man she had held in her arms in happier times. She must help him. But could she bring herself to face him once more?

John was watching her, as if trying to gauge her reaction. She turned to him.

'Do you think he wants to see me?'

John sighed. 'I think he thinks of nothing else.'

Roisin turned back to the window, in a quandary. She did not wish to picture Kit locked in a cell. Even less did she want to see it. Yet she must go to him. She was his wife, for better or worse.

'What do you think I should do?' she asked the man who stood before her, silent.

He brought his eyes up to meet hers. 'You need never see him again after today. Hear what he has to say, if anything.'

Another pause. He was right, and she knew it. 'Will you come with me?'

He nodded. 'I have a carriage waiting if you can come right away.'

Roisin steeled herself. 'Very well. Take me to him.'

So it was that, after a carriage ride that was too brief for her liking, she found herself walking under the forbidding arch and through the gates of Newgate, John at her side. The smell rose up to greet them as they descended—a smell of urine, rotten food, death and despair. Despite her best efforts, Roisin's skirts trailed on the dirty flagstones, in she knew not what. She tried not to think about it.

The gaoler, after accepting a coin from John,

turned and led them down a narrow, damp-walled passage. He breathed heavily as he walked, and she could smell alcohol on his clothes and on his breath. She supposed that if she worked in such a place she too would be a drunkard.

A rat ran over her foot, startling her. The gaoler ignored her cry of surprise and dismay, but John stopped in his descent and turned to her, concerned.

'I'm fine,' she said, hurrying onwards. The sooner she got into this place the sooner she could leave.

As they walked, Roisin was telling herself firmly to be strong—not to let her husband see the effect his betrayal had had on her. She was not here to weep at his feet like Mary Magdalene at the foot of the cross. If he wanted to be a martyr, that was his own business. She would help him, she knew that much, whether he asked her or not. But she would not forgive and forget. Nothing he could say would make her.

She straightened her shoulders, preparing herself for what lay ahead.

They stopped before a door, deep in the bowels of the prison. John stood back, allowing her to pass him, an encouraging smile on his face. 'I will remain outside.'

She did not envy him, waiting alone in the dark while their greasy companion returned to his room and his ale. But she only nodded, and went through the door the gaoler held open for her.

She stood for a moment as it swung shut behind her, her eyes adjusting to the sudden semi-darkness, trying to find her bearings.

The room was lit only by a few small rays of sunlight that filtered through a tiny barred window, very high up the wall. Leaning against the wall opposite her was a man, his legs shackled together. Shadows covered his face, and only his eyes were visible. Looking at him, she saw only the highwayman she had kissed so long ago, and wondered how she could not have done so before.

'Ewan Hamilton, I presume,' she said drily.

'Well timed, lass,' he said, and that rich, strong accent curled around her as it had when they first met, and she had held a gun to his crotch. And he had touched her skin. And it all had gone wrong, once and for all. 'You get here just in time for my demise.'

Roisin felt a chill run along her spine as she heard again the man who had lived in her mind all this time. Her husband was no longer a simple landowner, but a knight of the road once more, facing her again as he had on that fateful night. Her mind wandered back there, of its own accord.

'You *were* kind to me,' she said absently, far away. 'Whatever they may suggest.'

In the dark, he smiled. 'I had to be. You'd've blown my brains out else.'

Roisin frowned, blinking. It was like the dream she

had been having had come true. He was alive again. Yet it was wrong. *This* was wrong.

'Stop it, Kit!' she snapped, turning away from him, one hand over her eyes. 'Why must you play with me?'

He stepped out of the shadows, once again her husband. Except that his shirt was filthy, as if he had been held against a slime-covered wall, or flung to the floor. His eyes were the only things that seemed alive about him.

'What are you doing here?' he asked, his voice normal once more. Normal, yet different, as if he had seen things since he had been here that he had not seen before.

She stared at him. 'Do you think I make a habit of tramping through prisons, husband? I came because I heard you were to hang.'

'So I am.'

She stared at him, and his hopelessness made her feel stronger. 'No,' she said simply.

A small smile curved his lips upward. 'Not broken, yet.'

'It will take more than you to break me,' she assured him coldly.

The smile died. His jaw tightened. 'Where are you staying?'

'I have a suite at a hotel in town. My brother sent me some money.'

It was a lie—she was using her title as credit until

she could pay the bill with the sale of her jewellery. Her family, in truth, had no idea what was happening. But it had the desired effect. Kit felt the sting of her words, just as she intended. There was a silence. Water dripped from the walls. He watched her with an unblinking stare. Roisin sighed.

'How long have you been here?'

'This is the third day.'

She was amazed. 'Were you going to send word to me?'

No answer. There were shadows under his eyes. She glanced about her, at his prison. There was no chair in the room—he must have spent most of the night sitting on the floor. Yet still his eyes met hers, unmoving. Unreadable as ever.

She said, 'Well, I am here. What would you have me do, Kit?'

He rubbed a hand over his face, making it dirtier than it already was.

'Roisin. I did not ask you to come.'

'Please!' She held out a hand. 'You need my help, Kit. Swallow your foolish pride!'

He leant his head back against the wall. 'I have very little pride left, I assure you.' His voice was low, as though he spoke to a stranger.

He moved towards her, the leg irons hampering his movement. Looking down she saw that his ankles were rubbed raw.

They stood, distant as strangers, the air around them alive with questions.

He said, 'I thought you never wanted to see me again.'

'I did not,' she told him. 'But I cannot pretend we are not still married.'

'And you wish we had never met, as you said before?'

Roisin gazed upon him, caked in filth. He was here because of her. His brother was dead because of her. If she had passed along a different route… or just sat and allowed herself to be robbed… 'Of course.'

Finally his eye contact broke. His shoulders sagged a little and he coughed—a dry, raking sound that tore at her, almost breaking her cold veneer. Her arms ached to be around him, pulling him to the ground, cradling his head in her lap. She wanted to stroke his hair and tell him that she would get him out while she still had breath in her body to fight with.

Instead she stood, back rigid, chin raised, wordless.

The silence between them grew again. She shifted her feet, uncomfortable.

Kit raised his eyes. 'I love you,' he said simply.

She frowned. It was the last thing she had expected him to say; a thing he had never said before. It made her want to weep—to both embrace him and pound his head against the stones of the wall in fury. Her throat constricted. Why must he say such a thing now?

'You do not love me,' she said. 'You love the chance I represent.'

Silent, he shook his head.

'You used me to save your home,' she told him, 'as you now can use me to try and save your skin. You do not have to placate me with words, Kit. I'm a grown woman.'

He came closer, his jaw set, touching her for the first time: one hand on her cheek, his thumb playing across her lower lip. 'I know it sounds false within these walls,' he said gently. 'But if I get me out of here, I will prove it to you.'

She stood, unflinching. How could she know what he felt for her? If she tried to think about it, it would drive her mad.

'Roisin,' he said, eyes bottomless, 'if you do not want it, I will never come near you again, you have my word.'

Her fists clenched at her sides. Should he not be vowing to fall at her feet, to follow her to the ends of the world? She supposed not. Extravagance had never been his way.

His hand stayed where it was, the area of skin he touched suddenly the most sensitive place on her body. He came closer still, bending his head towards her. Her eyes closed as his lips touched hers.

'No.' She stepped backwards, away from his kiss.

She kept her eyes closed until she was sure she had control of herself. Then she met his gaze.

'I know what you feel for me,' he told her.

She looked away, at the bars on the windows with the sickly light falling through them; at the slime-covered walls. Anywhere but at him, for if he met her eyes now he would know. Another silence stretched between them. She could think of nothing to say.

At last, he said, 'I feel very near Jamie here. He must have been very frightened.'

Roisin sighed. 'Why must you skirt round the issue? Why can you never say what you feel to my face? You love me—conveniently—but you still cloak yourself from me! If you are afraid, say it!'

He was very close, so she could feel his breath on her cheek. 'I am afraid,' he said quietly.

'Of death?'

Kit nodded. 'Of death. But also that you will hold me to my word, as my brother did, and that I will never see you again.'

Their eyes met. She said, 'Kit, you should have told me.'

'And every second I did not weighs on me.' He put his hands on her shoulders. 'I need your help. There is no one else to ask.'

'And what of John?' Her eyes blazed. 'He has stayed near you, with not a thought for himself, his reputation! He came to ask me for my help because he knew you would rather die than humble yourself to ask!'

'That is not true.'

She nodded, eyes narrowed. 'No? Perhaps you would have asked, once you knew there was no way around asking. Because you owe it to Jamie.'

'And because I wanted to see you again.'

It was becoming difficult to stand so near and not touch him. Roisin wanted to be away, to nurse her broken heart. Perhaps he spoke true—and that almost made his betrayal worse. She wanted to slap him, to kiss him. Outwardly, she remained calm.

'I have to go,' she said.

His face was a mask. 'Will you come back?'

She shook her head. 'I don't think so.'

He nodded. 'It seems you are avenged.'

Roisin sighed. 'I am still your wife, am I not? Let me see what I can do.'

She took another step back, knocking on the door. His eyes followed her.

'Thank you for coming.'

Suddenly, she wanted to laugh. He sounded like he was seeing her off after a garden party. The door opened behind her.

'Goodbye, Kit,' she said.

He did not reply. But she felt his eyes on her back as she left him, and could not turn for fear of what she would do.

John waited outside. Roisin met his questioning eyes and, as the door closed on Kit behind them, she dissolved into tears. She put both hands over her mouth, trying to hold back the sobs and the rising panic within. He watched her, brown eyes helpless, as if he was wondering what to do.

'He looks dreadful,' she said, voice shaking. 'Have you seen him?'

He nodded. 'Earlier today.'

'We have to get him out.' She tried in vain to wipe her eyes, ashamed suddenly of herself. She was evidently not the only one hurt by events. There were shadows under John's eyes and the way he carried his body told of total exhaustion.

He nodded. 'Come, let us leave this place.'

The gaoler, who had appeared again behind them, grunted and led the way.

By the time they were out of Newgate, Roisin felt less hopeless. In the pocket of her dress lay the pouch of jewellery Kit had given back to her.

'John,' she said, touching his arm. He turned, opening the door of the carriage for her. 'I'm sorry— I know you're tired. But…will you take me to the jewellers where Kit sold his watch?'

He nodded. 'Of course.' She suspected that he would rather go home and get some sleep, though it showed not a jot on his face.

When they had started to move, and he was staring out of the window at the passing streets with a glazed expression, Roisin said, 'How long have you known Kit?'

'Since he was thirteen and I two years younger. I came from a rich family, but when we lost our money I was forced to seek employment.' He smiled at her surprise. 'Yes, I was a gentleman's son, once upon a time.'

'What happened?' Roisin leant forward, fatigue temporarily forgotten.

He shrugged. 'My father was a merchant. We had a large house in town and the best of everything. Then one day two of his ships were lost in a storm. The expense was more than he could cover. He fled abroad, leaving my mother, Annette and I. The house and everything we owned was sold. I was eleven then and had never worked a day in my life. I was trained to nothing and had not yet learned my father's business. The only option for me was to go into service. I started as a kitchen boy and worked my way up. Kit and I always saw eye to eye, since the day he caught me up a tree in the orchard, stealing apples.'

'What did he do?'

A fond smile. 'He joined in. We ate until we had to hold our bellies to stop them bursting.'

'And Annette?' Roisin could not help asking.

John sighed. 'Our mother was never the same.

Annette worked for a dressmaker and cared for her until she died a year ago. Then she asked me to get her a position with Kit. Fool that I was, I agreed.'

Roisin said nothing to this, seeing the guilt on his face. 'What was Jamie like?' she asked instead.

He smiled fondly. 'Jamie was always a law unto himself. I don't know how many times his father administered the strap in our youth. He lived for the good things in life. He never had a sense of responsibility like Ki— Lord Westhaven had. Not until their father died. He was my age.'

'You have done much for them both,' she told him.

He sighed. 'If it was in my power I would have done more.'

'We will save Kit,' she assured him. 'Fear not.'

He looked at her. 'I should be saying that to you, I think.' He smiled. 'Lady Westhaven—'

'Roisin,' she interrupted. 'We have seen enough together now to be on first-name terms, I think. And I never asked your permission to call you John, either.'

John seemed a little taken aback, but nodded. 'Roisin. I wished to say that I think you make a perfect wife for Kit—exactly what he needs. Though he has not done right by you, I know that he feels…abysmal—'

'So do I,' she said, not wanting to discuss Kit further. 'And I will not act hastily, believe me. But for now we must concentrate on his release.'

He nodded. 'Forgive me. I speak out of turn.'

'Never.' She laid a hand on his arm. 'It is not only Kit who has you to thank for your friendship. And your loyalty.' She lowered her eyes. 'I know not what the future holds for him and me, that is all.'

He nodded.

All of a sudden, Roisin had to ask, 'Speaking of loyalty, where is your sister?'

John's jaw tightened in the way Kit's did when he thought of something unpleasant. He did not meet Roisin's gaze. 'I care not. Annette has done much for which I am ashamed—on her behalf,' he added, 'for she is unashamed herself. She is gone from Oakridge.'

Roisin hesitated, then asked, 'Did you know...that she and Kit...?'

He nodded. 'Though he never spoke of it to me, he knew I knew.'

'You did not disapprove?'

He looked uncomfortable. 'I was, I must admit, surprised at him. Yet, though it pains me to say it about my own sister, she has a way about her... She bewitches men, I think, and she saw in him a way to regain what she had lost. I think that was her plan all along—and I cannot believe I did not realise until now. She was never able to accept our fall from grace, you see.'

Suddenly it all made sense to Roisin. Annette's

seemingly ridiculous expectations, her impassioned anger towards the new Lady Westhaven: *You think your wealth makes you better than me?*

'I do see,' she said, almost to herself.

'And Kit…' John continued, pulling a wry face, 'this year past was not an easy one for him. But let us say…it was not one of his most enlightened decisions.'

She smiled. 'An understatement if ever I heard one. You will not speak ill of him, will you, John?'

He merely shrugged. 'We have been friends a long time. It is not my place to say so, but he has been more like a brother to me. I did not speak about Annette to him because I trusted him to do what is best. I am sorry she treated him so, now.'

Roisin raised her eyebrows. 'I am glad to be rid of her, though I should not say so to you.'

He shook his head, frowning. 'I do not think that anyone will be sorry to see her go, even if she is my blood.'

Roisin gave him a tentative smile, which he returned. She could only guess what he had said to his sister of the subject of herself and Kit.

She looked out of the window as the carriage slowed. 'We are here.'

Sure enough, they had arrived at the jewellers. He alighted, helped her down, and led the way inside.

She explained her purpose to the elderly man behind the counter, tipping out the pouch of jewellery before him and saying that she wished to sell it all. She had removed only a couple of pieces—those left to her by her grandmother, for example. Other than those, her complete jewellery collection lay there. She examined them, glittering in the light. They seemed from a life very far away, when she had been so young. Hard to believe it had been little more than two months ago that she had seen Kinsale for the last time.

She had given these jewels up for lost long ago, she reminded herself, when they had been stolen by Ewan Hamilton. It was only right they should go towards freeing Kit. It was the others to which she felt attached—the mahogany box filled with his mother's collection was still at Oakridge. She had looked forward to wearing them for him.

Jerking her mind back to the present, she listened to the price the jeweller was offering. It seemed fair to her—nothing like the true value, of course. But, judging by what she knew of past high-profile ransoms, it should be more than enough to free Kit. There should be a substantial amount left over, and that was all she needed—some money of her own to fall back on, come what may.

They bargained for a time, haggling over particulars while John browsed goods displayed elsewhere in the shop. Finally, however, she accepted the jeweller's offer, and was paid in cash, which she secreted away in her hidden pocket. She thanked him, and turned to look for John. He was standing at the other end of the shop, gazing into a cabinet. She joined him.

'Something you like?'

He looked over his shoulder at her. 'Jamie's watch.'

'It is still here?'

He nodded, pointing. 'There.'

A gold pocket-watch lay there, chain coiled round it. It appeared old, and valuable. Roisin leant closer. As if by magic, the jeweller appeared at her elbow.

'Interested?'

She nodded. He unlocked the case, taking out the watch and handing it to her. His asking price made John draw in his breath beside her. It was clear the jeweller was making a substantial profit on the price he had given Kit.

Roisin thought about it. Even with the purchase of the watch, she would still have more than she needed to buy Kit's freedom. What was left would not be much—but enough to get by on, for now.

'I'll have it, please,' she told him.

He smiled. 'A gift for someone?'

She nodded. 'My husband.'

The jeweller smiled. 'He will get years of pleasure from it, madam.'

She returned the smile politely. He would, indeed. But she would not be there to see them.

* * *

Back in the carriage, John looked at the small flat package wrapped in paper that Roisin held, in which lay the watch.

'Will you give it to him for me?' she asked, holding it out to him. Her eyes were sad. He shook his head.

'You should give it to him yourself, Roisin.' It felt strange calling her this, but it seemed to bring her comfort. It occurred to him that this woman had no one to talk to now.

'I cannot.' Again she offered it. 'Please, John. Just leave it where he can find it, in the library. I owe it to him. Now my debt is paid and I can leave.'

He suspected this was not the whole reason for her purchase of Jamie's watch. He was glad, however, that it would be back where it belonged. He took the box from her.

'I will make sure he gets it.'

She nodded. 'My thanks.' She watched him put the box away, in an inside pocket where it would be safe. Then she set her shoulders and raised her chin. 'Now, John, the work begins,' she said, her voice steady. 'I have to talk to my uncle.'

Her uncle was at home although, as Simpson told her, her aunt and cousin were out calling on friends. Roisin was glad. She was curious as to how Cathy's *amour* with Mr Jonstone was continuing, but this was not the time for such things. Later, when this mess was cleared up and she had a place to call her own, she would be available for gossip. As it was she was free to deal with the business in hand.

Colonel Penrose rose from his desk and smiled at his niece. 'Roisin. Do take a seat. Can I offer you some tea?'

She shook her head. 'No, thank you, Uncle. There is a pressing matter I want to discuss with you, if you have the time.'

'Ah,' he said quietly, 'I wondered if I might be seeing you. How is your husband?'

She dropped her eyes from his. 'You know, then, that he is in prison?'

He nodded. 'It is, I am afraid, the talk of the town.'

She gave an exasperated gasp. 'Have people nothing better to do? How goes the story this time?'

Her uncle shrugged. 'That Ewan Hamilton had an accomplice, and that the man in question is a well-known aristocrat.'

'Do they know it is Kit?'

He considered. 'I think people are beginning to suspect, although the matter is being treated with some delicacy. He resides at Newgate, I understand?'

She nodded. 'They have not been kind to him.'

'My dear,' he said gently, 'they are kind to no one, regardless of birthright.'

Roisin leant forward. 'Uncle, can you help me?

There has been a mistake. The girl who brought the story to the authorities is a delusional liar. My husband is not guilty of this crime.'

He looked at her levelly, as if wondering whether she was trying to deceive him, or had been deceived herself. 'I think we both know that something is going on at Oakridge,' he said softly. 'If one brother is involved, will not people start questioning the mysterious death of the other brother? The same day, I take it, as Hamilton was hanged?'

It was no good—she was not fooling him for a moment. Pretence flung aside, Roisin leant across his desk. 'Uncle. You have to help me. This cannot happen. Please. It was a misunderstanding. I have a thousand pounds here that says so, that must be enough to buy his freedom. If it is not, I can get more.'

He frowned at the purse she threw on to the table. 'Where did you get this?'

'I sold my jewellery.' She cast her eyes down. 'Some of it was very old, please don't tell my mother.'

For the first time, he smiled. 'You interfere in things you do not understand, child.'

'No.' She shook her head. 'You can help me—I know you can. Talk to the Lord Chief Justice for me, I believe you know him well.'

'Indeed I do.' Her uncle's gaze was beginning to hold a respect that had never previously been there. 'We served in the army together, years ago. I saved his life once.' He smiled. 'But that is another story. You wish me to ask a favour of him?'

She nodded. 'Please, make him see that Kit has been wrongly arrested—his reputation is beyond reproof! That it was all a mistake, and the maid was lying. That there is no evidence that he ever had anything to do with Ewan Hamilton.' She clasped her hands together. 'Please.'

'Roisin. Although I admire your husband greatly—' began Colonel Penrose.

'I know you interfered before,' she said quickly. 'You can do so again.'

He stopped. She could see him thinking about it.

'Uncle, highwaymen buy their freedom every day—and for much smaller sums than this,' she said. 'All I need you to do is convey the request for me and ensure he is freed. I will do the rest.'

'And if I do?'

'Then you will have done me a great service. And you will have saved the life of a man who was desperate and reckless, but never dangerous. And he will never do anything so foolish again, you have my word. What do you think?'

'I think,' he said quietly, 'it is a good thing Robert Webbe is such a good friend. Nevertheless, I fear this can be the last favour I ask of him.'

'Then you will do it?'

He nodded.

'Is it enough?'

'I should think so.' He took the purse from the desk. 'I will do as you ask, and deliver this. But I cannot promise there will not be damage to his reputation. If you want a story circulated, you must think it up yourself.'

She nodded, tears of gratitude coming to her eyes. 'Thank you. I hope you do not think less of me, Uncle, for this.'

'On the contrary,' he said softly, honestly, 'I never knew you had such mettle in you.'

She smiled. 'I will never be able to repay you.'

'If you are happy with your husband, then that is enough. My sister, your dear mother, would be pleased to know that I have had a hand in it. Although,' he added, seeing her look, 'there is no need for her to actually find out.'

'We will be happy,' she assured him, hoping fervently that it would, one day, be true. They would be, eventually. Only, not with each other. She knew not what they would do about the bonds of state and God that tied them together. And not even Colonel Penrose could help her with that. So she simply smiled, kissed him—fervently, several times—and left the house.

Kit would not hang. That was enough for now.

Chapter Fourteen

Dawn came quietly to the cell in Newgate, only a few rays coming through the small barred window. Kit, sitting against the wall, knees drawn up to his chest, raised his head and looked up.

It had been the longest night of his whole existence, worse even than the night Jamie had died. He knew now what his brother had felt, and could not believe the courage it must have taken to go to the scaffold the way Jamie had. Kit closed his eyes, his head aching. It was cold in the cell, the walls radiating a damp chill that penetrated his clothes and settled on his skin. He had developed a cough that tore through his chest, burning his throat. He had not slept.

He hated this, having nothing to do but explore his thoughts again and again. He kept seeing the face of his wife in his mind's eye—cold and impenetrable. He had hurt her beyond measure, he knew that now. Perhaps she would never forgive him. She had been beautiful, standing in his cell last night. More so because it had been days since he had seen her. Beautiful like a statue carved from marble, he reflected wryly. Like ice. She had seemed to feel nothing for him. He could not decipher where her anger ended and what she felt for him began, if there was still any genuine feeling underneath.

It was driving him mad, slowly, sitting here and wondering. There had been points last night when he had almost wished they would hang him and get it over with.

Even as the thought passed through his tired mind, there was a noise at the door—someone turning a key in the ancient lock. Kit sprang to his feet, finding a new strength. Thoughts of hanging were far from him now—let them try it. He would put up a fight.

The gaoler entered, grinning sarcastically, his lank, greasy hair falling around his face. Kit watched him approach with contempt.

'Good news,' said the old man. It was impossible to tell from his voice whether the news was good for prisoner, or for captor.

'Yes?' Kit was wary. Was he to go to trial now? Would Roisin be there?

The gaoler was nodding, obviously determined to eke out every morsel of suspense in whatever piece of news he bore. He sidled closer, still grinning like a loon.

'Well?' Kit was in no mood for guessing games.

The pain in his chest and head would have shortened his temper even if he did not have a profound dislike for this man.

The gaoler's smile turned bitter. 'You're to go free.'

There was a pause. Kit stared at him, dumbstruck. Was this some sort of game—to be played with prisoners before they were hanged? Did he do this often, just to drive the condemned mad? He was approaching now—for what purpose? Did he want to add to this mental torment with another beating?

But, no, now the man was bending over, unlocking the shackles at his ankles. Unbelievably, he was unchained. Kit breathed a sigh of relief as they came off, the metal parting from his rubbed-raw skin. They had been his bane for days. But, go free? Just like that? It seemed too simple, somehow, that he could just walk out of this place, when everything he could do was insufficient to secure Jamie's release.

A thought occurred to him. Roisin had been at work.

A surge of gratitude went through him. She had done it, despite her feelings for him. But how—what had she told them?

'Why am I being freed?' he asked, as he was pushed towards the door.

'"Misunderstanding", apparently,' said the other man dismissively. 'Makes no odds to me. There's 'undreds of your type buy themselves out of here, gentlemen and otherwise.'

Kit nodded, still dazed. His legs carried him along familiar corridors after the gaoler, their weakness countered by the thought of fresh air and light. It occurred to him, as they grew closer to the gates, that the only time Jamie had seen this light before he was hanged was on his way to Tyburn. The knowledge was no comfort.

'Off you go, then,' said the gaoler almost cheerfully, gesturing towards the street as they stood under Newgate's entrance arch. Kit looked at him. It seemed at any moment guards would burst out from hiding, take him by the arms and drag him into the depths of the prison once more. He took a step forward. Nothing happened.

Then he was shoved roughly from behind, the huge studded door banging shut behind him as he stumbled into the yard. Kit wheeled round, but his gaoler was already gone into the depths of the prison from whence he came. He stood, breathing in the air, eyes sore with the light, clothes and body filthy, telling himself to get a grip on reality. He had not eaten in a couple of days.

'Kit.'

Someone was calling him. He glanced up and there was John, coming towards him across the courtyard. For a moment he thought he was seeing things, imagining his friend. He blinked. John was still there, drawing closer. He took Kit by the arm, gently, and began to lead him away from the towering prison behind him.

'Come, I have a carriage waiting. I'll take you home.'

Kit nodded. His throat was dry, his tongue sticking to the roof of his mouth. He turned to where the carriage stood, and spoke with an effort. 'Is Roisin here?'

John shook his head. 'No. Sorry.'

'She did this?'

'Yes.'

Kit nodded. 'Thank you.'

John was handing him into the carriage. There was a blanket over him. He was not sure where it had come from. 'Why do you thank me? Your wife did all the negotiating.'

Kit smiled. 'You brought her to me.'

His friend sat beside him as the carriage began to move, shoulder to shoulder, his solid presence holding Kit upright.

It seemed an interminably long journey, during which he drifted in and out of sleep. He was only slightly more coherent by the time they reached Oakridge Park, the familiar sight of the house through the carriage window going some way to heal the ache within him.

John helped him upstairs, into his room. There a bath waited, the water steaming. The sight of it was like a blessing, and Kit went forward, fumbling with the buttons on his soiled, stinking shirt, eager to get it away from his body. His fingers were still stiff with cold, and refused to work as his mind ordered them to.

'Here.' John came forward, deftly unbuttoning the shirt. 'I think I'll just tell Cook to burn this,' he said, as he removed the garment. 'It is long past...'

Kit lifted his eyes to his friend's face as his voice trailed off. John was looking in horror at his chest. Kit followed his gaze down, fingers exploring the huge bruises that covered him. His dry lips parted in a mirthless smile.

'Peine forte et dure,' he said softly.

They had strapped him to the ground and placed weights on his chest, in the hope of obtaining a confession. He remembered the gleeful face of the hated gaoler bending over him, enjoying every moment. He had said little, despite the pain, and at last they had ceased. A suspected highwayman was too big a crowd-puller at Tyburn day to risk killing through torture. It had not been a pleasant experience.

John swallowed. 'Forgive me for taking so long to get you out.'

Kit put a hand on his shoulder. 'You got me out. That is all I care about. It is more than I could do for...' He sighed, head light, heart heavy.

'I'll leave you to your bath,' said John.

He left, and Kit spent long in the bath, scrubbing

the smell and the dirt and the feel of Newgate out of his skin. He sat there until the water lost its comforting warmth, thinking of his brother, and his home. And of his wife.

Of Roisin, until the water went cold.

When he finally reached his bed it was to almost fall upon it, stretched out full-length, clawing the covers over himself, exhausted.

He slept and, had he been aware of it, would have been thankful he was too tired to dream.

It was over twelve hours later when he awoke, and the early evening light fell through his window in such a different way to how it crept into the cell. He lay, eyes fixed on the ceiling, examining the different aches in different parts of his body.

He felt better. Rolling on to his side, he coughed harshly for a few moments, chest tightening. Mostly better.

He got out of bed, pulled on the clean clothes that lay ready, and went in search of food—because now the most pressing thought was that of his immense hunger.

A fire burned in the library—trust John to know it was the first place he would go. And—thank God—a plate of fresh baked scones and a pot of jam stood upon his desk. Eagerly, Kit made his way across the room.

He stopped as he saw something else. An unfamiliar box, on his desk beside the scones. Frowning, he picked it up, his interest piqued. It opened easily.

Kit froze. There, nestled in velvet, his brother's watch. It lay so he could see the initials JW inscribed into the gold. He had thought it gone for good. He did not know what to think now it was here again.

Reaching out behind him, Kit found the bell-pull without looking and rang it long, eyes fixed on the pocket watch. Within a minute John entered, stopping in the doorway.

'You're up, then. Shall I bring a pot of—?' He broke off, one glance at Kit's face telling him that tea was not the reason he had been called.

Kit watched him. 'Jamie's watch.'

John nodded. 'Yes.'

'Where did you get it? How…' Kit knew the question was tactless, but he did not care '…how did you afford this, John?'

'I did not.' His manservant looked levelly at him. 'Your wife did.'

'Ah.' Kit touched the watch with a hesitant finger. 'Why?'

'She said she owed it to you,' was the reply.

'I see.' He took the watch from its box, feeling the weight of it in his hand, then slipped it into his pocket. 'She has more than repaid anything she owes me,' he said softly. 'It is I who will not be able—or allowed, it seems—to repay her.'

For a few seconds he was lost to his surroundings as he heard her voice again at Newgate, telling him that she did not want to see him—that she wished she had never met him. He deeply regretted not telling Annette to leave the night she had attacked his wife. But then, the maid was not solely to blame in this. He should have been honest with Roisin—then there would have been no secrets to expose.

He sighed heavily, head aching. 'John, am I the most damnable fool on the face of the earth? What must I do? What do you think would be the best way to—?'

John cleared his throat. 'With respect…'

Kit smiled. 'You have never said anything to me with respect. Please do not start now or I truly will lose my mind.' He waved a hand at his friend. 'Go on.'

John returned the smile as Kit perched on the edge of his desk. 'I think you and Roisin should stop asking me what I think and talk to each other.'

'Roisin?' Kit could not resist. 'Now you are on first name terms with my wife, Farham?'

'She asked me to call her Roisin,' John said, refusing to be riled.

'Rightly so.' Kit slapped him on the back. 'You have been invaluable to us both.'

'Hardly.' John crossed his arms. 'Kit, she sold her jewellery. Everything you gave her back. She bought you out of Newgate, and she bought the watch. And she would not give details, but I think she more or less begged her uncle to help her. My part was to circulate rumours, that is all, so now all London talks about the injustice and offence done to you by your spell in Newgate. I merely salvaged your reputation—she saved your life.'

There was a pause while Kit took this in. 'Yet she would have me believe she does not love me.'

'Whatever her reasons,' said John, 'she did as much for you as could be done.' He paused. 'And she comes tomorrow morning to collect her clothes.'

Kit's head snapped up. 'Why?'

'She intends moving out at the first opportunity. Possibly returning to Ireland.'

That could not be allowed to happen. Kit thought of Oakridge as it had been while Roisin had lived as his wife. He could not go back to the emptiness again—to the silent, echoing corridors. The room seemed to close in on him, suddenly insufferably hot.

'Kit?' John was watching him with concern.

Kit ignored the dizziness that assailed him as he pushed himself away from his desk and stood upright. He must talk to her. Running a hand along his brow, he felt beads of sweat there. John must have stoked the fire too high, he thought, forcing his mind to attend to the matter at hand. His wife was leaving the country. She must be stopped.

'Tomorrow, you say?'

'Yes.' His friend took his arm. 'Kit, I think you should—'

'Then I will be here,' he said firmly. 'Inform me when she arrives.'

'You have my word. Now I think you should rest. Or at least sit down.'

He was right. The room had started to move around Kit. 'Very well.' He smiled at his manservant. 'I'm going back to bed. But remember—the minute she gets here I want to know.'

When Kit awoke next it was to a pounding headache and a dry, aching throat. Squinting in the late morning sun, he shut his eyes again, a small groan escaping him. It was so *cold*. His body ached in the same way it had last night, only worse. He felt like he could happily sleep for ever, if this headache ever allowed him to sleep again.

There were footsteps in the hall. Kit swallowed. He did not wish to be disturbed now, he just wanted to close his eyes and forget that the last few days and everything with Roisin had ever happened. Perhaps, he thought, this apparent illness was some form of divine retribution.

The door to his room opened and John entered, a tray in one hand. He placed it on Kit's bedside table and crossed to the window, pulling open the curtains. As the light hit him full on, Kit groaned again, rolling over.

'Leave me be,' he said, voice husky.

John crossed to the bed. 'Kit? Are you ill?'

'I don't know.'

John's hand was cold against his forehead. 'You've a fever. I'll call the doctor.'

Kit pushed him away. 'I don't want a doctor.'

'Very well.' His manservant considered. 'But Newgate has taken its toll, I fear. If you don't improve by midday, I will ride for him myself.'

Kit frowned, raising himself on his elbows. 'I'm not a child, John. I don't need to be coddled.'

'Nevertheless.' John crossed back to the window and re-pulled the drapes. 'You should rest. I'll send word to Roisin to call another day.'

Kit muttered something rude and closed his eyes.

'Do you want her to see you like this?'

'No.'

'Then you can wait until you feel better.'

He was right. Kit knew he was in no state to receive any callers—even his wife. The thought of her made his stomach ache in a way that had nothing to do with the fever coursing through his blood. But he wanted to have his wits about him when she came.

He nodded. 'Very well.'

'I will send a message then.' John nodded towards the tray. 'Eat your breakfast.'

Kit looked mournfully at the tray. There was little he wanted to do less.

* * *

Breakfasting with Cathy in her hotel room, Roisin found she had no appetite. The thought of returning to Oakridge later in the day made her feel strange, though she could not describe how. She did not want to see her husband again, at the same time as she wished to be in his arms, as they had been before everything had fallen down around their ears. She had asked Cathy to come with her for this reason—as a buffer between herself and Kit. She did not feel ready to discuss with him what they must do about the way he had lied to her, about her refusal to live with him— or about the shell of their marriage.

After the initial shock at discovering Kit's past, Cathy had accepted the situation surprisingly well. She had listened as Roisin told the whole tale, shaking her head in disbelief—but less in disapproval. He would not have considered such an option if there was another way, she said stoutly. Her regard for Kit was undamaged by recent events, it seemed. He was a good man with good intentions. Cathy, Roisin realised with a jolt, was more worldly than she had assumed. It was the way of things, her cousin told her, and Kit was not the first nobleman to have been so tempted from the path of lawfulness. She did, however, agree that he should not have lied, and Roisin was glad to have an ally in that at least.

As it was, Cathy seemed determined to cheer the

situation up. If she had noticed her cousin's mood this morning, she was ignoring it so far. She chattered about Mr Jonstone—how they had driven in Regent's Park together, how grateful he was to her for showing him around her home city. How handsome he was— how kind, how thoughtful. How honest as well, Roisin was willing to bet. There had been a time when she would have said those things about Kit. It was barely believable to think that that time was mere days ago. She had been Lady Westhaven for barely a fortnight, and already she had been estranged from her husband for almost a week—as long as they had lived under the same roof together.

Cathy drew to a halt in her verbal flow without Roisin noticing. She sighed.

'You're thinner. Are you eating?'

Roisin looked down at the cup of tea before her. 'Yes. Of course.'

Her cousin was not convinced. 'Will you not come home?'

'It is not my home,' Roisin told her.

'It could be. My parents liked having you there before. You need not discuss Kit with them—they will be discreet.'

'I cannot.'

'And I still may not tell them you are here? They would want to know. My mother keeps asking if I have been to see you at Oakridge—they think that is where I am now! I had to tell them that Jane returned to us because you had appointed your own maid—and I had to have a word with *her* to make sure she keeps anything she knows to herself!'

Guilt washed over Roisin. She had abandoned Jane without a second thought. 'Is she all right?'

Cathy suppressed a grin, not really put out. 'I think, in truth, she had more excitement in a few days with you than in twenty years with my mother. And she is not given to idle chatter—your secrets are safe there.'

Roisin smiled back wanly, taking Cathy's hand across the table. 'I'm sorry you have to lie,' she said slowly. 'It seems unfair, I know... but I promised your father I would be happy with Kit. It seems wrong to tell him I am not.'

'If you are moving out of Oakridge, you will have to, sooner or later.' Cathy leant forward, pressing her cousin's hand gently. 'Roisin, surely you cannot afford to stay here much longer?'

Roisin did not meet her eyes. 'For another week. Longer, perhaps, if I can get smaller rooms.'

'Then what are you going to do?'

'I was thinking...' She sighed. 'I mentioned to John that I was thinking of returning to Ireland.'

'And are you? Seriously?' Cathy's eyes were wide.

'I suppose I will have to.' Roisin's eyes filled with tears, despite herself. 'Though that is not my home now, either.'

'Roisin.' Cathy moved around the table to drape an arm across her cousin's shoulders. 'You miss him, don't you?'

'Of course not.' Roisin turned her face away. 'You must forgive my foolishness. I do not sleep well.'

Cathy was about to say something reassuring when a knock sounded at the door. Roisin glanced up sharply, brushing the tears from her cheeks.

'I'll go.' Cathy rose, sweeping over to the door with the air of a woman in command of the situation. She opened it, speaking briefly to the porter who stood there. By the time she returned, having tipped him and closed the door again, Roisin had control over herself.

'A note for you,' she said. 'It is from Oakridge.'

'You read it.' Roisin poured more tea, eyes aching.

'Very well.' Cathy broke the seal. She stood silently as she read the short note, then looked up, brows knitted together.

'What is it?'

'It is from John. He says we must come another day to get your clothes.'

Roisin sighed. 'Why, when we are ready today?'

'He says Kit is ill.'

Her heart seemed for a moment to stand still. 'Ill?' Cold fingers ran up her spine. 'Ill how? Does he say?'

Cathy shook her head. 'Only that he cannot receive callers.'

Roisin rose to her feet, concern colliding with anger within her. 'I am not a caller—I am his wife! I am not asking to be *received*, I simply want back what is mine.' She stopped. 'It says nothing? Only that he is "ill"?'

'Only that.' Cathy regarded her anxiously. 'What shall we do?'

'We shall go now.' Roisin drew herself up. 'He need not see me. I cannot wait.'

She turned and went into the bedroom that adjoined her sitting room, to ready herself. As she did so, thoughts churned in her mind. Kit was ill. Could it be serious? She remembered him coughing in Newgate, and the creeping chill of the cell. Her breath stuck in her chest. She *would* go to Oakridge today, despite his letter. She needed to be sure he was all right before she left for Ireland. Also, she reminded herself, she needed her things. The two reasons combined were good enough ones to ignore the note.

She returned to the sitting room, where Cathy had put on her outdoor things, obviously expecting a hasty departure.

'Are you ready?' Roisin asked.

Cathy nodded. 'I rang for the porter and asked him to hail us a cab.'

'Thank you.'

They went down to the vestibule together, where a cab waited outside the hotel's grand frontage.

Climbing inside, Roisin was suddenly glad to be on her way. There was nothing worse than sitting in a hotel stewing over events. She needed to find out for herself what was happening at Oakridge.

The journey seemed to take an age, however, now she was so impatient to get things over with, and it was with a profound relief that she finally spied the gate-posts at the end of the long driveway. The house was just the same as ever, she thought, with a wave of what could not be homesickness because she cared not about the place. She was merely glad to be here so she could take her things, she assured herself, nothing more.

As Cathy and Roisin alighted on the front steps, instructed the driver to wait, and began to ascend, the front door opened. John appeared, confusion apparent on his face.

'Roisin.'

'Hello, John.' She went up the steps towards him.

'Did you not receive my message?'

'I did. Thank you.' She carried on, Cathy behind her, determined not to ask about her husband. 'It is not Kit I have come to see, thankfully, so I will not disturb him.'

He looked as if he could think of nothing to say to that, holding the door open for her and following her inside.

'I will let him know you are here, nevertheless.'

She shrugged. 'As you wish. This is his house.'

She swept upstairs, Cathy on her heels, leaving him standing in the hall.

'Roisin,' hissed Cathy. 'You were very short with him.'

Her cousin sighed. 'I know. I hope he understands I am not angry with him. I just want to get my clothes and leave this place.'

They hurried to Roisin's bedroom and she pulled out her large trunk. Together they packed her clothes, folding and arranging them carefully but quickly, speaking little. It felt strange to be back here in her room, which was not really hers any more. Roisin tried not to think about it.

When they had finished and the wardrobe stood empty, Roisin stood back, hands on hips. The trunk was too heavy to lift.

'I'll get John,' she said, making for the door. 'He can help us.'

He was already on his way, however, as she stepped out into the corridor. He stopped as he saw her, smiling slightly.

'I was coming to search for you,' she said awkwardly. 'The trunk needs taking downstairs. Could you help?'

He nodded. 'Of course.'

'Thank you, John.' She gave him a small smile, then, because she could not wait any longer, she asked, 'How is Kit?'

'He has a fever. It does not seem too serious.'

'Has a doctor been sent for?'

He smiled wryly. 'You know Kit. He will not hear of it.'

She nodded. 'He is safe in your care, I know.'

She turned to go back into her room, her relief palpable. He was not seriously ill. She could leave without worrying, in the knowledge that John would do what needed to be done for him.

John cleared his throat. 'Roisin?'

She faced him. 'Yes?'

'He wants to see you.'

She dropped her gaze from his. 'Why?'

'He did not say.'

She had been foolish to think she could avoid him. She sighed. 'Very well.'

'He is in the library,' John told her. 'I will see to your cousin and the trunk.'

'Thank you.'

Leaving him, Roisin made her slow way to the library. She could have refused to see her husband, she knew—could have left without giving him the satisfaction of seeing the pallor of her complexion and the faint but visible shadows under her eyes. He would know the effect this was having on her if he so much as laid eyes on her. Yet she wanted, deep down, to reassure himself that he was all right. So she went, trying to plan what she would say and failing to think of anything.

The library door was open, the sound of his rasping cough reaching her as she approached the doorway. He sat with his back to her, in his wing-backed chair in front of the fire, one hand to his chest, as if it hurt.

She stood, suddenly engulfed in a tide of sympathy, concern and sorrow for the man she loved and the circumstances that had brought them here, so that she must knock at his door like a stranger. She did just that, rapping her knuckle against the doorframe.

He turned, making it halfway to his feet before she said, 'Don't get up.'

She moved into the room, face warmed by the fire, as he sank back into his chair. There was a blanket over his knees, she saw, knowing John must have brought it for him. He was flushed, eyes bright with fever, though he seemed to be cold.

He said, 'Sit down, Roisin.'

There was another, smaller chair facing his. She settled herself on it, perched on the edge, uncomfortable. His eyes were on her face, watching her every expression, as usual.

'How are you?' she enquired politely.

He shrugged. 'I've been better. But there is worse.' He paused. 'I have you to thank for saving me from that.'

'I am your wife,' she said simply.

He nodded. 'Well, wife, you do not appear exceedingly healthy yourself.'

'I am perfectly well, thank you.'

'I see.' There was a pause as he coughed into a fist, breathing heavily when he was able to stop.

'You should see a doctor,' she admonished despite herself.

'So John says.' His eyes bored into hers. 'It isn't a doctor I want, Roisin. I want my wife with me.'

'Well,' she said stiffly, 'your wife does not wish to be here.'

'You should be at Oakridge. It is my duty to provide a roof over your head.'

She looked away. 'Your *duty*?'

'Yes, apart from anything!'

'You need not trouble yourself,' she told him. 'I am going back to Ireland.'

He leant forward in his chair. 'I had not thought you would run away.'

'I am not,' she objected. 'I…'

His voice was gentle as she lowered her eyes. 'You have nowhere else to go? Then come home.'

'This is not my home.'

'It is where you belong.' He reached out a hand to her, and his flesh was very warm where it touched hers. 'You are my wife.'

She broke free, standing up. 'Stop reminding me, Kit! That is no reason to come back to Oakridge! You did not treat me like your wife when you lied to me!'

'Then what will we do? People will start to talk.'

She regarded him coldly. 'I care not what people say. We will not be the first married couple to live apart! Tell them my health is poor and I go to Ireland to recover—or that I am visiting my mother. Tell them I have been carried off by brigands—I care not! I cannot live here.'

He sighed. 'You expect me to believe you do not love me?'

Tears stung her eyes. 'What does it matter?'

'It matters a great deal.' Slowly, he raised himself to his feet. 'Roisin, why did you buy back Jamie's watch?'

'Because I did not want to feel indebted to you.'

'That is all?'

She shrugged. 'I would not want to know that something I held dear sat in a jeweller's cabinet.'

There was a pause. 'Thank you,' he said at last.

She inclined her head, and when she raised it again he had moved closer.

'Will you never forgive me?'

His fingers brushed her cheek and she had not the heart to remove them. Her body responded to his touch in the same way it always had, something unfurling slowly in the pit of her stomach. She lifted her gaze to his.

'Kit. Don't.'

As their eyes met, his hand dropped to his side.

'Come. One kiss goodbye.'

Roisin looked at him, wondering what it would do

to her. Already she wanted to feel his arms about her, his body against hers. But she could not forget the feeling of his betrayal, the cold chapel floor under her as she gazed upon the painted face of his brother. She could not forget the sickening panic of finding out the truth.

She wanted to go home, yet half of her felt she was here already.

She turned her cheek towards him. 'Very well.'

Gently, with one finger under her chin, he turned her head back to face him and touched his lips to hers. She could feel the heat of fever radiating from his skin, and, without thinking, put up a hand to his cheek.

'You should take better care of yourself.'

His eyes were unreadable, but she knew where his thoughts lay as he covered her hand with his, then turned his head to kiss her palm.

She pulled away, freeing herself from his grasp. 'Goodbye, Kit.'

He said nothing, but she knew his eyes were on her face.

She turned, tears blinding her, and fled, through the winding corridors of Oakridge and out into the light, where the carriage stood waiting, with Cathy already inside. Kit had not followed her, she knew. She was grateful.

John stood by the cab, awaiting her. His brown eyes were liquid with sympathy as they met hers.

'You are ready to go?'

She nodded. 'Yes, thank you.' She took his hand and pressed it in hers. 'Thank you for everything, John. Goodbye.'

The cab drew away from the house as soon as she stepped inside, looking away from Cathy's pained face and the view of Oakridge through the window. She had to leave. She would not think about the alternatives, because there were none. Despite the fact that she loved him—that she desired him—every bit as much as she had by the shores of the lake only a matter of days ago, she could not go back. She would not.

But she could not keep herself from weeping.

In his chair before the fire, Kit sat, burning with fever and frustration and desire. He knew that she still cared for him just by seeing her. But she could not bring herself to forgive him. The knowledge, he knew, would work itself under his skin and haunt him for ever more. Unless he did something about it.

Throwing back his head, he roared for his manservant, the effort bringing on a fit of coughing. By the time he had stopped, John was in the doorway, regarding him reproachfully.

'Use the bell,' he said. 'It will be less hard on your throat.'

Kit ignored him, throwing off his blanket and shoving himself to his feet. 'This will not pass. She wants to come home, I can see it. Something must be done.' In frustration, he cast his eyes over the shabby room, suddenly intensely displeased with what he saw. 'Who would wish to come back to this?' he muttered. 'John.'

'Yes, Kit?'

'Hire some more servants. It is disgraceful of me to expect you and Cook to wait on me single-handed. And we will open up the house—the whole house. Order some new rugs, and have the paintwork in this place touched up. The roof is fixed now—let us get to work inside. I will make Oakridge fit for my wife, and then I will prove to her that I am worthy of a second chance.'

John inclined his head, expressionless. 'I will make arrangements.'

Kit thought awhile. 'We have little time—only a few days. But be sure to have the piano retuned, and pay special attention to the ballroom.'

'The ballroom?' His friend looked confused. 'Why?'

Kit smiled. 'Because I'm going to hold a ball.'

Chapter Fifteen

Within a week Roisin was tired of staring at the walls of her hotel suite. She had been to the shipping office to buy her ticket to Cork, only to be told there would be no places aboard any vessel for at least another week. Now, pulling on her gloves, she was on her way out to try again. She could not stand London for much longer like this, with Cathy as her only link to the world. She headed for the door, just as someone knocked on it.

A porter stood there, holding a large white box. He smiled.

'This was just delivered for you, ma'am.'

'Thank you.' She took it, shut the door and placed it on the *chaise-longue* that stood by the window. It must have been delivered by hand, for the box was unwritten-on. Roisin regarded it with suspicion. It could only be from her husband. She was not sure she wanted it.

Another knock at the door.

'Roisin?' Cathy's voice. 'Are you there? Open the door, quickly—I have such news!'

Again, Roisin went to the door. Cathy was flushed, fanning herself with one hand.

'Come in,' she said, wondering what social miracle had occurred now.

'It's all over town,' Cathy began, short of breath.

Roisin rolled her eyes. 'Something always is. What is it this time?'

'You'll never guess. There is to be a ball at Oak-ridge!'

'A ball?' Roisin shut the door in case any gossips lurked in the hall—knowing this town it would not be unlikely.

Her cousin nodded eagerly. 'Kit celebrates his birthday the day after tomorrow—everyone is invited.' She stopped, flushing as she saw Roisin's surprise. 'You…have not received your invitation?'

'I am not exactly on speaking terms with Kit,' Roisin said shortly. 'I didn't even know it was his birthday. It does not surprise me that he does not want me there—and I would not wish to go.' She paused. 'He has invited your family?'

Cathy nodded. 'And Mr Jonstone. So thoughtful of him.'

'I see.'

'I am sure you are to be—' Cathy spied the box. 'What is that?'

'I don't know.' Roisin shrugged at it. 'It arrived just before you did.'

'Well, are you just going to leave it there?' Her cousin sighed. 'Roisin, open it!'

Despite herself, Roisin smiled. Cathy seated herself with a sigh in readiness as she untied the string around the box and lifted the lid. Inside was a mass of silk and a small white envelope.

'What is it?' Cathy leapt to her feet again.

Roisin reached into the box and pulled out an evening gown. It was a light sky blue with lace at the cuffs and the wide neckline. The white underskirt was embroidered with silver thread, picked out on the rest of the dress with silver piping around the bodice and sleeves. There were matching shoes in the box as well.

'Ohh,' said Cathy, reaching out a hand to touch the skirt. 'Roisin. This must have cost a fortune.'

Roisin was silent. She had never owned a gown so fine. The card lay unopened in the now empty box. Picking it up, she broke the seal—Kit's seal—and read the invitation contained within.

'See!' Cathy was beside herself. 'He *does* want you there!'

'It makes no difference.' Roisin laid the dress across the back of a chair. 'I will not be there. I will send this back to him at once. He knows I cannot be bought.'

'Roisin!' Cathy looked shocked.

'I am serious.' Roisin, turning the card over, saw Kit's handwriting on the back.

Do this one last thing for me—my wife should be by my side at my birthday ball. Then you are free. Kit

She held it, staring at his bold scrawl. Social blackmail—she should have known. It was true enough—her absence would cause tongues to wag. He could, she supposed, tell them she was ill.

'What is it?' Cathy came forward.

'Read for yourself.'

There was a pause. 'Are you going to go?'

Roisin stared at the dress. She had no doubt it would fit perfectly—her husband was too organised to have made a mistake. She sighed. His birthday... He had never mentioned it to her. She supposed he had other things on his mind at the time.

'I don't know,' she said honestly.

'He clearly wants you there.'

'I care not what he wants.' As she spoke, Roisin knew she did not sound convincing.

'It is a beautiful dress. You will be splendid in it.'

'The perfect accessory,' she muttered.

'That isn't what I meant.' Cathy touched her arm. 'Roisin. If this is to be the last time you see him—'

'I *have* seen him for the last time!' Exasperated,

Roisin sat down beside the dress. 'I have said good-bye—why must he ask me for more?'

'Perhaps he just wishes to have something to remember you by,' suggested her cousin sweetly.

Roisin's forehead creased into a frown. 'Cathy?'

'Yes?' A pink flush stole up Cathy's neck as Roisin looked hard at her.

'You have not happened to bump into my husband, have you? You seem to know exactly what he wants.'

Cathy lowered her eyes. 'He dropped by the house. He said he was on his way somewhere and had…' She flushed further, and shook her head. 'All right. He came to ask me to make sure you came. I have never seen him so determined, Roisin.'

'Determined not to be made a fool of.'

'Perhaps that is all it is.' Cathy sighed. 'Perhaps it is more. Will you go? For the sake of appearances at least? You may even enjoy yourself—they say balls at Oakridge were once the best in the county, when Kit's father was alive.' She smiled encouragingly. 'Then you can be away.'

Roisin pursed her lips, arms folded. 'Must I be a puppet on his arm, even for only one night? He said he married me because I was not such an ornament.'

'People will talk,' Cathy said gently.

'They will always talk!' Exasperated, Roisin shrugged. 'But I suppose I shall have to. I will never hear the end of it if I do not—from you at least.'

Her cousin smiled. 'That much is true. But, Roisin, I think you will enjoy yourself. End your time here properly. If he wants to see you one last time, then show him what he has lost, if nothing else!'

Roisin frowned. 'It is not my intention to toy with him. But I shall go, because he asks me to, as husband to wife. Then I will leave this country once and for all.'

She hoped, even as she spoke, that—this time—she could stick to her intentions.

Cathy, stepping out of the hotel entrance on to the street, immediately felt that someone was watching her. She turned her head and, as she had expected, saw Kit. He was leaning against the wall, eyes following her. As she approached he pushed himself upright, straightening his wig, and came to meet her. There were shadows under his eyes. He did not bother with a greeting, but the pained anticipation on his face told her why he was there.

'Well?'

'Well what, Kit?'

'Is she coming?'

She lowered her eyes. 'I think so.'

'You think so?'

'She seemed to think it was her duty to do so. She is less than happy about it.'

'But she will come?'

He was unbending in his determination, she

thought, a man who could not fathom an answer other than the one he needed to hear. If by force of his will alone, he would ensure she was there.

'Yes,' she said quietly. 'She will come.'

He nodded. 'Thank you. Did she like the dress?'

'I think she was impressed, despite herself. It was well chosen.' Cathy looked at him, guilt rising in her. Though Roisin had guessed her part in this, she still felt she had duped her cousin. 'I hope your intentions are honourable, Kit.'

'When have they not been?' He gave her a faint smile, coughing slightly.

She chose only to give him a reproachful glare in answer to this. 'You should be at home, in bed.'

'There are more important things to attend to.'

Again, she looked into his face. 'She is badly hurt, Kit.'

'I know she is.' He sighed. 'I want to make things right, that is all. She will not regret she came.'

'All right.' Cathy put a hand on his arm. 'I will see she is there. Now get you back to Oakridge.'

He nodded. 'I will see you on Saturday, in your finery. Thanks again, Cathy.'

'I hope only that she will thank me also,' said Roisin's cousin. 'You have long been my friend, Kit, but she is family. If you make things worse—'

'Trust me.' He was very serious, suddenly. 'I love her.'

'Very well—we shall see. Take care.'

With that she kissed him on his pale cheek and climbed into her carriage. When she glanced back he was gone.

Saturday evening, the night of his birthday ball, and Kit was having second thoughts. He sat in the library, eyes glazed, swinging Jamie's watch on its chain before his face, and thinking.

He had spent a considerable amount of money on this ball. Money that he still felt guilty about spending. He had the dowry still, but where was his wife? Would she take exception to these frivolities, planned to show the world how he was renovating his family home? Oakridge looked better than it had in years, she would have to admit that. And it almost operated like a proper household again.

Except that it had no mistress.

Kit traced his brother's initials. He had kept one promise, perhaps at the cost of another. He had told Roisin he would provide for her, and he was not unaware of what she had given up for him. Her future, her dowry. Not to mention her family jewellery. And he had lied to her in return.

If he admitted it to himself, that was the real reason for this ball. Next year, when he came into his own money, things would be better. He would be able to give her the life she deserved—if he could only get her to give him the chance. He wanted his wife back, and he needed to show her why she should trust him again.

A knock at the door brought him out of his reverie. John stuck his head into the room.

'Is everything ready?' asked Kit.

'Of course. We're all prepared. I've laid out your clothes upstairs.'

'Thank you.' Kit looked around the room. 'Is there anything I've forgotten?'

John grinned. 'Just to breathe. Good luck.'

Kit returned the smile. 'Thank you.' He stood up as his friend left the room, and tucked the watch into his pocket. He had closeted himself in the library long enough. Now it was time to show his wife the man she had truly married. He only hoped it was not too late.

Roisin was barely ready when Kit's carriage arrived for her on Saturday evening. She did not recognise the man who drove it—it seemed Kit had hired himself a new coachman. He was courteous and well mannered, helping her inside and addressing her as Lady Westhaven. It sounded strange to her now, without her husband in attendance.

She settled herself inside, spreading out the skirts of her new gown. It fitted perfectly, as she had expected—the bodice enclosing her snugly, framing the tops of her breasts. The feel of it as she moved was so luxurious… Roisin smoothed the silk, taking pleasure in the precise stitches of the embroidery. She hoped her husband considered his money well spent—she certainly looked the dutiful, loving wife, even if she did not feel exactly that.

Still, it would be good to see Oakridge again. She did not like to admit it to herself, but she had missed it.

There were people standing at the top of the steps, she saw, as the carriage drew up to the house—had Kit's guests started arriving so soon? She leant forward, trying to get a better view. No, these were not guests. They stood, lined up, hands folded, eyes fixed on the carriage. Apparently waiting for her. John stood to one side, smiling at her as she stepped out of the carriage. Roisin took the steps slowly, suddenly self-conscious under the many pairs of eyes that watched her. The last thing she wanted was to trip over her dress and fall flat on her face.

'What's all this?' she asked John.

His smiled widened. 'Allow me to introduce the new staff.' He turned to the line of servants. 'You know Cook, of course.'

'Yes.' The two women exchanged smiles.

'And here are our below stairs maids, Mary and Evie,' he went on, as two girls who could not have been more than seventeen curtsied shyly. Mary was tall, slender and blonde, Evie a tiny, freckled redhead. John winked at them and moved on. 'For above stairs, Henrietta and Harriet.' Two practically identical maids smiled at Roisin, dark-haired and plump-cheeked. 'Hetty and Hatty—twins,' he added under his breath. Roisin grinned.

'You've already met Robert, the coachman,' John continued. 'Which leaves only Dick, the head gardener.' A tall, weatherbeaten young man grinned at her. 'He has already worked wonders on the box hedges.' John faced the servants. 'This is Lady Westhaven, your mistress. Now, you can all get back to work—there is much to do before the guests arrive.'

'Lovely to meet you all,' Roisin said as they dispersed, shy smiles tossed in her direction. When she stood alone with John, she said 'What was the reason for that?'

'Kit wanted you to meet the servants.'

She nodded. 'I see that. I only wonder why, since I am not going to be living here.' She looked around. The place did seem more cared for, somehow. 'Still, I am glad your workload has lessened.'

He seemed pleased with himself. 'Kit has put me in charge of running Oakridge. Hence the new clothes.' He was, in truth, much more smartly dressed than usual—the sackcloth apron and leather jerkin replaced by a waistcoat, complete with lace collar.

Roisin nodded, eyes sparkling. 'Very grand. Should I bow?'

John grinned. 'Not at present.' He gestured towards the door. 'Come, I should not have to usher you inside. Kit thought you might like to join him for a drink before the guests arrive. He is in the—'

'Library?' She rolled her eyes. 'Nothing changes.'

'Drawing room,' he corrected. 'He awaits you, unless you wish to refresh yourself first after your journey?'

Roisin raised her chin. She could well imagine Kit sitting in the drawing room, a glass of port in his hand, awaiting her for a civilised conversation to pass the time. Well, that was not what she was here for.

'I do not feel like drinking. Tell Kit I have gone upstairs to ready myself.'

He nodded, face giving nothing away. 'Your room is ready for you.'

'Thank you.'

As she started to walk away, he cleared his throat awkwardly. 'Roisin?'

She turned. 'Yes?'

'I thought you might like to know…I had a letter from Annette.' For a moment there was pain in his eyes.

Roisin moved closer. 'How does she?'

'She has found a new position in a house in Hertfordshire. A wealthy family.'

'Well. I am pleased that she is…comfortable,' said Roisin with an effort. 'She is your sister, after all.'

John raised his eyebrows. 'A wealthy family with three unmarried sons.'

'So. She is up to her old tricks.' *And I am here in the mire she has made of her last adventure.*

'I should not have told you,' said John, stricken.

'No, it is good to know.' She put a hand on his arm. 'At least she is safe away from here. Will you see her again?'

He shook his head. 'I know not. As you say, she is my sister, though I feel little love for her at the moment.'

'I wish you well,' she told him, giving his arm a squeeze.

'And you will not join Kit?'

She smiled at him, but there was little mirth in it. 'I am only here for the sake of appearance, John. I see little point in drawing it out. Let me know when the first guests have arrived and I will join them then.'

'Very well.'

She knew he watched her as she went up the stairs, and wished she did not feel the lead weight that was in her chest. But she had spoken the truth, and if she was to play a role for society, she would wait until it arrived. Until then she would be in her room.

The evening was going well, young as it was. Kit, standing by the entrance to the ballroom greeting guests, glanced around furtively. People were standing and talking, drinking punch and listening to the musicians he had hired. The dancing had begun, a sarabande proceeding nicely on the dance floor behind him. Everything seemed to be getting along perfectly, judging by the smiles on the faces of his guests.

Still, his smile was forced. He identified the feeling in the pit of his stomach as nerves, with surprise. He had nothing to feel apprehensive about—this was his party. So why wasn't he having any fun?

Kit scanned the large room again. They had opened it up after years of dust and neglect, polishing the floor until it shone and repairing the ancient chandelier. It hung now in the high ceiling, reflecting light down upon the floral arrangements in every crevice.

Still no sign of his wife.

He knew she had arrived, because she had spoken with John. The house was slowly filling with guests—outside, society's finest alighted from their carriages and glided up the steps. Everyone was here, including Cathy and her American, Phineas Jonstone, and Roisin's aunt and uncle. He was telling everyone who asked that his wife was still readying herself upstairs, with a light chuckle as he lied, as if such things were to be expected of women. In reality, he was beginning to suspect that she had lost her nerve and would refuse to come down.

He need not have worried. A ripple of voices by the door signalled Roisin's entrance. He stood straighter, running a hand over his wig. There was a pause, then she approached him through the crowd, and he saw what everybody was looking at.

His wife was beautiful, even more so than usual, tonight. The dress he had agonised over was a perfect fit—and she was wearing his mother's pearl and diamond choker, he saw. Her hair was piled upon her head, padded and powdered, held with pearl-headed pins. A few tendrils hung down the back of her neck, teasing the eye, inviting the finger to coil them, to stroke them. Kit's mouth was dry suddenly. He was aware that, despite the hum of conversation and the music, everyone was watching them from the corners of their eyes.

Roisin came to a halt before him, looking up into his face. Kit smiled—a smile that did not reach his eyes, however, for he saw the distance in hers.

'Thank you for coming,' he said, too softly for anyone to overhear.

Her eyes were cool. 'You gave me little choice.'

He inclined his head. 'True enough, I suppose. You are beautiful tonight, Roisin.'

She shrugged daintily. 'It is your dress, the compliment is yours. You have exquisite taste, apparently.'

Kit wanted to take her in his arms and kiss her until she thawed.

'Happy birthday, by the way,' she said.

He nodded. 'Thank you. Yesterday, in fact.'

'How fortunate. Another year gone, then. Less than a year left until you have your inheritance.'

She was not in a good mood.

Kit took her by the hand. He could feel her displeasure radiating through her glove, but she too was aware of their surreptitious audience. 'Do you not have a birthday kiss for your husband, Roisin?'

For a moment she only stared at him. Then, reaching up, she kissed his cheek, her lips barely brushing his skin. It was, he supposed, all he could expect.

'I have not brought you a present,' she told him. 'I had not the time or inclination to find one.'

'I don't care.' His eyes were drawn to her lips, full and soft, despite her cold expression. He could not lose her. 'Will you honour me with a dance? I believe they are about to play a minuet.'

'Must I?'

He wanted to kiss her, here in front of everyone. 'It is expected.'

'Very well.'

He offered her his arm, which she took. Then, as the minuet began, he escorted her on to the dance floor and they took up their positions. Roisin did not seem happy, but, as the dance began, her body moved automatically in steps learned from childhood. She barely met his eye, despite his efforts to catch her attention.

The floor filled up with couples around them. Kit mentally crossed his fingers and prayed for a miracle.

Roisin was having trouble keeping her mask from slipping. She had determined to be polite but distant with her husband—to keep things civilised—but things were not turning out as she had imagined. She had not expected him to look so handsome, for a start. The sight of him in his finery took her breath away, even as she walked towards him determined to be implacable. He seemed taller, making her feel tiny when they stood together. The lace at his throat only emphasised the hard line of his jaw, and his dark eyes were just as piercing as ever, yet gentle too, tonight. As usual, he was up to something.

Now, dancing with him, his statuesque form moving alongside her, Roisin was having trouble remaining icy. His closeness was awakening the usual tingling sensations. Something must be done—she must distract herself. She cleared her throat.

'How is your health?'

He smiled. 'Very much improved, thank you.'

Roisin nodded. 'I am glad to hear it.'

'Are you?' He lowered his chin, looking into her face even as she turned her head away.

'Of course.' Her eyes did not meet his. 'You have done wonders with the house in the time since I left.'

'Spending your father's money again.'

She looked up at him sharply. 'You wanted it to renovate Oakridge, did you not?'

'Indeed.'

She gave a curt nod. 'Then what you do with my dowry is none of my business. Especially now.'

Those eyes still bored into hers. Roisin licked her lips. 'Cathy is here with Mr Jonstone, I see.'

'Mmm. Roisin?'

'Yes?'

'Be quiet a moment.'

She complied only because she could think of nothing else to say. She tried not to concentrate on the way he 'accidentally' brushed her as he passed. She told herself to listen to the music and not meet his eyes. His steady gaze unsettled her. She tried to move back a little, hoping no one had noticed that she was not quite in time with the music.

Around them, the dance floor was full of chatting, laughing people. Cathy was dancing with Phineas, their eyes locked as they moved around each other on the floor. Her aunt was by the punch bowl…

Roisin kept her gaze on the assembled company, avoiding his eye. His shoulders were impossibly broad beneath his new waistcoat. She felt suddenly like she needed to grip his arm for support, so strong was the urge to reach out and—

Roisin stumbled, stepping hard on Kit's foot as they came together and nearly pushing him into the man behind them. She broke away from the dancers, breathing shallow.

'Excuse me. I am very warm—I think I need some fresh air.'

She fled through the nearby terrace doors, open to

let in the evening air. Outside the sun was setting, turning the sky crimson and gold. Roisin leant on the balustrade, lowering her head and breathing deeply. What was she thinking? She wanted nothing from Kit—she only wished to return home. What was she doing here?

She sighed. Except, in her heart, she already was home, and her feelings for him seemed not to have changed one jot. She let out a frustrated sigh. She had been a fool to come here, to expose herself to his unique way of breaking her heart once again.

'Roisin?'

Just the voice she did not want to hear. He stood in the shadows behind her, as he had the night she met him.

'I do not feel well,' she said. 'Please, lend me your carriage again. I need to rest.'

He came towards her, steps light on the stone. 'You do not seem ill.'

'Well, I feel it!' It was not a lie. Her stomach was fluttering uncontrollably. Her whole body was acutely aware of him—she could feel him coming closer.

His hands caressed her shoulders and upper arms. 'Perhaps you are cold.'

'Kit.' Roisin closed her eyes. She had not the strength for this, again. 'Why do you do this?'

'I wanted to see you one last time.'

'Do you think I am a fool?' She turned to face him.

'How many one last times will there be? Must I always be at your beck and call?'

'I wanted you to see what Oakridge could be, if run properly.'

'I have seen it. Now, may I go?'

His fingers played with the curls at the nape of her neck. 'Why must you go? I told you I would prove that I loved you when you came to Newgate. Will you not let me try?'

'How?' She stiffened at his touch.

His hand left her neck abruptly and his forehead creased. 'Perhaps first of all by finding the woman I married. She was full of fire and life—you look as if someone's rammed a poker up your—'

'Kit!' Roisin's eyes opened wide. 'You are not in one of your roadside inns now—kindly moderate your language! You are addressing a lady and—' She stopped, hearing herself. 'Oh, God, you're right.' She clapped a hand over her mouth and regarded him, eyes wide.

Kit's deep chuckle reverberated through her as he began to laugh. Despite herself, she gave him a sheepish grin.

'I married you to escape becoming my mother,' she said, half-laughing, half in dismay. 'Now look at me.'

'It was not my doing,' he said, eyes sparkling.

There was a silence in which the laughter died, seemingly swept away in the light summer breeze that fanned Roisin's hair around her face. She faced her husband, no longer angry. She did not know what she was feeling—only that it was a type of calm.

'Why am I here?' she asked again, not unpleasantly.

He regarded her. 'Because I need you to be. Because I love you.'

The words wound inside her and pierced her through. 'Kit. You married me for money, we both know it.'

He folded his arms. 'Do you love me?'

She met his eyes. 'Yes. I loved you as Ewan, and I love you still.'

Kit smiled. 'Then why do you not allow me such a liberty?'

She sighed. He knew she had no answer.

'Roisin.' He took her by the shoulders. 'I have felt this from the moment that pistol ball entered my body. You were not a simpering socialite—you were something quite different. And you were beautiful, all dishevelled and shaken.'

'Is that why you kissed me so?' The memory lit something within her. He had not kissed her in quite the same way since.

He let her go, and gazed out over the darkening grounds. 'I kissed you because I could not stop myself. I thought I was never going to see you again, and I forgot to be a gentleman.' A small smile flitted across his lips. 'It was all I wanted to do the second time I saw you—looking bored at the theatre. The only things that stopped me were the people watching—and the fact that you would have had no idea who I was.'

She frowned. 'I did know who you were. But I managed to convince myself it could not be.' She sighed. 'I should have listened to my instincts. Perhaps you should have told me, Kit.'

'Would you have married me?'

She thought, her mind weary of the question. 'We will never know, I suppose.'

Kit, brow furrowing, turned to her. 'Kissed you so…how?'

Roisin dropped her eyes. She had thought he had not noticed. 'With such…passion, as if you wanted something desperately from me.'

'And I have never kissed you that way again since?'

She thought. 'Perhaps the night we were married.'

'Ah. Yes.' He glanced down at his hands. 'Another lapse in propriety.' He smiled at her. 'My father always used to say that was the way a man ought to kiss his mistress, not his wife. He knew better than most—he had three.'

'Wives?'

Kit shook his head. 'Mistresses. I do not remember him kissing my mother.'

Roisin studied his profile. 'Did you kiss Annette that way?'

He turned his head towards her. 'Annette… Yes and

no. Yes, because I desired her physically. No, because I had such respect for you. You impressed me with your will as well as your beauty. I suppose I did not care what sort of a person Annette was. That, I fear, is how all this ended up so…unhappily.'

Roisin met his eyes. 'Are you unhappy, Kit?'

He turned to face her, hip leaning against the stone balustrade. 'Not in this instant.'

'But, in general?'

He shrugged. 'Very. You?'

She smiled. 'I'm miserable.'

Kit sighed, went to run a hand through his hair and encountered his powdered dress wig. He groaned. 'Confounded thing!' Pulling it off, he flung it as hard as he could over the balustrade with feeling. Roisin watched it disappear.

Kit ran both hands through his flattened hair, making it stand on end. 'See? I cannot cope with this rigmarole alone! I need my wife!'

She sighed. 'You need a wife. And it was your idea to have a ball.'

'For *you*!' His jaw was set. 'And now I have ruined a perfectly good wig and a perfectly good marriage.'

Roisin frowned. 'Perfectly good?'

'Were you not happy? In that small instant before—'

'Before the truth came out? Yes, I was.'

Serious suddenly, he came closer. 'As was I. Can

you not do the undoable and forgive me? I was a fool, Roisin. Do not ruin both our lives because of it.'

She half-turned away, blinking. 'What makes you think my life is ruined?'

'You remember how I kissed you.'

'How could I forget?' She drew herself up. 'It does not mean—'

She never finished, however, for he took her waist in his hands and covered her mouth with his. She let out a muffled cry of protest as, lifting her off her feet, he sat her on the balustrade, mouth hard against hers. He kissed her as he had in the woods, when he thought he was never going to see her again, fiercely and unreservedly, his fingers stroking her hair and her neck. Roisin placed her hands on his shoulders, fingers splayed against the muscles beneath his shirt, mouth exploring his as he explored hers, until her lips were deliciously tender. Her hands crept around him, pulling him closer until their bodies touched, her breasts against his chest, his legs lost in her skirts as he pressed against the stone and against her. She slid off her cold seat, her body rubbing along his as she did so, arms locked around him. All the time he was kissing her as if the world would end any moment. From the almost painful pleasure coursing through her, Roisin was not sure that it would not.

'Kit,' she whispered against his lips, pulling her

mouth away for a moment. 'Kit, there are people inside. They will—'

'I care not,' he muttered, lips on her neck and the tops of her breasts.

'Please, stop.'

With an effort that surprised her, she ignored her body's urgings and pushed against his chest, hard. He stepped back, fully aroused, jaw clenched.

'God's *teeth*, woman! Are you trying to kill me?'

She bit her lip, inappropriate mirth suddenly taking hold of her as she beheld him, clothes mussed, hair sticking up…

'What?' His eyes were wild. He glanced down at himself, at the obvious evidence of his passion. 'See how you affect me, Roisin?'

She felt a wave of love for him as he stood, glaring at her. 'Kit—'

'Did you come here just to taunt me?' His eyes blazed with the anger of frustration. 'You wear my dress and tease your hair into that…that concoction, and you talk of kissing me, yet I am not allowed to touch you! Do not torment me! Go back to Ireland if you must—remove yourself from my sight. Roisin, I am only a man! I cannot be expected to—'

'I forgive you,' she said softly.

'—carry on as if nothing has happened between us when you insist on—' He stopped, as if suddenly struck mute. 'What?'

'It is done,' she said. 'You cannot undo it, you are right.'

He stared at her. 'Am I?'

She nodded. 'I want to come home, Kit, if I can have your word that you will never lie to me again.'

Her husband stood, stunned. 'Why?'

Roisin shrugged. 'I have only loved two men, Kit, and you are both. I am more sorry than I can say about all that has happened, but I played my part in it. And…' she looked over the grounds, then at him, as he came closer '…we have been through so much.' She met his eyes. 'Was that the whole truth, Kit, that you told me?'

He nodded. 'There is nothing else. I never meant to hurt you, but I could see no other way. You must believe me.'

'Then let us be as we were. That is all I want. I am so tired of feeling betrayed.' She came forward and took his hand. 'Let us mourn your brother, and keep his secret together.'

'He wished he could have met you,' he told her softly. 'I think he would have tried to steal you from me.'

Roisin smiled. 'He may well have tried. But it would not have worked.'

He tipped up her chin and kissed her, very gently. 'There is one more promise that I made to him, Roisin.'

'And what is that?'

'That I will have sons for both of us.'

'Sons?' Head against his chest, she looked up at him. 'What about daughters?'

'He did not say I should not have daughters.'

She smiled. 'Then we will see what comes. And, Kit?'

He kissed the top if her head. 'Yes?'

'We will live for ourselves, not for others. We have both spent too long trying to be—or trying to escape—what those who love us wanted.'

'Agreed.'

'Having said that…' she grinned up at him '…our guests will be wondering where we are.'

'I can't go back.' He kissed her mouth, then the tip of her nose.

'Why?'

'No wig. Not socially acceptable.'

She broke away, kicking off her shoes. 'That is no excuse to slight your guests. I'll get it.'

With that she was away, off into the gathering dark in her stockinged feet, to retrieve the hated wig. Kit stood a while, watching her disappear into the twilight, a smile playing about his lips.

Her voice floated back on the light breeze, calling him from wherever she was. With a grin, he picked up her shoes and gave chase. Down on the lawn the shadows were growing, and the party would go on all night.

They had time.

* * * * *

Editor's Note

THE romantic figure of the highwayman has always played a part in British folk history. The first—admittedly mythical—highwayman was Robin Hood: stopping the carts and carriages of the rich on the road through Sherwood Forest, and robbing them to give the money to the poor. Later in the medieval period it was suggested that Prince Harry—the future King Henry V—himself played this Robin Hood role.

Mary Wollstonecraft explained the polite nature of the highwayman as part of the English character: 'In England, where the spirit of liberty has prevailed, it is useful for an highwayman, demanding your money, not only to avoid barbarity, but to behave with humanity, and even complaisance.'

The mounted chivalrous highway robbers of the seventeenth and eighteenth centuries took such a hold on the English imagination that thousands would flock to see them executed at Tyburn. Printed ballads about their crimes and their true confessions sold inordinately well, and still survive to this day.

One among these courtly rogues was Claud Du Vall who, in holding up a coach containing a knight and his lady, invited the lady to dance. He later refused to accept more than £100 of the £400 carried by the knight. Du Vall's epitaph reads: 'Here lies Du Vall. Reader, if male thou art, Look to thy purse; if female, to thy heart.'

Dick Turpin must be the most famous highwayman of all. Although in reality Turpin was a brutal murderer, his exploits and *politesse* became legendary. He inspired John Gay to write *The Beggar's Opera,* in which highwaymen and their mistresses behave like lords and ladies of the *ton.*

The last highwayman in Britain is thought to have been hanged in 1831. But the ghost of the gentlemanly rebel, capable of stealing both a lady's jewels and her heart, still has the power to capture our imagination.

'Bring my purse back.'

'Why?'

She frowned, frustration taking hold. 'Because I will shoot you!'

'Of course you will.'

He turned and began to walk away. Roisin took a deep breath and pulled the trigger.

She was not expecting it to be so loud. The force of the huge bang threw her backwards against the carriage, smoke issuing from the barrel of the gun. Gasping, Roisin threw it from her. It landed on the ground with a heavy thud.

Silence.

A long, horrible silence.

Then an almost inaudible groan.

Roisin forced herself to look over at the heap on the ground that had been her attacker. He lay, half on his back, half on his side, and she could see the rise and fall of his chest as he took deep, gasping breaths. He was not dead, then. She was not sure if that was a good thing or not...

'God's death...' he murmured, raising his head. 'You shot me!'

Emily Bascom lives in London with her boyfriend, a sunflower and a dog named Giles. She has a degree in English and Drama from Royal Holloway, London. In her quest to find a real job, she has been a milk(wo)man, a charity fundraiser and a Station Assistant on London Underground— all of which she loved. She craves olives, hates cricket, and dreams of retiring to Uganda.

The Rogue's Kiss is Emily Bascom's début novel for Mills & Boon® Historical Romance™. It captures the spirit of Georgian London in a dramatic, passionate love story.